Also by Patricia Paris

A Murderous Game
Run Rachael Run

THE GLEBE POINT SERIES
This Time Forever
Letters To Gabriella
Return To Glebe Point

THE BONAVERAS
Lucia
Caterina
Coming Soon

Lucia

A BONAVERA NOVEL

PATRICIA PARIS

Windswept

Livonia, Michigan

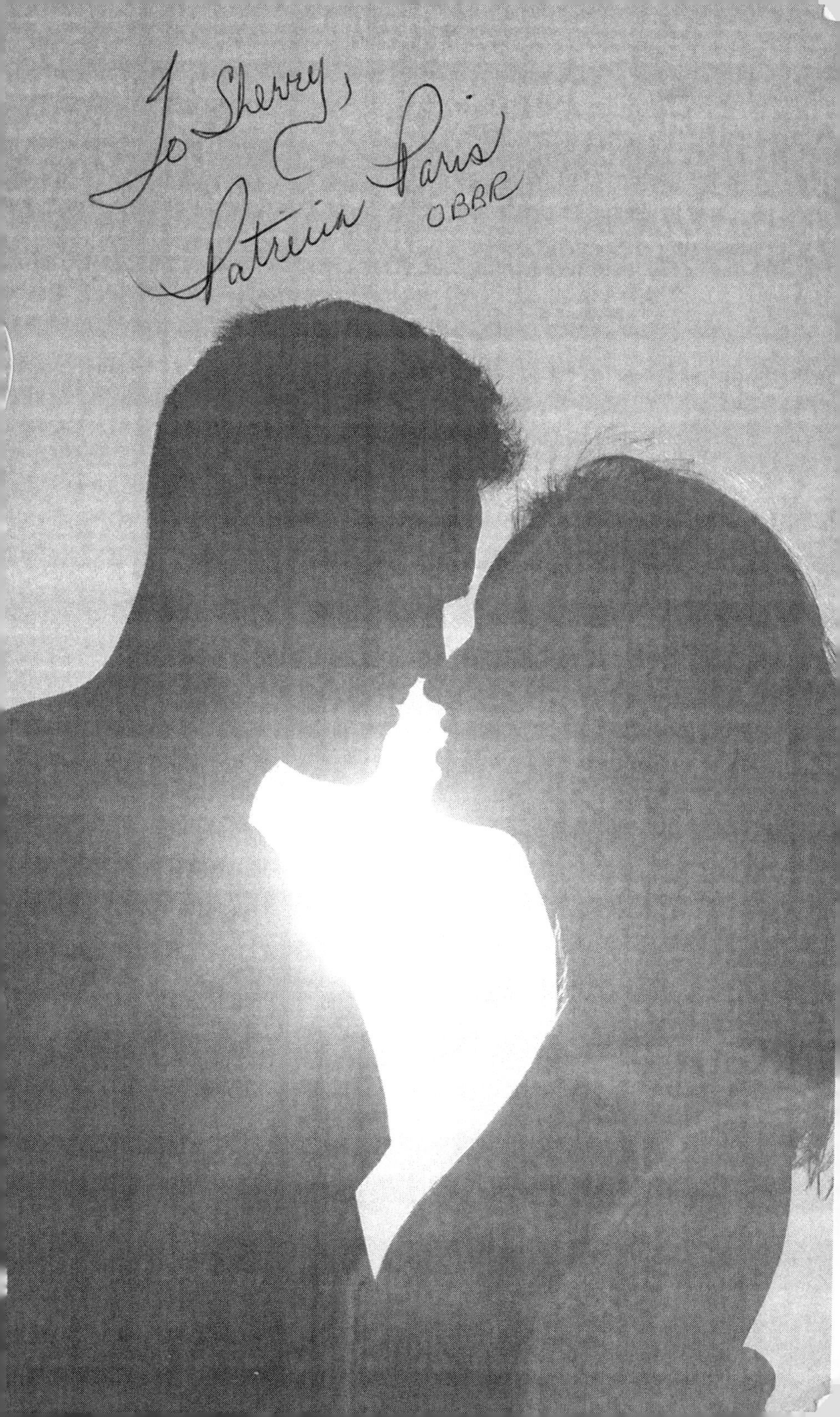
To Sherry,
Patricia Paris
OBBR

Cover design, interior book design,
and eBook design by Blue Harvest Creative
www.blueharvestcreative.com

Edited by S.M. Ray

Lucia

Published by Windswept
an imprint of BHC Press

Library of Congress Control Number:
2016954221

ISBN-13: 978-1-946006-12-7
ISBN-10: 1-946006-12-2

Visit the author at:
www.authorpatriciaparis.com &
www.bhcpress.com

Also available in eBook

Acknowledgments

Thank you to the special five who have endured countless winery visits and wine tastings with me in the quest to learn about Virginia's amazing wine industry. You know who you are!

To my earliest readers, Nette Boliver, Sophie Moss, and Nadine Schneider, I can't thank you enough for the time and thoughtfulness you put into reading the first drafts of this book and giving such wonderful feedback and insights. You are all awesome!

Special thanks to John von Senden, for leaping into a new genre by reading his first romance novel to consult with me on architecture, licensing, and building materials. If I got any of it wrong, the fault is mine, not his.

As always, I am extremely grateful to my editor, Sandra Ray, for the care and meticulous attention she gives to my work. You're the best, Sandra!

To my publisher BHC Press, thank you for your dedication to your authors, your guidance and support, and for turning my books into such beautiful works for my readers to enjoy.

And to my husband John—you are the wind in my sails—thank you for believing in, and being there for me, always.

Lucia

Prologue

*The days of wine and roses
Smile and run away like a child at play...*
Johnny Mercer, "Days of Wine and Roses"

Cortona, Italy 1986

*A*utumn drenched Cortona, rich, warm, golden beneath a Tuscan sun that painted the valley below in shades no artist brush could duplicate, no man with a soul could witness that his heart would not weep at its beauty.

Rodrigo Bonavera and Vincenzo DeLuca sat at one of the two small iron tables nestled close together on the gravel courtyard situated on the side of Rodrigo's villa. It was their habit to do so, just as they had many other evenings too numerous to recall, discussing the harvest, politics, family, or whatever took their fancy in the moment.

From this perspective they could appreciate the gently rolling hills, so much a part of the countryside, the fields, and the mountains beyond, for they were men of the land. It fed their spirits as much as the air fed their lungs.

"*Mio bel paese*," Rodrigo murmured, as he was known to do when he was in an appreciative mood of his homeland, which was often. He picked up the wine glass in front of him and raised it to the light.

The liquid nectar turned a rich, jewel red in the evening's waning rays. He regarded Vincenzo, a man he had known since he was a mere lad of six, born on the same day, in the same year, fifty-eight years to the day.

They had much in common. Both embraced tradition and held family close to their heart. Each had dark hair, peppered now with grey, and the weathered skin of men who worked long days in the sun.

Rodrigo's eyes were dark, black pearls his Sophia called them, for there was almost no brown in them, and when he laughed, she said they shown like jewels. Vincenzo's were an unforgettable shade of blue, clear as a cloudless summer sky, rich and pure, and many a girl had fallen for those eyes before they did the man in his younger days.

"You are the brother of my heart," Rodrigo said, "no less than if we had sprung from the same womb. That we would each be blessed in such a way, it cannot be coincidence. Destiny, Vincenzo, it can be nothing less than destiny."

He brought the glass to his nose, scented the ruby ambrosia inside, and then tipped it toward his friend. "Your grandson, my granddaughter, born these many years later each on the same day as you and I. I believe we are right in this, my friend. It is a sign—a sign our families are meant to come together as one."

"We are agreed then." Vincenzo tapped the rim of his glass to Rodrigo's. "To our grandchildren. May they marry and prosper, and may our blood blend and flow through their children's children."

"Yes, we are agreed, and although they may not be happy with us when they discover what we've done, they will thank us one day."

Each man drank, sealing a pact that bequeathed their first-born grandchildren, Lucia Bonavera and Antonio DeLuca, neither more than five hours old, one to the other.

"When will your son and his wife return from the States, Vincenzo?" Rodrigo inquired. "They're planning to come home soon, are they not?"

"Yes. I asked him the same question when he called to tell me of Antonio's birth this afternoon. I told him I did not want to wait until my only grandchild was walking before I laid eyes on the lad. Their visas expire in a month and they will be returning then."

Rodrigo nodded. "Your grandson, he will be American as well as Italian."

"What are you saying?"

"I believe because he was born in the States he will automatically be a citizen of that country as well as our own."

"That may be, but he will be Italian first, in his heart."

"Of course he will. *In Italie!*"

Vincenzo raised his glass again. "To Italy!"

Rodrigo heard the crunch of gravel and looked around to see Michele, his only son, walking toward them with a grave look upon his face.

"Father." Michele stopped next to the table, his eyes a mirror of sadness. "We've just received horrible news."

Rodrigo stood up, concern flooding him, and put a hand on his son's shoulder. "The child...is she—?"

"No, no, Lucia is fine," Michele assured him, but his tone held much grief. "It's Uncle Gino. He...he's dead, and Aunt Rosa, too. They were murdered, Father."

Rodrigo clapped a hand against his stocky chest. "*Mio fratello.*"

Shock and disbelief swirled in his brain. How could his brother have suffered such a fate? Why would anyone harm him? And his lovely wife, so young—only thirty-two—too young to be lost to them.

He didn't want to believe, but Michele's shattered expression dismissed any hope there'd been a mistake. Rodrigo hung his head, pain filling his heart, tears flooding his eyes.

THEY HAD BEEN in this place called Virginia for two months, arriving within days of Gino and Rosa's passing, and Rodrigo longed to go home. His wife Sophia was even more anxious to return to their beloved Cortona.

They were strangers here, and he knew she missed the familiarity of their little village, of walking to the square to pick up some bread and fish, some cheese and fruit, and perhaps a bit of gossip from her friends.

Michele had arrived a few weeks ago, bringing Isabella, his young wife, and their infant daughter, Lucia, with him. He had come to help Rodrigo sort through Gino's affairs, but Michele and Isabella had wanted to wait until the child was a little older before making the journey to the States. Their presence soothed Rodrigo and his Sophia through this difficult time, for there was no greater comfort than family when the heart mourned.

Rodrigo walked alongside Michele, in front of the rows of vines Gino had planted in the hope of establishing a successful vineyard. The sun had begun its climb, illuminating the haze that hung over the low foothills and valleys of the Blue Ridge Mountains, giving them an ethereal quality ripe for mystical imaginings.

At the sound of their approach, five deer that had been enjoying a breakfast of spring's tender new grape leaves, bolted into a copse of trees on the far side of the property, their white tails flicking in retreat as they disappeared into the protective veil of the thicket.

"I think my brother would have been wiser to invest in a few cows rather than trying to turn this land into a vineyard." Rodrigo gestured toward the retreating deer. "The only thing these vines will ever be good for is foraging by the local wildlife."

Michele took in the acres of vines, planted in neat rows that marched all the way to the wood line bordering his uncle's land. "It's what he knew, Father. You always said he was a good wine-maker. Who's to say he wouldn't have been successful establishing a winery here?"

"He was better than good, but that was when he was making wine in our country. Have you tasted what's in the cellar? I've had better vinegar," Rodrigo said, thinking the problem lay with the land and not his brother's skill. "These grapes will never produce wine that tastes like what we have in Italy."

"That isn't necessarily bad. I've been reading uncle's journals. He was experimenting, and given time he might have surprised you. His wines may be different from what you're used to, but good in their own right. That is the beauty of wine, is it not, Father?"

Rodrigo shrugged. Perhaps Michele was right. The vines were still young. They needed to mature before they could produce quality grapes. Only time would tell, he supposed, but unfortunately, Gino would never know if his gamble would pay off.

"Maybe the new owner will carry on with what your uncle started." Rodrigo put an arm around his son's shoulder. "I think Gino would want that, that his dream be given a chance."

"Would you consider not selling?"

"No." Rodrigo didn't have to think about it. Cortona was his home, the home of his heart. He did not want to live anywhere else, nor would he want to be a long-distance landlord.

He had no use for his brother's house, or this land, but he was a man of duty, so he and Sophia would stay until they settled the rest of Gino and Rosa's affairs. Once they did, then they could go home.

He felt his son shift beside him and eyed him curiously. "Why do you ask?"

Michele looked down, kicked his shoe against the ground still damp with morning dew. "Isabella and I, we've been talking...we thought we might stay in the States a while...get a better feel for the area."

Rodrigo gaped at him. He knew his son well. His heart tightened over the thoughts racing through his head. "You want to stay here, make a new life here? You want to move from Cortona?"

"Nothing's definite, Father," Michele was quick to respond. "We were just...talking. Neither of us has ever been more than fifty miles from our little village. Since we're already here, we thought we should take advantage of it to see other places, consider other possibilities."

"Other possibilities? I know what you mean by other possibilities, Michele. I can see the truth of it in your eyes. And what of your mother and me? You give us our first grandchild and now you want to move some five thousand miles away and set up house in a foreign country before we even get a chance to spoil her?"

"It would just be a trial, Father. We may decide we don't like it well enough to stay, and if we do, it wouldn't be like that. You would come visit, and we would come home to see you."

Rodrigo looked away, toward the mountains, his heart heavy in his chest. He had always known his son would leave one day. He had the spirit of an adventurer flowing through his blood, but he had not imagined the day would come so soon, or that Michele would set his sights on a land so far from home.

What could he do? What could he say? Michele and Isabella were young and full of life, excited about the possibilities of all that lay ahead of them. It would be selfish to try and make them feel guilty in order to change their minds. And even then, they might not, which would only make everyone feel worse.

He sighed heavily and closed a brawny hand over his son's shoulder. "Will you keep the vineyards?"

"I'd like to try. I've discovered they've been making wine in Virginia for a long time. Their industry's young by our standards, but a few vineyards have shown strong promise. There's speculation they could be producing award-winning wines someday."

Rodrigo was skeptical about that, but he heard the excitement in Michele's voice, and his brother had possessed an uncommon oneness with the grape—the growing and turning it into wine that sang to the soul. If Gino believed this land held promise for a successful vineyard, perhaps his dream just needed more time and nurturing to become a reality.

"You have not mentioned anything to your mother yet?"

Michele shook his head. "No. It was difficult enough telling you."

"She has a strong heart. It will heal." As would his own, Rodrigo told himself.

He turned and embraced his only child, holding him close as the sun rose higher and washed the tips of the new spring vines in soft, golden light that, despite the sadness weighing on his heart, whispered of promise.

One

Journeys end in lovers meeting,
Every wise man's son doth know.

William Shakespeare, *Twelfth Night*

Present Day

I'll take care of everything, Mr. Swan; just don't let your wife go to your room until I give you the signal." Lucia Bonavera gave the man standing beside the reception desk a conspiratorial wink.

Carl Swan nodded and then turned to go rejoin his coworkers who were mingling in the solarium where the winery usually conducted tastings.

"Oh." Swan spun back around. "What's the signal?"

Lucia grinned. Swan was adorable. He'd sought her out shortly after checking in to enlist her help with an anniversary surprise for his wife of thirty years. She didn't get to play cupid every day, but was happy to do so if it made her guest's stay a more memorable one.

"A nod and a wink." She gave an exaggerated wink and nod. "Just like that."

Swan rubbed his hands together, clearly anticipating his wife's reaction when she discovered his surprise.

"I better get back in there before Sue comes looking for me. I don't want her to get suspicious."

Lucia watched him go. *Love, it must be wonderful.*

"What are you looking all dreamy about?"

Lucia turned at her sister's question. "Hey, Marcella. It's Mr. Swan. He's so excited about surprising his wife for their anniversary. It's sweet. The guy's still crazy about her after thirty years."

"Listen to you sounding all romantic."

"Hey, I appreciate a good love story as much as the next person."

"Oh yeah, since when?"

"Since always. It's just, well—true love is a rare thing. That's why it's nice to see a couple like the Swans who still try to make each other happy after being together so long."

Lucia glanced at her watch and mentally calculated how much time she'd need to set everything up. "Speaking of which, were you able to get the chocolate and flowers when you went into town?"

"I got them. They're in your room." Marcella nodded toward the solarium. "How late are they scheduled for?"

"Until eight thirty. They were just served dinner, so they're in Cat's hands for now. Since you're here, I'll go set the stage in the Swans' room and be back with plenty of time to spare."

"Okay, go." Marcella walked around behind the reception desk and waved her off. "I don't want to get stuck making small talk with a bunch of forensic accountants. Their social skills are probably worse than mine."

"You're stereotyping. They're just ordinary people who happen to be extremely analytical, suspicious, and probably think everyone they meet is embezzling something."

"Yeah, just the type I want to chink glasses with over dessert."

"Don't worry, little sister, I'll be back before they get to dessert, so you don't have to stress over having to converse at any length with the guests."

After gathering everything she'd need, Lucia went up to the second floor where the guest rooms were located and slipped into the Swans' room.

Eliana, the marketing muscle of the family, had recommended naming the inn's rooms after different grape varietals. She'd said going with a wine theme would add to the fun for guests, and she'd been right. Most people got a kick out of it when Lucia told them they would be in Cabernet Franc, Petit Verdot, or whichever of the six guest rooms she put them in.

She'd originally scheduled the Swans in Seyval Blanc, but switched them to Viognier when Mr. Swan called her the day before their arrival to tell her he and his wife would be celebrating their thirtieth anniversary while they were there, and he wanted to surprise her. Viognier was the largest, and in Lucia's opinion, most romantic room—perfect for celebrating a milestone anniversary.

She took the vintage, white French water pitcher from the top of the antique bureau and filled it with water from the adjoining bath. She wanted to make an arrangement that would be as full and lush, as dreamy and romantic, as one in a Parisian oil painting.

Selecting twelve pink and twelve white roses from the three dozen Marcella picked up in town, she began inserting them into the pitcher, trimming some of the stems so they weren't all the same height, then rearranged and fluffed until she got the effect she wanted. She positioned the arrangement in front of the bureau's mirror so the lustrous display would reflect in the sparkling glass along with the flickering candles she intended to light just before the Swans returned to their room.

After a quick search online earlier in the day, she'd discovered lilies were the traditional flower for a thirtieth anniversary, but Mr. Swan told her roses were his wife's favorite, so Lucia had foregone tradition. The woman should have what she loved most, and really, did anything beat roses for romance?

Stepping back, she angled her head left, then right, studying the arrangement with a critical eye.

"Perfect."

Next, she filled the clear glass votive holders she'd brought up with fresh candles. She put a few on the bureau, the fireplace mantle, and a couple on each night table. Taking the remaining roses, six pink and six white, she pulled off the flower heads, scattered a handful of petals across the bed, and then, while walking backwards toward the door, tossed them into the air, a few here, a few there, to fall where they would, like blossoms scattered on a breeze.

Before going back down to the main level, Lucia took one final look from the doorway, and smiled at the results. *Happy Anniversary, Mr. and Mrs. Swan.*

WHEN SHE GOT back down to reception, Lucia poked her head into the solarium to see how things were progressing. Caterina hovered over the dessert table, checking to make sure the presentation met the same exacting standards her sister insisted on with whatever came out of one of her kitchens.

"Everything looks delicious, Cat." Lucia sidled up next to her. She plucked up a miniature cheesecake that had been topped with burnt sugar, a small piping of crème fresh, and a slice of kiwi, split and arranged *just so* on the crème, and took a bite. "And tastes amazing." She licked a stray speck of the decadent cream from her upper lip.

Her sister promptly rearranged the remaining cakes to fill the hole left by Lucia's pilfering.

"Thanks. The waitstaff's clearing dinner now. Dessert's self-serve, and Carlos will be on hand if anyone wants more wine."

"Okay. How'd things go?"

"Good. We only had one minor incident when a guest knocked his wine over and spilled it on a woman's dress. Fortunately, it was white and cleaned up with some club soda."

Cat leaned closer and lowered her voice. "I think the guy had too much to drink; unfortunately, it's made him think he's a ladies' man. It doesn't seem like he's had much practice, though; he's not very smooth—*hey babe*."

Lucia arched a questioning brow.

"We dubbed him *hey babe*. That's been his come-on line with all the female staff."

Lucia gave her an eye roll and popped the rest of the miniature cheesecake into her mouth, finished it off. "I'll let the group know they can help themselves to dessert and then—"

"Hey babe."

The two sisters turned in tandem to face the man who'd spilled the wine. Lucia recognized him from when he'd checked in—Bill Riley. He'd seemed quiet and shy, and, although she was doing exactly what she'd accused Marcella of by stereotyping, he'd fit her preconceived notion of someone who analyzed paper trails for a living, right down to the two mechanical pencils he'd had in his shirt pocket when he arrived.

He looked between the two of them and did some weird thing with his lips and eyebrows.

Lucia suspected the wiggling brows and quirking lips were an attempt to look sexy, but in his inebriated state he'd taken it beyond slightly amusing to ridiculously comical. She covered her mouth and faked a cough to disguise the laugh that slipped past her lips before she could stop it.

Cat cleared her throat and faced Lucia. "I've got to get back to the kitchen." Humor danced in her eyes but she kept her composure, at least until she walked away and Lucia saw her shoulders shaking.

Hey babe still stood in front of her.

"Is there something I can help you with?" Lucia asked.

Riley wore a goofy-looking grin, likely the result of an alcohol-induced brain fog. She didn't think he was a bad guy, or a letch. He was just Bill, a forensic accountant who'd had one too many drinks and would regret it in the morning.

"It's Mr. Riley, correct?" Lucia gave him a pleasant, but professional smile.

"You can call me Bill, babe. I was just going to get another drink. Why don't I get us both one?" He leaned toward her and she leaned away.

"No drinks for me, Bill. I'm working. In fact, I need to make an announcement about dessert." She stepped sideways, picking up a plate as she did, and held it between them. "Here, you can be first in line. Help yourself to some coffee to go with it."

She left him standing there, and after addressing the group, made a beeline back to reception.

MARCELLA LOOKED UP from her book as Lucia approached the large antique desk that served as command central for the inn. Lucia had refinished the ornately carved piece, a family heirloom that had belonged to their great-aunt Rosa whose parents had built the original house in the 1930s.

Rosa had travelled to Italy the summer she turned twenty-eight, supposedly to visit a childhood friend who'd moved there a number of years earlier.

Their parents told them the real reason was that Rosa was having doubts about her fiancé, a local Virginia man she was to marry that fall, and the trip was an excuse to put distance between them while she tried to figure out what was in her heart.

While in Italy, Rosa met their great-uncle Gino and the two fell deeply in love. He returned with her to the States, where she broke her prior engagement and shortly afterward married Gino.

The newlyweds lived with Rosa's parents, inheriting the house when the older couple died. They lived there five more years, and by all accounts were very happy. Unfortunately, their happiness ended abruptly when Rosa's former fiancé snapped one day and murdered them both in what was believed to be a crime of passion.

Lucia's parents, who'd come from Cortona to help her grandparents settle the estate, fell in love with the area and remained in Virginia to start a new life. Had it not been for Rosa marrying her uncle and the tragic consequences of that action, her parents might never have left Italy, and her life would probably be very different.

Her parents built on to the house in the mid-nineties, adding the large solarium where they did wine tastings, and removed the wall between the original parlor and study, opening the rooms up to each other. At that same time, their mother, who'd always loved a house full of people, converted the second floor of their family home into guest rooms and opened a bed and breakfast.

The current reception area had little in the way of furniture: the main desk, a tall wooden swivel rack that held brochures of local attractions and restaurant menus, and next to the solarium doorway, a large buffet with storage cabinets on the back side and a wide marble countertop that served as a refreshment bar.

When guests were in residence, they could help themselves to complimentary coffee, tea, fresh fruit, bagels, as well as Caterina's homemade muffins or scones. From noon to four, there were cookies, tea, and the inn's signature lemonade with fresh mint.

"The group finished dinner," Lucia told Marcella. She thought of Riley and frowned. He was a guest, and she always tried to make every guest's experience with them a positive one. It was clear he'd overindulged and she had a suspicion he'd probably regret his actions when he sobered up. She was hopeful that she wouldn't have another encounter with him when she went back into the solarium. She didn't want to have to say or do anything that would add to his embarrassment tomorrow if she could avoid it.

She gathered her long hair and twisted it into a loose braid, securing it at the end with a hair band she had in her pocket. "I'll need to run up to the Swans' room before they break up to light the candles. Are you good here until the group wraps up?"

"I'm fine." Marcella gave her a quizzical look. "Everything okay? You seem distracted."

"I was just thinking about one of the guests." Lucia told her sister about *hey babe*. "I'm pretty sure it's the alcohol doing the flirting, though." She sighed lightly. "If he persists, I'll need to find a way to discourage him without making too big a deal of it. I don't want to hurt his feelings."

"Why not use your trump card? It's usually effective when you're trying to turn down someone gently that you've just met."

"I've never used it with a guest, but I suppose I could." Lucia slapped a hand over her heart and drew the other across her forehead. "I'm flattered, Bill, I am, but alas, I can't get involved with you. I'm betrothed—promised to another—I'm sure you understand."

"Are you going to get all breathy and sigh like that?"

"Too heavy on the drama?"

Marcella sniggered.

"Okay." Lucia switched gears. "I'm back in there to watch over things, and if need be, try to salvage a man's pride for when he comes to his senses."

Just before she reached the solarium, Lucia heard the front door swing open and looked back over her shoulder. A man stepped inside, looked around, and then approached the front desk.

Everyone staying with them for the conference had checked in, so if he was with the forensic accountants, he must be staying at one of the other hotels they'd coordinated with to accommodate the rest of the group. If he was coming for this evening's kick-off dinner, he was getting to the party late since the main course had already being cleared.

Marcella set down her book. "Good evening, how can I help you?"

"Good evening," the man returned, and Lucia detected a slight accent.

He was tall, with dark hair that was pushed back over his forehead, a little longish—black silk, straight and thick, roguish as hell—hair that made a woman's fingers itch to run through it and muss it up.

He was angled toward the desk so Lucia didn't have a good view of his face, just a partial glimpse of a patrician profile. She hoped he didn't want a room because they were fresh out.

Marcella glanced at her and hiked a brow, as if to ask if Lucia wanted something. The man turned his head, his gaze following Marcella's. His eyes connected with Lucia's and she tumbled into them.

Everything around her blurred. The rest of the room faded. There was only he, only she, staring at each other as if seeing something they couldn't believe existed. A ripple of energy shot through her, unexplainable, unsettling, yet as real and undeniable as the air around her.

Lucia looked away, a bit dazed. She turned back toward the doorway and, shaking the residual haze from her head, walked into the solarium.

She spotted Caterina across the room, but as she set off in her sister's direction, her thoughts remained on the man in reception. Who was he...and what had caused that bizarre, overpowering attraction to a man she didn't even know?

25

"UMM, EXCUSE ME? Can I help you?"

Antonio forced his eyes from the woman walking into the adjoining room. He turned back to the one who greeted him. She bore a strong enough resemblance to the one who just left to guess they were related...probably sisters. She looked slightly younger, but had the same chestnut hair and dark eyes.

Fortunately, when he looked at this woman, the floor didn't seem to give way and make him feel like he was free-falling the way it had when he'd locked eyes with the other one.

"Yes, hello." He extended a hand and she took it, gave it a firm, no-nonsense shake. "I'm looking for Lucia Bonavera. Are you she?"

"No, I'm her sister Marcella."

"And the other one, she's one of your sisters as well? You resemble each other." From what he knew, there would be four of them, four sisters who owned and operated Bonavera Winery and Guest House.

"Yes, she is." Marcella seemed to be fighting a smile. No doubt she'd observed whatever that was that just happened between him and her sister and found it amusing. "That was Lucia, the person you said you were looking for."

And that's what he'd been afraid of.

He hadn't wanted to come to Virginia to search her out, but his grandfather had him over a barrel. He'd been planning a visit to the States for months, and since DC was on his list of places to visit anyway, he'd agreed to stop by the winery to meet the Bonaveras with the hope he could debunk the old man's superstitions and convince him to see reason once and for all.

He hadn't anticipated he might be attracted to Lucia. *Physical...it was purely physical. It had nothing to do with fate or any other nonsensical notion.*

Marcella cleared her throat, bringing him back to the moment. When he looked at her again she asked, "Are you with the forensic accountants group?"

LUCIA

"Forensic accountants?"

"I didn't think so," she said with a soft chuckle. "Then, how can I help you?"

"I'm travelling through the area and was hoping to get a room." He didn't know if the Bonaveras had ever heard of him or their grandfathers' ridiculous betrothal contract. Either way, when he told them who he was, they were bound to wonder what he was doing here now.

Marcella pulled a large leather registry from the desk drawer. "There's a group here for a two-day conference and I think we're booked tonight and tomorrow, but I don't usually work in reception so I'll double-check. If we don't have anything, I can call around to see if someplace nearby has availability." She flipped open the book. "What's your name?"

"Antonio. Antonio DeLuca."

She started to write it down on another piece of paper. Her hand froze midstream and her eyes flew up to his face. "Antonio De-DeLuca?" Her lips parted, her expression mirrored disbelief, and he had his answer—they knew who he was.

Marcella started to laugh, and then slapped a hand over her mouth. "Did you know that was...before you asked...that she was—?"

"No."

"Oh, this is too rich. Wait until Cat and Eliana find out."

"Your other sisters, I presume?"

"Yes." She eyed him a moment. "What are you doing here? Did she know you were coming?"

He shook his head. "No. I'm in the States on holiday. My grandfather asked me to look up your family and give you his regards while I was here. He and your grandfather were very close, like brothers."

"Yes, I know." The corners of her mouth twitched humorously. "Your visit doesn't have anything to do with that old marriage

27

pact they made, does it? I mean, you're not...like...here to claim your bride or something, are you?"

"Hell, no!" He assured her, dispelling the possibility. Claiming Lucia might be what his grandfather intended him to do, but Antonio had a different agenda.

He pulled a frown. "I'd venture to say that agreement came about after our grandfathers consumed a couple of bottles of heady wine that took the wishful thinking of two old men too far. They got it into their heads that because your sister and I were born on the same day, the same one they both were, it was a sign of some kind. Fate, destiny, all that nonsense."

"You're not a believer?"

"No. Are you?"

Marcella shrugged.

"Is Lucia?"

"God no! And she'd never let anyone dictate how or with whom she spent her life."

A wave of relief flowed through him. "That's good. I wouldn't want her to think...never mind." If what Marcella said was true, maybe he could use this detour to his advantage. "Does it look like you've got a room?"

Marcella glanced back down at the registry. "No. I'm sorry, I don't see anything."

"Well then, since I'm not familiar with the area, I'll take you up on your offer. I'm sure it will be more efficient than me trying to find something else."

"No problem."

"Thank you. Would it be okay if I stepped into the other room and said hello to your sister? I promised my grandfather I'd look her up, and I may not have another opportunity to come by."

Marcella glanced toward the room where Lucia had disappeared into earlier. "She's overseeing a function, but they're winding down so there's not much for her to do now. Go ahead. I'm sure she'd be disappointed if she found out her fiancé came all the way from Italy to see her and she missed him."

A MAN IN khaki slacks and a white dress shirt and holding two glasses of wine staggered up to Lucia. He pushed one forward, tilting it precariously toward her dress.

"Hey babe, you're back," he slurred. "I saw you come in again so I got us each a drink." He swayed, looking unsteady on his feet. "Did you miss me? I missed you."

Lucia stepped backward, toward a table with desserts that she'd been straightening when Antonio entered the room. She hadn't seen him yet, and he held back to gauge the situation.

"I'm working, so I can't drink, remember?" he heard her say. She took both glasses before he could object and set them down next to the desserts. "But I'll tell you what, let's just leave these here and I'll get us both a cup of coffee."

She gestured toward an empty table a few feet from where they stood. "Why don't you go sit at that table and I'll bring it over."

The man leaned in again, closer than appropriate if he was a guest, and wagged his head mere inches from her face. "Why don't you bring it up to my room instead, babe? We can have our own party, just you and me."

Antonio took a few steps forward but stopped again when Lucia placed a hand against the man's shoulder, holding him at bay. "I can't do that, Mr. Riley. No fraternizing with the guests. House rule. You do understand, don't you?"

The guy pouted. "Don't you like me? You were being so nice. I thought you liked me."

"Of course I like you, Mr. Riley, but I'm afraid you mistook my friendliness for more than it is, and I'm sorry for that. You see, the truth is—I'm engaged."

Riley wrinkled his brow. "You are?" He looked at her hand. "But...but you're not wearing a ring."

"No, I'm not, but that's because...well...I haven't found the right one yet."

The guy seemed to mull that over then said, "You're not just making this up because you don't like me, are you?"

"Of course not. I...I..."

Antonio closed the distance between them. "Good evening, darling." He leaned in from behind and kissed Lucia on the side of the cheek. "I'm sorry I'm late. I got held up on a call."

She spun around, wobbled on her heels, and stared up at him with huge, startled eyes the color of jet black ink—liquid ebony.

He reached out and took hold of her elbows, steadying her. Registering her stunned expression, he gave a subtle wink.

She caught on and he felt her relax under his touch. The shock ebbed from her eyes and he detected a flash of relief in their fathomless depths.

"Who are you?" Riley asked.

"I'm her fiancé." Antonio extended a hand toward the other man. "Are you a friend of hers?"

"N-no, I'm...I was j-just t-talking to her." It took several seconds before he noticed Antonio's outstretched hand and tentatively took it. "Bill Riley," he said, and started to back away just as another man walked up to them.

"We're going to be going up to our room in about ten minutes," the newcomer said, addressing his comment to Lucia. "You told me to give you a heads-up."

"Okay, great, Mr. Swan. I'll go put the final touches on everything now." She looked at Antonio, gave him an almost imperceptible nod of thanks, and then glanced at Riley. "If you'll excuse me, gentlemen, I need to go take care of something."

She hurried from the room, leaving the three of them standing there to watch after her.

"I didn't know she was engaged." Riley sounded a bit nervous, as if he were worried Antonio might be upset.

"I'm sure you didn't. No harm done." Antonio patted him on the back.

Swan studied Riley with a look of concern. "Bill, how much have you had to drink? You don't look well."

Riley squeezed his eyes shut. Although he didn't know the man, Antonio had to agree with Swan that Riley looked a bit green.

"I'm not sure." Riley rubbed his forehead. "I think I might have overdone it, though. You know I'm not much of a drinker, Carl."

Swan put his arm around Riley's shoulder and turned him toward the dining area. "Let's get you some water and then maybe you should go to your room and lie down. Our meetings start at eight tomorrow and you don't want to show up with a head banger."

He led Riley away, sitting him down at the nearest table and pouring him some water. He signaled another man over and said something to him. The new guy nodded and sat down at the table with Riley, probably charged with making sure he made it to his room okay.

Antonio slid his hands into his pockets and strolled back out to the lobby. Marcella still sat at the desk, reading a book. Lucia was nowhere in sight and he assumed she'd gone to take care of whatever final touches she'd been talking to Swan about.

"Oh, hey," Marcella said when she looked up and saw him. "How'd it go with Lucia? I'll bet you floored her."

"Well, actually, I don't think she realizes who I am, even though I said I was her fiancé. We didn't really get a chance to talk; she was...occupied when I went in."

"Really? I didn't think she'd be too busy."

"There wasn't a lot happening, but she was busy. Busy trying to fend off some guy who'd indulged beyond his limit and mistook your sister's friendliness for something else."

"Oh." Marcella chuckled. "*Hey babe.*"

"Excuse me?"

"The guy. My sister Cat dubbed him *hey babe* because that's what he'd say whenever he approached any of the women in there tonight."

Antonio heard the unmistakable click, click, click, click of spiked heels announcing a brisk approach down the hallway on the other side of the open French doors to the left of the inn's main entrance.

His pulse quickened as their staccato rhythm echoed crisply against the wooden floorboards. Lucia had been wearing high heels—a delightful pair of black strappy stilettos that showcased her long legs to perfection.

He turned toward the sound. A rush of anticipation sped through him as quickly as a flame would engulf a rope that had been soaked in kerosene.

Lucia breezed through the doorway and into the reception area, a classic beauty with a confident gait, and the flame spiked hotter.

She saw him almost immediately and her eyes widened. Antonio heard her quick, sharp intake of breath and swore he felt a jolt of desire slam into her as strongly as the one that smacked into him, as if they were somehow connected and he was experiencing it with her.

"You." She slowed her pace, and he wondered if she did so to ground herself before crossing the room. She stopped in front of the desk and glanced at her sister, a smile flirting with her lips, and then nodded in his direction.

"My hero." The smile gave way to a lighthearted chuckle. "He came to my rescue with *hey babe*."

Lucia set the small box she'd been holding down on the desk and turned to face him. "Which I didn't get to properly thank you for. So thank you."

He gave a mock bow. "Happy to be of service." He straightened, caught a whiff of her perfume—subtle, sophisticated, and haunting. It reminded him of the jasmine growing on the trellis at the little trattoria back home where they made his favorite minestrone. It suited her.

"The man seemed determined," Antonio said, not able to blame the guy for trying. What man, especially one whose courage had been bolstered by the fruits of the vine, wouldn't be tempted to try their luck with her? "When he started questioning your story, I thought it might be a good time for your fiancé to materialize."

"Well, you played it nicely. He clearly had too much to drink. You saved me from having to get too heavy-handed with a guest, so I'm grateful."

Lucia walked around and behind the desk and picked up a pad of sticky notes. Antonio saw Marcella looking between them. Amusement danced in her eyes, as if she couldn't wait to see what would happen next.

"I hope you weren't looking for a room." Lucia jotted something on the pad, pulled off the top piece of paper, and stuck it on top of a stack of folders that were piled neatly on the desk. "We're booked for the next two nights."

"Marcella already explained the situation. She found something for me in Middleburg."

"Oh, okay. Where'd you book him?" Lucia asked her sister.

"The Hunt and Hound. Since it's his first time to the area, I thought he might enjoy staying someplace that oozed history."

Lucia nodded. "Good choice."

She regarded him again. "You'll like it there. It's charming, and if you're around for lunch, you might want to try their Peanut Soup and spoon bread, my personal favorites."

Their eyes held for several seconds before she laughed somewhat self-consciously, and said, "You know, the least I can do to thank you for coming to my rescue is offer you a glass of wine before you leave...if you're not in a rush. And there's plenty of dessert left over from our group's event if you'd like some. I can promise our sister Caterina's desserts are worth a try."

"That isn't necessary, but I'm not one to turn down wine and sweets. I have a fondness for both." He did, but he also had a fondness for intriguing women, and she intrigued him.

He saw no harm in joining her for a glass of wine and dessert, and doing so would also give him an opportunity to gauge if she might be an asset in dealing with his grandfather.

"Good. I'm Lucia, by the way." She thrust a hand toward him and he took it. Her palm felt warm, silken, her fingers long, and he wondered what they might feel like if she were to lay them on other parts of his skin. It was a natural reaction. She was a beautiful woman, and he was attracted to her; there was no denying it, but he wouldn't let a physical attraction get in the way of his plans, no matter how strong.

"And you are?" Her eyes delved into his and she cocked her head, waiting for an answer.

Marcella laughed, and he and Lucia both shot her a look before reconnecting.

"Why, I'm your betrothed, darling."

Lucia pinned him with a look of amusement through siren's eyes that sparkled like black onyx jewels. "And does my betrothed have a name?"

"He does." Antonio searched her face, absorbing every nuance, and despite his agenda couldn't help but be enchanted. "Antonio," he said, watching for her reaction. "Antonio DeLuca."

She blinked as his name must have registered and then her lips parted.

"Wait." She gave a slight shake of her head and stared up at him with the same expression of incredulity he might have been wearing if their situation were reversed. "You mean, you're...then you really are—"

"Your fiancé," he finished for her.

SHE AND ANTONIO had been sitting in the solarium for the last hour, sharing in a little flirtation and a bottle of Seyval Blanc, one from their cellars, and a lovely vintage at that. Lucia held up the bottle and he nodded. She poured them each some more.

It would be evident to anyone who saw them together they were attracted to each other, but nothing would come of it. They were the proverbial ships in the night, and within days at most, he'd be hoisting his sails, steering a course that would eventually take him home, to another country, another life, and one that had nothing to do with hers. Too bad—she enjoyed his company and wouldn't mind sharing a bit more of it—perhaps because she knew he *was* safe, posed no risk to her heart.

She watched him as he talked about the betrothal contract their grandfathers had drawn up almost thirty years earlier. Watched his expressions, took in the contours of his cheeks and strong jaw, breathed a little heavier over his gorgeous mouth...oh, he was easy on the eyes.

"They were convinced we were meant to merge our families' bloodlines." He shook his head and grinned at her. "I don't remember your grandfather, just stories, but if he was still alive, I have no doubt they'd be double-teaming us."

He swirled his glass and took a sip of wine, rolled it in that gorgeous mouth. "I see by the label it's one of yours. I wasn't sure what to expect from Virginia wines, but I like it."

"Thank you. Virginia's putting out some wonderful wines right now, has been for years, but people are just beginning to discover how good. This is one of last year's vintages. Marcella oversees the wine production, and she knows her stuff. We've won a couple of awards."

"That's impressive. What about the rest of you?"

"We inherited the winery from our parents. They died in a car accident just over three years ago. It's our primary source of revenue right now, so that's the main focus, but we've each got specialty areas we'd like to utilize more.

"Caterina's the chef at Caulfield's. It's a restaurant in Ashburn, one of the local towns. She also does catering, mostly here at the winery, but other events when she can.

"She and Marcella are twins, and the youngest. Cat used to be the sous chef for a five-star restaurant in New York. After our parents died, we weren't sure what to do about the winery. Marcella and Eliana were the only two still living here at the time, and Eliana was on the road a lot. Marcella was adamant against selling. The winery and the vineyards are her life, the only one she's ever known, and we all grew up here, so none of us were keen on the idea of selling the family house. We agreed to keep it running on a trial basis, three or four years, to see if we could make a go of it on our own."

A lock of hair fell down across Antonio's forehead. Lucia watched with some fascination as he reached up with long, lean fingers, brushed it back, and resettled his hand on the table. She wanted to reach out, run her own hand over his head, feel the thick, silkiness of his hair wrapping around her fingers, and the desire to do so surprised her.

The attraction that tugged at her wasn't natural. It was too strong. It went beyond the physical awareness, and it didn't make sense to her, the way it seemed to consume her so quickly and completely. She'd never experienced anything like it before, and if she didn't know he'd be leaving soon, it might give her cause for concern.

She shifted and crossed her legs, took a moment before continuing. "Eliana left her job with a marketing firm in DC, and now she handles all the marketing and event planning for us. She oversees the wine tastings, too. Marcella didn't want to be involved with them, even though she's more knowledgeable than any of us, so she only conducts tastings when she has to; she prefers to talk to vines, not people. Eliana thrives on social interaction, and with her experience in sales and marketing the tastings fit logically under her wing."

"And what about you?" He forked a piece of cheesecake from his plate. He popped it into his mouth and then angled his head, watched her.

Lucia traced the tip of her index finger around the rim of her wine glass. She'd never once imagined what he might look like, be like. In her mind, he hadn't been real, just a convenient excuse she could whip out as needed. But, here he was, and in the brief time they'd spent talking, they seemed to share an undeniable connection.

He interested her. And the longer they sat there talking, the more she experienced of him, the stronger her desire to crawl into his lap and taste their Seyval Blanc on his tongue, to see if she could detect the citrus notes lingering on that velvet temptation. It was crazy!

A dangerous man, indeed...and, of course, she wouldn't give in to it, despite the unexplainable pull he exerted over her. She didn't know him, and once he moved on—in a day, two, three, however long—the probability of seeing him again were about as likely as a heat wave in January. Not impossible, but she'd never experienced one in Virginia in her lifetime.

Lucia uncrossed her legs and cleared her throat. "I used to work at a boutique hotel in New York, but like Cat, I moved back home when we agreed to try to make a go with the winery. Our mom converted the second floor here to guest rooms and opened the inn about fifteen years ago, so that was already established, and since I had hospitality experience, we agreed I'd take that over. I also pinch-hit for Eliana with some of the events she can't cover, like the one tonight."

They chatted for another ten minutes or so. When he finished his second glass of wine, he pushed back from the table and stood up, roughly six-feet-two inches of *off-limits* male that made Lucia want to cluck her tongue with disappointment over the fact.

"I should get going. Thanks for the wine and the dessert. It was nice meeting you."

Lucia stood as well and stuck out her hand. "Nice to meet you too." They shook, and she half-wished he'd tug her forward—close—to test the waters, to play with the fire. He didn't. "And thanks again for earlier, with *hey babe*."

"No problem. If I can't rescue my fiancé from groping drunks, what good am I?"

They walked outside together, onto the inn's large, wrap-around front porch. Lucia wished they'd had a vacancy, that he could have stayed with them and she might be looking forward to seeing him again tomorrow, just once more, instead of saying goodbye tonight. She'd enjoyed their brief time together and was sorry to see it end.

"I'm glad you looked us up. If you ever plan to come back to the area, let us know in advance and we'll hold a room for you."

He nodded and then fixed his eyes on hers. Sinfully sexy, cobalt blues under lashes so thick it should have been illegal they belonged to a man. "I feel like we should hug goodbye. After all, we are engaged." He opened his arms—an invitation—and Lucia stepped into them without thought, without hesitation.

She was cautious with men, ever since Brad. Their grandfathers had been like brothers, though. She and Antonio were, in a way, almost family. A brief parting hug seemed appropriate, as appropriate as if she were saying goodbye to any other relative. But it wasn't brief, and the desire to nuzzle against him was an enticement she never felt when she hugged one of her sisters.

Antonio tightened his hands on her shoulders and pulled her in closer. His heart beat strong, steady, and hauntingly welcoming where her cheek lay against his chest. To Lucia, it felt like an embrace—more comfortable than she'd expected, more intimate than intended, and sadder than it should because really, it meant nothing.

The sadness surprised her, that she would feel it so deeply, that a stranger could stir such a reaction within her in such a short amount of time.

He let her go and Lucia took a couple of steps backward. She wrapped her arms around her waist, missing the physical comfort of him. He was broad, his chest firm, she'd felt the hard muscle of him under his shirt. What woman wouldn't have felt good leaning into that?

She cleared her throat. "So, enjoy the rest of your time in the States."

"I will try to." He turned around and walked purposefully away—out of her life—his long legs making quick work of the winding slate walkway that led from the main building to the drive and the large gravel parking area beyond.

Lucia remained on the porch and watched his car turn out of the winery's entrance onto Old Sanders Road, until she could no longer see the receding taillights.

Safe journeys, Antonio DeLuca. Buon viaggio...I think I am going to miss you.

Two

From wine what sudden friendship springs!
John Gay, "The Squire and His Cur"

Antonio tucked the tails of his white shirt into his jeans. He snagged his wallet and keys from the bedside table, exited the room, and jogged down the stairs to the first floor of the Hunt and Hound Inn and Tavern.

He'd read in their brochure that a fire destroyed most of the original building in the early 1800s. It was rebuilt shortly afterward but suffered another in the 1920s. The current building had been erected on the same site shortly thereafter, at which time the owners expanded on the original design to include more guest rooms and a larger dining room. The fieldstone walls, large fireplaces, and artwork, all contributed to the sense that one had stepped into the past.

For convenience sake, Antonio decided to have breakfast at the inn's restaurant. He'd looked over the menu after checking in and found the selection to be quite extensive, the prices very reasonable.

The hostess greeted him immediately and led him into a cozy dining area, seating him at a table next to a massive fireplace. The scent of smoked bacon mingled with that of fresh-baked biscuits, coffee, sweet maple syrup, and his mouth salivated in anticipation.

He scanned the menu, several items tempting him, and after going back and forth a few times, decided on pecan French toast with caramelized bananas and a side of Applewood smoked bacon, neither of which he'd ever had before but was anxious to try.

After giving the server his order, he pulled out his phone and scrolled through the dozen or so new messages for anything requiring his attention.

He'd entrusted the running of his architectural firm to the other two architects on staff, Rick and Maria, both capable of handling any of their projects, but asked them to let him know if anything major came up.

Seeing nothing urgent, he put the phone away and settled back in his chair, the low lighting, soft music, and casual atmosphere of the inn's tavern infusing him with a sense of calm.

In the six years since he'd started the firm, this was the first time he'd taken any extended time off. He'd worked hard to make it a success, and although he hated being in his debt, especially now, he wouldn't have been able to do it without his grandfather's help.

His grandfather had convinced Antonio to let him give him a loan for the start-up. Antonio hadn't discovered until recently that he'd lent the money under false pretenses. That didn't change the fact that if he couldn't get the old man to see reason soon, he could lose everything he'd worked to build.

Antonio frowned. He didn't plan on letting that happen, and if making a pit stop in Virginia to meet the woman who stood in the way of his financial independence could help his cause, then spending a few extra days in this area to get to know her would be worth it.

He'd always wanted to see more of America, to experience firsthand the country of his birth. After all, although he considered himself Italian, he was also a U.S. citizen.

He'd travelled to Florida every year on holiday to visit with his mother's family until about the time he turned twelve and his parents had been killed in a freak boating accident off the Florida coast. As an adult he'd returned to attend conferences and to work on a project in upstate New York a couple of years ago. He had an NCARB certificate, which he'd needed for a state to license him, and since the company he'd been working for had told him they might want him to work on something else for them in the DC area, he'd gotten licensed to work in New York as well as the Commonwealth.

Those visits had all been work related though, and he hadn't had time for sightseeing. Since he'd agreed to his grandfather's mandate that he come here, he might as well take advantage of what the area offered. DC was a hotbed of museums, including the Museum of Natural History, part of the Smithsonian's cluster, and the International Spy Museum, which he'd always wanted to visit. If he stuck around a few more days, he could squeeze in one or two.

Perhaps Lucia would go with him to some of the local wineries. She'd know which ones had the best reputations. Afterward, they could get dinner—someplace unhurried, where they could linger over the possibilities the night held. Sharing an intimate meal with a woman was a sensual experience he always enjoyed—good food, good wine, easy conversation—they were aphrodisiacs he never tired of. Throw in Lucia Bonavera and—. It was a recipe for seduction.

Antonio drummed his fingers on the tabletop. Their grandfathers' agreement meant nothing to him, nothing more than a pact between two lifelong friends—a product of superstition and a bit of wishful thinking.

What person in their right mind would expect him to honor a thirty-year-old agreement that he'd had no say in?

His grandfather.

Not only had the old man insisted he make this detour to meet and try to woo Lucia, he'd maneuvered him into a position that his financial independence could be threatened if he didn't. He knew his nonno believed what he'd done was for Antonio's own good, but he was being irrational and nothing Antonio tried had been able to get the man to see reason.

Antonio poured himself more coffee from the carafe the waitress left on the table.

When and if the time came that he fell in love, he would choose his own wife. He had no intention of trying to court the woman; still, he'd agreed to look Lucia up, if for no other reason than to debunk his grandfather's beliefs. To prove there had been no karma, no kismet, no attraction whatsoever when they met, and fate could not care less if they ever saw each other again.

Unfortunately, that wasn't completely true. He'd definitely felt an attraction. It was an interesting development, unexpected certainly, but truth be told, she intrigued him.

Antonio finished his meal and exited the restaurant a short while later, a frown tugging the corners of his mouth. Fate might not care if he ever saw Lucia again after meeting her last night, but he wasn't as anxious to continue on to New York as he'd thought he'd be.

If he stayed a few more days, it would be entirely his choice. He didn't have a set schedule, and the more he knew about Lucia, the better he could use that knowledge to argue marrying her would be a mistake for both of them. And if he could prove somehow that Lucia was just as dead set against it, then surely his nonno wouldn't hold Antonio to the agreement he and Lucia's grandfather made that had him by the balls.

It was a beautiful spring morning, and after eating such a large breakfast, Antonio was in the mood to walk it off and stretch his legs.

The Hunt and Hound was on a quiet side street on the outskirts of the quaint village. He walked down to the main street and headed into town.

Middleburg was steeped in history. Many of the buildings that housed the wide assortment of shops and restaurants, like the inn he'd stayed at last night, displayed plaques identifying them to be on the National Historic Registry. Everywhere he looked he saw something to do with horses, fox, and the hunt. If he'd woken up here and didn't know where he was, he might think he was in an English village.

He walked under a cherry tree. Its pale pink blossoms sprinkled down around him on the morning breeze, carpeting the brick sidewalk under its umbrella. The town was small and it wasn't long before he found himself back where he'd started.

When he returned to his room a few minutes later, he noticed the brochure he'd taken from the Bonavera Winery & Guest House the night before laying on the bedside table. He picked it up and leafed through it. As he did, his mind conjured an image of Lucia, the way she'd watched him, humor in her eyes and a smile on her lips as they'd chatted.

He heard the husky timbre of her voice in his head, the way it had resonated along his nerves every time she spoke or laughed... and how much he'd wanted to lean forward to taste the flavor of her words, that laugh...and yes, to feel them vibrate against his tongue as they rolled into his mouth and faded into a kiss. It had been a struggle not to kiss her when she hugged him goodbye.

He tapped the brochure against his other hand, and with only a passing thought about the repercussions, made a change in plans.

44

LUCIA BUSIED HERSELF straightening magazines, fluffing the floral arrangements, and restocking brochures while she and her sisters waited for Eliana to arrive for their Tuesday morning update and planning meeting.

Cat and Marcella lounged in identical wing chairs flanking the stacked-stone fireplace in the library, arguing over the best romantic comedy ever made. Marcella thought nothing came close to *Princess Bride*. Cat insisted it was *Love Actually*. They each had their reasons, and Lucia thought both had valid ones, but she didn't see the point in debating it. Neither would convince the other to their way of thinking and in her mind they were both great movies, so what did it matter.

If they were dressed alike, and if Marcella cut her waist-brushing hair to match Cat's sleek shoulder-length bob, and bothered with makeup, her sisters would look like matched bookends. It always amazed her how two people who were so alike in every physical feature could be so different otherwise. But she loved them both the same and appreciated that they were unique in their own ways. Marcella, ever reserved, sensitive, thoughtful, a bohemian child of nature, felt more comfortable in the fields tending her vines or making wine than interacting with people.

Her twin preferred to be wielding a whisk in the kitchen. Caterina was the most exacting person Lucia knew, a creative perfectionist with a flair for the exotic, which she exhibited not only in the presentation of her wonderful dishes, but in her style choices as well.

"Hey, sorry I'm late." Eliana blew into the room like a gust of wind whipping down the mountains. The black leather purse slung over her shoulder swung freely, slapping against her hip with each opposing step. Her face, her hands, the tone of her voice, all told their own story. She was energy in motion and could raise the oomph meter in any room just by her presence.

She sat down on one of the three over-stuffed couches that formed a U-shaped seating area facing the wing chairs and the fireplace. Leaning forward, she poured herself a cup of coffee from the Wedgewood china pot that had been their mother's, and topped it off with a healthy dose of crème fresh.

"Man, you wouldn't believe the summersaults I had to do to line up Toby Knight and the Chugalug Boys for the fall festival. They're so hot right now they only had two open weekends before Thanksgiving that they hadn't committed to, one of them being the weekend of the festival. They had three other requests for gigs that weekend. But—" Eliana flashed them all a huge, beamer of a smile. "I worked my magic and convinced them to book with us. So major score for the Bonaveras!"

She pumped a celebratory fist in the air, took a sip of coffee, and sighed. "Thanks for this, Luch; I was hoping you'd make some. So what did I miss?"

"Nothing but the great rom-com debate," Lucia informed her, and reached for one of the cranberry-orange scones Cat had made for their meeting.

Eliana sat back and crossed her legs, one of her ankles immediately set to spinning in a circle that wouldn't stop until she stood back up. "Okay good, so nothing new."

"Nada," Lucia assured her.

"I'd like to set up some meetings with a couple of architects next week," Lucia put forth, getting down to the business at hand. "I know it may be premature since we haven't checked with the county yet, but it might help when we do to go in with some plans. I checked the calendar and it looks like everyone's free Tuesday, Thursday, and Friday mornings, so I'll see what I can arrange during those times."

They spent about ten more minutes discussing business, and when they were done, Cat zoomed in on Lucia. "Okay, now that

that's settled, what's this Marcella told me about Antonio DeLuca coming here from Italy to meet you?"

Eliana nearly spilled her coffee in her lap. "What! DeLuca was here? When did this happen? Why am I just hearing that your mythical fiancé showed up to collect you?"

Lucia laughed around the bite of the scone she'd just taken before swallowing it. "He didn't come to collect me. The real and more boring story is that he came to the States on holiday, and his grandfather asked him to look us up while he was here. He merely stopped in to say hello at the man's request because he and Nonno Bonavera were so close. He came by, we shared a bottle of wine, a few laughs over our grandfathers' archaic betrothal contract, and then he left."

"I can't believe we all missed him." Eliana put her cup on the large square table that anchored the seating area and then stood up. "Is he coming back to meet the rest of us? I'm dying to know what he's like."

Lucia shook her head. "No, he said he'd probably be leaving today or tomorrow morning to drive to New York. He was hoping to get a room here last night, but with the accountants' group we didn't have any availability. Marcella got him one at The Hunt and Hound."

Eliana swung her head in their sister's direction. "You met him?"

Marcella curled her mouth into a smile that begged explanation. "Oh yeah, I met him."

"Annnnd," Cat prompted, just as curious for details as Eliana.

"And if there'd been a pile of logs in the middle of the lobby, they would have spontaneously burst into flames with the sparks that were flying between the two of them."

"She's exaggerating," Lucia said, her lips twitching. *But not by much.* There had definitely been some strong chemistry between her and Antonio.

"I'm not exaggerating," Marcella countered. "You were practically drooling, and he looked like he'd been zapped with a stun gun or something."

"It must have been so weird to actually meet him when he's always been this—I don't know—kind of an imaginary person. He was gorgeous, wasn't he? I'll just bet he was, and you couldn't believe it because you never gave him any real thought and he walked in here last night and he was mouthwatering. I'm right, aren't I?" Eliana looked between Lucia and Marcella, clearly wanting the scoop.

"Pretty much," Lucia conceded. "But he was also funny and interesting. It would have been nice to have more time to get to know him a little better...you know, as friends."

"Yeah, right," Marcella said. "You wanted to suck tongue with him and you know it."

"You can be so crude, little sister."

"Deny, deny, deny." Marcella looked at the others. "She was all like...why don't you stay and have some wine?" She batted her lashes. "And dessert, there's plenty left over. It's the least I can do to thank you." She fluttered them some more.

Lucia rolled her eyes, and Cat and Eliana laughed.

"Thank him for what?" Eliana asked.

Marcella told Eliana the story about *hey babe*, how he'd started off hitting on Cat, then switched his attentions to Lucia, and how Antonio stepped in to come to the rescue when the man persisted.

"So did you really want to suck tongue with him?" Eliana's eyes gleamed with sisterly interest and a dash of humor.

Lucia ran her teeth over her bottom lip. "Okay," she confessed. "I'll admit I felt attracted to him, and I even wondered what it would be like to kiss him, but I also knew I'd never see him again. And you know what they say, sometimes not knowing is better."

The inn's phone rang and Eliana, who was closest to the desk, walked over and picked it up.

"Bonavera Winery and Guest House, how may I assist you?" As she listened, her lips curled and her eyes flew to Lucia's face. "Yes, let me see if she can take your call."

She put the call on hold and then cocked the handset in the air toward Lucia. Hiking a brow, she said, "It's Antonio DeLuca. Apparently, his plans have changed. He's going to be in town a few more days and he'd like to speak with you."

Three

Drink to me only with thine eyes,
And I will pledge with mine;
Or leave a kiss but in the cup,
And I'll not look for wine.

Ben Jonson, "Song to Celia"

O h, there you are, Lucia!"

Lucia turned away from the library's large fireplace mantle where she'd just placed the two large milk glass vases she'd filled with blue hydrangeas from the garden. She adored the luscious blossoms and couldn't imagine anyone not being enamored by them.

"Good morning, Mrs. Swan." Lucia picked up the ones she hadn't been able to fit into the vases from the coffee table as she walked past it. There were enough to make an arrangement for the reception desk as well.

"What can I do for you this morning?" she asked her guest.

"I want to thank you for everything you did to make last night so special. I thought Carl forgot all about our anniversary, but when we walked into our room, well, I just broke down and cried when I saw what he'd done. He told me he wouldn't have been able to pull off his surprise without you."

"I was happy to do it. It's nice to meet people like you and your husband who are still so much in love after thirty years. I hope I'll be as fortunate one day."

"Well," Mrs. Swan said, her perky voice reminding Lucia of the cheerful house finches that flocked to the feeders by the inn's side porch. "Carl told me that handsome man you were talking to before we left last night is your fiancé. I couldn't help but notice the two of you together. You make a stunning couple, and it was obvious you're smitten with each other."

"Oh, h-he...w-we," Lucia stuttered, not sure how to respond. She hadn't thought about the fact that Carl had overheard the conversation between Antonio and Mr. Riley the prior evening.

Not that it hurt anything for them to believe she and Antonio were really engaged. They'd all be leaving tomorrow, and she wouldn't want word to get back to Riley it had all been a ruse. When he'd come downstairs and had to walk past the reception desk this morning while she was talking to another guest, he'd looked mortified. She'd given him a friendly wave, as if nothing had happened, but she could tell he felt embarrassed and preferred not to add to his humiliation.

"No need to explain yourself, child. There's nothing wrong with letting the world know you're in love." Mrs. Swan winked at her. "Just look at Carl and me."

Two more women walked into reception, some of the other wives who'd accompanied their husbands to the conference.

"Good morning, Sue." One of the newcomers waved to Mrs. Swan. "You too, Lucia. We're all looking forward to our outing today."

Lucia had mapped out a tour of some local sites for the women to visit while their spouses attended meetings. She'd also arranged for them to have lunch at Twining Vines, a charming local restaurant that her best friend, Jenna, managed for her aging and eccentric Aunt Flora. It had a lovely outdoor patio, covered by a massive pergola planted with climbing roses and wisteria, and although the roses might not be blooming yet, the wisteria, with its showy, cascading purple clusters, should just be coming into full glory.

"Enjoy yourselves," Lucia said. "You have a beautiful day for it."

She followed the women outside, and after they drove away, pulled out the hose and started watering the potted plants in front of the inn.

Their guests were on their own for dinner. Most of them would be venturing out to try some of the area restaurants. Eliana had agreed to cover for her so she could go out with Antonio, insisted on it in fact, so Lucia couldn't use work as an excuse to turn him down.

Lucia grinned. Not that she would have. When he'd called to see if they could get together, she'd felt almost giddy, and she couldn't remember feeling excited about the prospect of going on a date with a man since...she actually couldn't remember when. And since she didn't have to worry there was any chance of falling in love with him and getting her heart broken...well, he was risk free.

She could enjoy the attraction for what it was, a delicious enticement, and be done with it when he was gone. Kind of like a scrumptious dessert, something she loved and would indulge in more often if she didn't have to deal with the consequences.

She pictured her pretend fiancé in her head: cerulean-blue eyes, jet-black hair, chiseled jaw, a killer smile, and strong arms that had held her a little closer than she'd expected last night...but not as close as she'd desired.

"Antonio, Antonio, wherefore art thou, Antonio?" Eliana's voice mocked from behind her.

Lucia turned and directed a spray of water from the hose at her sister.

Eliana burst into laughter and dodged out of the way. "I can't wait to meet this guy. I don't think I've ever seen you looking so dreamy-eyed."

"I don't get dreamy-eyed. That would be you, El." Lucia dangled the hose over a large, glazed, blue pot brimming with hardy red geranium, lobelia, curly parsley, and gave it a long drink.

"Oh yeah, well I'm beginning to believe Marcella that you dripped some drool over the guy. You were so wrapped up in your thoughts you didn't even hear me come outside."

"Maybe I was thinking about the architects we're going to meet with next week. We should probably make up an outline of everything we want done so we don't forget anything."

"I'm sure Cat's already done that." She eyed Lucia critically. "What are you going to wear tonight? Maybe your grey pencil pants...with that pale pink blouse, you know, the crepe one with the pearl buttons."

Lucia finished watering and walked over to the spigot. "I was thinking the white sundress you showed me last week, the billowy one with the back straps and rose sprays all over it."

"I haven't even worn that yet."

"Well, it's not like I'm going to be mucking a barn in it. We're just going to dinner." Lucia leaned forward and turned off the water. "It's the perfect casual date dress. If I'd seen it first, I would have bought it."

"Fine, you can wear it."

Lucia straightened and gave her sister a kiss on the cheek. "Thanks. What would I do without sisters?"

"Go naked?"

"Never on a first date," Lucia tossed back without missing a beat, causing her sister to snort as they linked arms and walked back into the inn together.

"SO WHAT ARE all of you supposed to be, the welcoming committee?" Lucia asked when she walked into the lobby that evening to wait for Antonio to pick her up for their date.

Eliana gave her a crooked grin. "We're just doing our duty and making sure he passes the sister test."

Lucia rolled her eyes. "Fine, but do me a favor and let him get inside before you launch an inquisition." She knew nothing she could say would convince her sisters to leave.

To them, Antonio was like a fictional character who'd only existed in their parents' stories. He'd never been real to any of them, including her. Now all of a sudden he was. She couldn't blame them for being curious. If it were one of them going out with him, she'd be curled up on the couch wanting to see what he was like too.

"We'll be good," Caterina promised, then grinned at the others and added, "at least we'll try." She wrapped her hands around her arms and gave a shiver. "Did one of you turn the air conditioner on? It's not even June yet."

Marcella pulled a throw off the back of the couch where she was sitting and tossed it to her twin. "It does feel unusually cool in here. Maybe Rosa dropped in to check out Luch's fiancé, too. See if she approves."

Cat glanced around the room and then frowned. "You're as bad as Mom, attributing everything from a misplaced set of keys to a low setting on the thermostat to our ancestor."

Marcella shrugged. "Just saying."

"Just not believing," Cat threw back.

Eliana cleared her throat. "Maybe Marcella's right. You know, Mom told me she saw her once."

"What? Oh, come on." Lucia usually stayed out of her sisters' debate about the existence of the family ghost. She'd always thought their mother had been enchanted by the idea of an ancestral spirit in their midst, and the story of how her aunt and uncle died was just the kind of fodder to fuel a mind that wanted to believe. This was the first time she'd heard anything about Mom actually claiming to see their aunt, though.

"She never said anything to me." She looked at Cat and Marcella. "You guys?"

Cat shook her head. "First time I've heard anything about ghostly sightings. How come you never said anything before this?"

"I didn't want any of you to think maybe Mom was losing it," Eliana admitted. "It kind of wigged me out when she told me, but there seem to be more unexplainable things happening around here than usual lately."

"She told me she saw her, too." Marcella got up from where she'd been sitting and went to stand in front of the fireplace. "More than once," she added. "I know Mom could be fanciful, but she wasn't crazy, and she wouldn't just make that up. If she said she saw Aunt Rosa, then I believe she saw...well, *something*. Maybe we do have a ghost, and that's why things go missing sometimes, or the lights flicker so often when no one can find a reason for it, or the temperature suddenly drops in a room...especially this one. It is where the murder took place."

"Let's not go there," Lucia suggested, and tried to ignore that the temperature seemed to dip a few more degrees. "It's a drafty house, it always has been, and that's all it is. I loved Mom as much as the rest of you, but we all know she had a vivid imagination. I don't know what she saw; maybe it was a shadow, the light playing tricks on her. What I do know is that there are no ghosts walking amongst us, and I think we should stop talking about it before one of our guests comes in and—"

The front door flew open with a bang. Cat and Eliana each let out a startled yelp. Lucia spun around, half expecting to see Antonio standing in the entryway. All four of them stared at the empty space a moment before Marcella looked over at Lucia and arched her brows.

"Oh, come on," Lucia said when she saw the look on her sister's face. "Don't tell me you think that was Rosa!"

Marcella shrugged. "I'm not sure what I think, but I'm not as closed to the possibilities as you are that more exists in this world than meets the eye."

Eliana leaned against the stone fireplace wall tapping a finger over her mouth. "You have to admit," she said after a moment, "the door just flying open like that when you said there weren't any ghosts, as if to disprove you, was a little spooky, Luch."

"Woo, woo, woo," Cat put in, wiggling her hands in the air.

Lucia shook her head and walked over to the door. "You're all being ridiculous. It was just the wind." She looked outside. There was no sign of Antonio yet, no sign of any life except a few birds flitting amongst the very still leaves on the vines that bordered the driveway. She closed the door and turned around. There *was* a logical explanation.

ANTONIO SHOWED UP about five minutes later. By the time her sisters got done with him and they were able to escape, Lucia hoped wherever they were going had a liquor license because the man was probably in desperate need of a drink.

"Sorry about that," she apologized as they pulled out of the winery's driveway. "I'm sure you weren't anticipating such an interrogation. We tend to be protective of one another, plus, they can't help but be curious about you."

She glanced across the front seat and took in his patrician profile. "I hope you're not feeling too battered."

"Not at all. What man wouldn't enjoy being the center of attention amongst four beautiful women?"

"We could go back and see if they want to join us for dinner. I'm sure they've got a million more things they could grill you about."

Antonio gave her a quick, questioning look. A thick lock of hair fell down over his forehead and he reached up and pushed it back.

"I was kidding," she said, amused he might think she'd been serious.

"That's good. I only brought enough for the two of us."

"Enough what?"

He curled his lips but didn't answer.

Lucia glanced out the window and then back at him. Her curiosity was piqued, and with it a sliver of doubt. He didn't know this area, so where would a stranger, someone from another country no less, whom she knew extremely little about, be taking her?

"You never told me where we were going. I hope I'm dressed appropriately."

He must have felt her looking at him and his smile broadened. He took his eyes from the road a moment, and she watched them travel over her. "Where we're going is a surprise—and you're dressed perfectly."

EVERYTHING ABOUT LUCIA appealed to him—her open, easy manner, the quickness of her smile, the way she moved. The physical attraction was strong, it pulled at him, the male side of him that couldn't help but imagine what it would be like to undress her slowly, run his hands up and down the long length of her, discover what brought her pleasure, how she made love to a man...how she'd make love to him.

He wasn't a believer in love at first sight. It was ridiculous to believe two people who didn't know each other could think they were in love when they knew little to nothing about each other. He did, however, believe one could be strongly attracted to someone, even a total stranger, someone you saw on the street or in a café, because there was something about them that clicked with your innate preferences—a pleasing voice, an air about them, a look across a crowded room that somehow felt intimate, a smile that offered just enough of a peek into their makeup to rouse one's curiosity.

He'd experienced it before. A few times such an attraction had evolved into introductions, one or two had led to a brief affair, most were lost after the moment—wisps in the wind. And now, with Lucia, he'd see where things led after this evening. Perhaps they would become lovers for a brief, sweet space in time before he got on with his life. Perhaps they would become no more than friends who shared a few laughs over their grandfathers' archaic betrothal contract.

He wondered how funny she'd think it was if he told her about the condition their grandparents had agreed on that was dangling over his head. Not very, he imagined, which was why he had no intention of telling her about it when doing so might only complicate things more.

Antonio slowed down to read the sign at the crossroads. There was little light here, but the woman in the cheese shop who'd given him directions told him the road he wanted would be about a half of a mile past an old blue water tower with a fox and hound painted on it.

"Ahh, this is it," he said, and made a right onto a gravel lane.

Lucia leaned forward and peered out through the front window. When she sat back, she looked over at him and said, "I've never been on this road before."

He could feel her studying him and wondered if the secluded nature of the place made her uneasy. He could understand how a man she'd just met, driving her to an unknown, isolated location, and being secretive about it might spur second thoughts.

"You look nervous. Let me assure you I am capable of protecting you from any small woodland creatures we might encounter when we reach our destination." He flashed a grin, hoping she'd see she had nothing to fear from him.

Her lips quirked and she seemed to relax again. "How are you at fending off a bear or mountain lion?"

Antonio put his foot on the brake and brought the car to a stop. "Maybe my plan for a moonlight picnic isn't such a good idea after all."

Lucia's eyes softened. "You brought me out here for a picnic? How lovely!"

He shrugged. "I'm Italian. We're romantics."

"Lest you forget, I'm Italian, too."

"Yes, but you were raised here. You've been Americanized, and there's a difference."

"I'm sure there's some truth to that," she agreed. "I'd love to visit Italy one day, see where I was born, experience it the way my parents did instead of just through their stories."

"You've never been?"

"Nope. I'll get there, though. It's one of my top five bucket list items." She glanced back out the window. "I'm guessing this road leads to Goose Creek, but how in the world do you know about it?"

"You're right. There's supposed to be an overlook that's the perfect spot to watch the moonrise, and tonight's will be full. The woman in the cheese shop I stopped into this afternoon told me about it, but she didn't mention anything about bears or mountain lions."

Lucia caught the corner of her bottom lip between her teeth and grinned. "I was joking. There have been plenty of bear sightings, and I've heard mountain lions have been spotted in Loudon County as well, but I've never seen either, and I've never heard about any cases of mauling or half-eaten bodies being found in these woods."

"That's comforting. Being mauled or having half of our bodies eaten off would definitely spoil the romance."

She laughed, low and throaty, a richly deep and seductive sound. The melody of it floated past his ears, resonated in his head, and stroked every nerve in his body to awareness.

Lucia Bonavera was unadulterated temptation wrapped in a white sundress that had been flirting with his imagination since he'd first seen her in it this evening.

When she looked across the seat, a mischievous glint in her eyes, the urge to pull to the side of the road, take her in his arms, and satisfy the desire she stirred in him burned hot in his blood. Temptation, indeed—she was the living, breathing, embodiment of the word—and he saw no reason to ignore the attraction when it appeared to be mutual. It wouldn't change their situation in any way, but it could certainly make it more enjoyable.

The gravel road ended at a dirt pull-off large enough to accommodate about four cars. Antonio was glad to see it was empty, and he hadn't seen anything parked along the mile or so they'd driven after the turnoff. They should have the overlook to themselves tonight.

He turned off the ignition. "We're here, and just in time. I wouldn't want to lose our reservation." He gave her a wink, then got out of the car and went around to the other side to open her door.

"I'd like to check it out before unpacking the trunk. There's no sense unloading it until we see if there's a suitable place to have our picnic."

Lucia gave a nod of agreement. He held his hand out toward her and smiled when she took it and then slid out of the car.

HE'D PACKED THEM an uncomplicated meal, cheese and prosciutto, fresh fruit and bread, and a bottle of wine. Of course there was wine, a blushing rosé that would complement the simplicity of the food perfectly.

He'd even thought to bring a blanket, and a large jar candle that they didn't need for the light, as the full moon illuminated the clearing well enough for them to see, but that added a lovely touch to their woodland repast.

"I borrowed these from the inn where I'm staying." Antonio unwrapped two wine glasses, nestled together in large white cloth napkins and set them on top of the lid of the wicker picnic basket he'd packed everything into that now performed double-duty as a makeshift table.

He uncorked the wine and filled the glasses one-third full before handing her one.

Lucia tapped her rim to his. "*Buon appetito.*"

His lips curled seductively. "*Grazie, altrettanto.*"

Antonio's eyes were such a deep blue in the fading light, so dark, and so intensely sexy, she could probably stare into them for weeks and not get bored, if it didn't mean she wouldn't get anything else done. And of course, they didn't have weeks to spend together. Days at the most, that's what they had. That's all they would ever have, so she decided she'd enjoy it.

Lucia brought her knees up in front of her. She balanced the foot of her wine glass on one of them and then picked up a piece of freshly cut mango. She might enjoy his romantic nature, but she was pragmatic enough to know this road they'd started down would come to a fork very quickly, with each of them veering off and going their own way. And that was a good thing; otherwise, she probably wouldn't risk spending this time with him.

"Mango is my favorite fruit." She slid it into her mouth, savoring the rich, creamy sweetness and unique flavor as she chewed.

"It's considered one of the royal fruits."

"Really? By whom?"

"People." He cracked a smile and then picked up the baguette and tore off a chunk. "I was a picky eater growing up. My parents had to bribe me to eat fruits and vegetables. They're the ones who first told me that. 'Mangos are a royal fruit, boy,' they'd say, 'and if it's good enough for royalty, it should be good enough for you.'"

Lucia tried to imagine him as a small boy being cajoled by his parents to eat his fruits and veggies. "But you like them now?"

"Love them. I developed a fondness for a lot of things as I grew older that I didn't appreciate as a boy." He spread some cheese on his bread, taking his time as if the baguette were his palette, the cheese his medium, and he a master artist.

"Here, try this." He held the offering in front of her, lifted it toward her mouth. "The woman in the cheese shop gave me a sample and I liked it. I think it'll complement the fruit."

Lucia opened her mouth and took a bite. The pad of his thumb brushed over her bottom lip when she did, soft as a satin negligee might whisper over heated skin when removed by a lover's talented hands and given leave to drift to the floor. Not an accident. An intentional stroke she wasn't immune to.

She chewed slowly. The tangy cheese hinted of fruit and herb, enhanced by the crisp, chewy crust and light airy center of the baguette. She swallowed and then took a sip of the rosé before giving him her verdict. "You're right. It's a nice pairing, and with the wine as well."

She tipped her head sideways and smiled into his eyes.

"What's that look about?" he asked, and she threw her head back and groaned.

"Ugh! I feel like I'm being seduced," she admitted, and laughed lightly because she rather enjoyed the feeling and, because neither of them had any expectations of the other, felt free to tell him so.

Antonio smiled broadly. "Then you need to catch up, Lucia. I was seduced the first time I saw you."

She bit back a grin. "Oh man, this is not good. Have some prosciutto and some cheese. Here...I'll make you one." She sat forward and took a piece of each, one on top of the other, and handed it toward him. "Now eat this."

He took it. "What? I bare my soul and you hand me meat and cheese? I thought doing so might at least earn me a small kiss." The corners of his lips tugged mischievously and she laughed again.

"Hey, you set the protocol with the one you made for me," she bantered, enjoying the interplay. "I'm just following your lead. It was delicious by the way—the cheese, what is it?"

"Brie, with fig and rosemary. Does that mean if I'd led with a kiss you would have followed suit?" He slid the tidbit she'd given him into his mouth and hiked an inquiring brow.

She debated her answer, knowing this kind of talk could easily lead them into more intimate territory. Could she have a brief fling knowing there was no chance it would lead to anything else? Could she let herself enjoy this man and still keep her heart out of it?

Degree was the key. There was no reason not to kiss him when she wanted to and knew in her bones she'd enjoy it. And it wasn't like he was misleading her. They both knew he was only passing through the area. She knew better than to mistake anything that might happen between them for more than a mutually enjoyable fling. Her heart was safe.

"What if I said yes?"

He swallowed his food and fixed her with a look that made her want to lie down on the blanket and say *whatever you're thinking, just do it.* Did that make her stupid or just horny? She took another sip of wine and eyed him over the rim of the glass instead, waiting.

"I'd put the rest of the food back into the cooler to keep for later and satisfy my taste for something else. Something I think we're both curious about."

"You know what they say about curiosity, right?"

He licked his lips and a pool of saliva gathered in the back of her mouth. "That if you don't satisfy it, it becomes an itch that will drive you crazy for the rest of your life?"

Lucia laughed. "Not the answer I was thinking of, but yeah, there is that."

"So?"

"So even though I admit I'm also curious, I think it would be nice to start with some basics first. For example, are you in a serious relationship with anyone, you know, a romantic one? What's your favorite food? What do you do for a living?"

"Okay, that's fair." He leaned back on his elbows and stretched out his long legs. "I'm not currently in a relationship, serious or otherwise." He paused and held her gaze, and she saw truth in his response. It was important to her. It didn't matter how strong the attraction or how fleeting their time together, if he was involved with someone else, she wouldn't encroach. She knew the pain of that kind of betrayal and would never knowingly want to cause it.

"My favorite food is pasta, done almost any way, but I probably enjoy it most with a simple marinara. And to your third question, I'm an architect."

"An architect!" Lucia sat up straighter. "That's such a coincidence. My sisters and I just talked this morning about meeting with some architects to discuss our expansion plans."

She pulled her hair around to one side. "It's too bad you're not from around here. If you were, I'd ask if you were interested. I'll bet you do wonderful designs."

"Thanks for the vote of confidence. My clients seem to like my work." He put some cheese and meat on his plate. "When you say expansion, what are you looking at doing?"

"That depends on what the county will allow. Cat wants to open a full-service restaurant. We also want to be able to accommodate more overnight guests. Right now we only have six guest rooms, but I'd like to increase that to fifteen, maybe twenty. When we have events, we don't always have enough rooms. The conference we're hosting now is a good example; some of the attendees had to get rooms off-site. If we could accommodate more people, we could attract more event business."

"Can you do all that at the winery?"

"That's part of what we need to find out. The bulk of our revenues comes from the winery, and we discovered there are restrictions to what percentages can come from where. I'm sure our parents knew all of this, and it may be why they never opened a restaurant on-site, but none of us ever had a reason to get involved with those aspects of the business before. There's a chance we may need to break the inn and restaurant off from the winery in order to meet the legal requirements."

"Are you talking about a different location?"

"Yes, but hopefully not far. There's a large piece of land about a half mile down the road from us that's for sale. It has been ever since I moved back, so if we're not able to expand on the winery's grounds, we might be able to work out some kind of arrangement where Cat and I purchase that property and open an inn and restaurant separate from Bonavera Winery.

"There's also a neighboring property that's been vacant for about three years that could be an option if we can't get the other one for a fair price. The owner inherited it from his uncle, but he moved away from the area about ten years ago and swore he'd never come back. It's not for sale, but if we approached him, he might consider it. He and I were friends in school. He was Marcella's first crush, but he's a year older than I and never thought of her as anything more than my kid sister. She was devastated when he moved."

"First loves can be crushing," Antonio said sympathetically.

"Yeah, especially for someone like Cel who doesn't impress easily."

Lucia sighed at the prospect of having to create a whole new business, but they might not have a choice. "We need to talk to someone from the county to find out what we can and can't do. We were planning to meet with some architects next week, and if we liked one of them, take their plan with us when we did. It seemed like a good idea, but now...well, I'm starting to think we might just be throwing money away to have plans drawn up when there's a good chance we won't be able to use them."

"I could go in and talk to them for you," Antonio offered. "I deal with local government and building codes all the time back home. I'm sure there are differences here, but it might be advantageous to have someone who understands the business talk with them."

"That's really nice, but do you really want to spend time trying to navigate the red tape of our county government when you'll only be here a few days?"

"I'll go by their offices tomorrow morning; I just need to find out where they are."

"Are you sure you don't mind?"

"I offered, so no, I don't mind, and I'm usually successful getting cooperation on my projects back home. Besides, I won't be trying to get you a variance, just information, so it shouldn't be too difficult."

"That's very generous. I know my sisters will all appreciate it as much as I do. If we're not able to move forward on either of those plans, I'm not sure what's going to happen, especially with Caterina. She's wanted her own restaurant since she was in high school."

Lucia finished her wine and Antonio immediately reached for the bottle and refilled her glass.

"Thanks," she said, grateful for more than just the rosé. "Do you need to know anything from me before you go see them?"

"You're just looking for clarification on land usage and what percentage of your revenue can come from sources other than the winery, right?"

"Pretty much. Once we know that we can decide how to proceed."

"Okay, then I'm good. If you're around tomorrow evening, I can come over and fill you and your sisters in on what I find out."

Lucia beamed at him. "Caterina isn't scheduled to work the restaurant, so everyone should be good to meet. You can come for dinner. I'll ask Cat to make something nice...as a thank you. Pasta. I'll ask her to make pasta marinara."

The moon rose higher, full and bright, illuminating the ripples on the river below as it flowed past the clearing where they sat sharing tidbits of this and that, things about themselves, each curious to know more about the other.

The evening raced by and Lucia wished she could slow it down, back it up, do it all over again. She hadn't enjoyed an evening so much in years and hated to see it end.

"I should probably take you home," Antonio said. "The air's getting chilly, and as good as you look in that dress, I doubt it'll be warm enough if it gets any cooler."

Lucia didn't disagree. The day had been sunny and pleasantly warm, reaching the low seventies, and she hadn't thought to bring a sweater, but she wouldn't mind having one now.

They packed everything back into the trunk and got in the car. Neither one said much on the drive back. They'd had a wonderful time, but Lucia now felt a touch of melancholy that cast a shadow over her good mood.

Despite what their grandfathers may have wanted, her life and Antonio's had taken courses of their own—like seeds carried on the wind that rooted and grew where they'd landed, on different soils, in different climates—not by chance but because her parents had made a conscious decision to begin a new life in a new country. No, she didn't believe in fate, no more than she believed the ridiculous notion her aunt's ghost inhabited their ancestral home.

67

ANTONIO AND LUCIA stood facing each other on the inn's wide wraparound porch. Silence encircled them, a cloak of anticipation warming her blood beneath its shroud.

Lucia shivered in expectation of what she knew was to come.

Antonio took hold of her hands and rubbed his fingers over them, the pads of his thumbs warm and gentle against her skin.

No words were needed to communicate their thoughts. Their eyes spoke their desire, locked on each other's gaze. He dipped his head, she lifted hers, and their lips met for the first time.

The kiss, the sheer perfection of it, overwhelmed her senses. Lucia wrapped her arms around his neck, abandoned herself to the glory of his mouth—giving, seeking, and hungry for hers—and knew to the depths of her soul the memory of this moment held the power to haunt her forever.

She didn't care. She had no more desire to deny herself this magic than she had to stop breathing. If all she was left with was a bittersweet remembrance, an unquenchable longing when he was gone, so be it.

Antonio held her tighter and she melted into him, their bodies molding together, moving against, and yearning for a completion they'd never know.

He groaned and broke the kiss, rested his chin on top of her head. "I knew I wouldn't be able to leave here without satisfying my curiosity about what it would be like to kiss you, but I have to admit I hoped it would be different."

Really? Lucia frowned. She'd never experienced anything as exquisite as their kiss. How could he not have felt the same rare perfection when their mouths joined? The magic of it had cast its spell over her, and she doubted any man would ever come close to making her feel that way again. It was impossible. There was no way she could have been so affected and he wasn't.

She leaned back and looked up at him. Antonio tilted his head down. Desire burned in his eyes as they roamed over her face and she saw the truth.

He rested one of his hands on her cheek. "How does a man settle for water the rest of his life after he's sipped from the sweetest, richest glass of wine? You've destroyed me, *cara mia.*"

In the next breath he was kissing her again, kissing her as if he'd been suffocating his entire life and she were the sweet air he needed to survive. He backed her up against the door frame and moved against her.

Temptation burned in her blood, incited her passions. It would be so easy to give in to it...too easy, and with little more inducement than another kiss she might be inviting him up to her room. It had been so long since she'd made love to a man, or even considered it.

Antonio pulled away again, cursing as he did, and took a couple of steps back. Lucia straightened, glad for the sturdy door frame to hold her up, and tried to steady her breathing. She'd never felt such consuming desire, and it caught her off guard that it flared to such a degree so quickly.

Antonio pushed his hands through his hair. "This is crazy." He shook his head and closed his eyes a moment. When he looked at her again, he was still shaking his head, and she suspected he'd been just as knocked off balance as she.

"I think I should say goodnight." She heard regret in his voice.

Lucia nodded. She'd rather he stayed, stand there and kiss her stupid crazy all night, but that would be...well, stupid crazy, considering. She smiled and gave a light laugh. "Thank you. It's been a night I won't soon forget."

"Yeah." His chest rose and fell as he drew in a deep, slow breath and let it back out. "Unfortunately, I'm afraid I won't either."

He held her gaze for several seconds then dropped his head and turned to go. "I'll be over tomorrow night to let you know what I find out from the county."

Lucia leaned her head back against the doorframe and watched him get in his car and drive away. She stood there for several minutes after he'd gone, hugging herself as the night air helped cool her passions and as it did, she wondered if it might not be better if she'd never met Antonio DeLuca.

Good wine is a good familiar creature if it be well used.
William Shakespeare, *Othello*

$\mathcal{L}$ucia woke slowly the next morning and stretched her arms lazily. Turning her head, she glanced at the clock on the bedside table and saw that she still had almost an hour before she needed to be downstairs.

The forensic accountants' conference was scheduled to end at two, and as they had no other guests arriving today, Lucia had told them they could wait until after they ended their meetings to check out rather than the normal eleven o'clock hour.

She slid out of bed and padded into the bathroom to wash up. After brushing her teeth, she studied her face in the mirror. What did Antonio see there when he looked at her? Had her eyes given away the wanting he stirred in her?

Reaching up, she touched her lips and rubbed the tips of her fingers over them. Lord. Would she ever forget the magnificence of their kiss? Would she now be cursed to compare every man she went out with to Antonio, measuring their kisses against his? Would she ever again experience anything even close to what he'd made her feel in those brief moments, or would all her future encounters with men seem like crumbs that left her hungry for more? Hungry for a man she'd never see again after a few more days.

How ironic that he should show up out of the blue and make such an impact on her. Two days ago if his name had come up, she would have spent no more time dwelling on him than she would any other stranger she'd never met. Now, she could think of little else.

She took her brush out of the bathroom vanity and pulled it through her hair. It wasn't just his kiss that had her thoughts scattering like a flock of ducks at the sound of a hunter's gun echoing over the lake; it was everything about him. She liked his humor, the way he moved. She liked the way he talked, found his accent sexy, and although she never considered herself a woman who needed to be romanced, she did enjoy his romantic bent.

"Hey Luch, are you in here?" she heard Eliana call from somewhere beyond the bathroom.

Lucia poked her head out to see her sister standing in the bedroom doorway. "Morning. What's up?"

"Cat's got one of her migraines. She was up early making scones and muffins, but I told her to go lie down before it got too bad. Can you help me pull this morning's setup together?"

"Sure. I just need to get dressed and I'll be right down."

Lucia hustled downstairs and into the solarium about five minutes later.

"I'm getting the coffee and hot water going." Eliana bent down and plugged the cord she was holding into the wall outlet behind one of the two buffet tables that had been placed against the side wall. "If you set everything else up, I'll take care of the food."

They worked quickly and quietly, and when they were done, Lucia and Eliana went into the kitchen where each of them helped themselves to some coffee and one of the scones from the plate of baked goods Eliana had set aside for the family.

The kitchen was long and narrow. It had originally been a side porch, but her parents had enclosed and converted it when Lucia was in college. The old wooden farm table where they were required to gather for family dinners every night when she and her sisters were growing up sat at one end of the room by a bank of windows that looked out over the back of the property.

Lucia took her breakfast there and sat down. The sun was just peaking over the top of the trees, painting the vineyard's newly emerging spring leaves with strokes of gold and reflecting off the early morning dew. Beyond, the mountains grounded all, low and ridged, cloaked in their famous blue haze, a comforting sentinel in their familiarity.

She bit into a still-warm almond scone and rolled her eyes in delight. "This tastes so good." She licked her lips and glanced up at Eliana who joined her at the table. "If you don't need help with anything else this morning, I've got some errands to run in town."

"I should be fine. We ordered box lunches from Kayla's for today since the group's finishing up early."

"That works, especially since Cat may still be out of commission. I should be back by eleven, so in plenty of time before they finish up." Lucia took a sip of coffee to wash down the pastry. "Oh, by the way, are you around this evening?"

"Yup. Why?" Eliana eyed Lucia with a grin. "You have another date with tall, dark, and sexy and need someone to cover for you?"

"Actually, he's coming over to meet with all of us. I told him about our plans to expand. It turns out he's an architect and deals with regulations and all that stuff back in Italy. He offered to check with the county to find out if we can do what we want and said he'd come by this evening to fill us in."

"That was magnanimous. First he changes his plans and stays a couple of extra days, and then he volunteers to go down to county and wade through their red tape to gather information for us..." Eliana arched her brows. "Hmm, interesting."

"He's a nice man, and he works with building codes all the time. He said it wasn't a big deal."

"Yeah, and he was probably so infatuated with you last night that he would have volunteered to do anything for you."

"He wasn't infatuated."

"Oh, really? Why do you think he's still here after telling you the night you met that he'd be leaving the next day?"

"Maybe after discovering there was so much to see and do in the area, he thought he'd tack on a few extra days to explore the sights."

"Yeah. I can tell you what sights he wants to explore." Eliana leaned forward and fixed her with a stare. "Speaking of which, sister, how *was* your date last night?"

"It was fine. We went on a picnic. We talked a lot. He's a great conversationalist."

"Umm hmm. Did he manage to kiss you at any point between all of his words?"

"Maybe." Lucia's grin betrayed her.

"Busted. You so kissed him. I can see it all over your face, and from the looks of it he knocked your socks off."

"I wasn't wearing socks, but okay, yeah, the man can kiss."

"And?"

Lucia glanced toward the doorway. "And I think I just heard some of our guests out in the dining room."

Eliana stood up and carried her dishes to the sink. "Fine, but I want details later. Since I'm currently not seeing anyone, I've got to get my thrills vicariously through you and Cat."

"I wouldn't count on it. Antonio will probably be leaving tomorrow or the day after, and although Cat hasn't said anything, I've got a suspicion there's trouble brewing between her and Mitch."

Eliana pulled a frown. "Can't say I'd be sorry if they split. Cat's seemed off lately, and I've developed some bad feelings about him."

"Same here. I've been biting my tongue because I haven't wanted to upset her, but I'd like to hear why you feel that way to see if my concerns are valid. Maybe we can grab a few minutes this afternoon when no one else is around."

"Okay, good. It wouldn't surprise me if he's the reason she's got a migraine."

A short while later Lucia sent texts to Marcella and Cat asking if they could get together for a family meeting at six. She'd promised Antonio pasta marinara as a thank you for helping them out, but if Cat wasn't feeling up to cooking, he might have to be satisfied with pasta à la Lucia.

She checked on a few odds and ends before leaving for town. As she turned onto John Mosby Highway, she was aware of an increased energy flowing through her, and there was only one thing she could attribute it to. She would see Antonio again this evening.

THEY WERE GATHERED in the library, flames licking over the logs in the fireplace, adding a touch of warmth to the cool spring evening, as Antonio briefed them.

"The code doesn't permit you to operate a restaurant as part of the winery if it generates more than thirty percent of your revenue. You can still offer complimentary breakfasts and snacks for guests, or cater on-site events like the one you had here this week, but you're limited beyond that."

"So if I were to open a restaurant, it couldn't be associated with the winery at all?" Cat's disappointment rang clear in her tone.

"If you want to open a full-service restaurant, then no."

"I was afraid the answer would be something like that, but a part of me hoped there'd be an exception that would let us do

what we wanted right here. I'd already envisioned turning the solarium into this wonderful dining area with stacking glass doors that would open to the terrace for alfresco dining. It would have been perfect."

Antonio scribbled a note on the pad he had on his lap and then glanced at Lucia. "I stopped to take a look at the land that's for sale down the road before I came here." He looked around at everyone and added, "Lucia told me if the laws didn't permit you to do what you wanted on-site you might consider purchasing it and building there. If you did that, you'd be working with a blank slate. You could do whatever you wanted in terms of the design."

"We might be able to get the land at a good price since it's been on the market for so long. If not, another possible option might be the Richards' property. It's been vacant since Jordan's uncle died and left it to him. If we were able to get in touch with him, he might consider selling," Lucia said.

"If he wanted to sell it, I think he would have put it on the market by now," Marcella threw out, and Lucia thought her tone sounded almost defensive. "Buying the property down the road and building what you want there sounds like the best alternative to me."

Caterina must have picked up on something as well and frowned, then said, "It has been for sale a long time, so if we can get it, we'd all be able to stay put and keep the family home." Always one to need some kind of plan, even a loose one, she added, "We'd have to hire a lawyer to get all the legal stuff figured out since Lucia and I wouldn't be able to keep our interest in the winery, but we can work all that out if we decide this is how we want to proceed."

She looked over at Antonio. "Based on what you found out, that could work, right?"

He leaned back in his chair and Lucia followed him with her eyes. He might be one of the most beautiful men she'd ever seen, and she enjoyed looking at him, but beyond that he had a casual elegance she found irresistible, in his style, his gestures, the way he moved.

He nodded in Cat's direction. "As long as the inn and restaurant aren't a part of the winery and don't contribute to its revenue, then yes. It's a good piece of land," he added, offering his opinion. He looked thoughtful for a moment. "There's a lot of potential to create something very special."

Eliana leaned forward and rested her elbows on her knees. "Lucia told us you're an architect. It's too bad you're leaving soon or we might have been able to convince you to give us some ideas." She looked at Lucia and winked.

"When are you leaving?" Caterina asked him. "Any chance we'd have a little time to pick your brain before you do?"

"I hadn't planned on staying beyond Friday." Antonio glanced toward Lucia and their eyes connected; it was a brief meeting, but long enough for her to feel the tug.

"I don't have a fixed schedule, though, so I suppose I could stick around a few extra days and put together some concept drawings. That is, if you're serious about wanting my ideas."

His offer surprised her, and Lucia's heartbeat tripped at the prospect of him staying a while longer. "That's really nice but we wouldn't want to inconvenience you."

"It won't. I'd already considered staying a few extra days. There's a lot more to do and see around here than I realized."

"That'd be great," Caterina said. "We'll pay you, of course, whatever your hourly rate is. Just let us know up front and if it's too steep, we can fire you before you get started."

Antonio chuckled. "We'll work out some agreeable terms. It would help if you and Lucia each put together a list of anything specific you'd like incorporated into the design, the feel you're going for, how you need it to function, general size. I won't be doing any detailed drawings, but it'll be useful having an idea of your vision even if they're only concept sketches. I'll give you my email and as soon as I get them, I can start working on something."

"If you'd like, you could have a room here now since the accountant group is gone," Marcella offered. Everyone looked at her and Lucia was surprised she hadn't thought of it herself. If he wanted to walk the property, or take measurements, or whatever else architects did when they were designing a project, it made more sense for him to stay there than to drive back and forth from Middleburg.

Antonio glanced at her, raised his brows as if he wasn't sure how she felt about it. Of course it made sense since one of the reasons he'd be staying longer was to do some drawings for them.

"Good idea, Marcella," she said, and then turned back to Antonio. "If it would make it easier for you and you want to make the move, I'll schedule you into a room."

Antonio nodded. "It would be convenient. I'll stay where I am tonight and check in here tomorrow."

With that settled, they went into the solarium to have dinner. As promised, they were having pasta marinara. While Cat put the finishing touches on the meal, the rest of them gathered around one of the tables that had been set up for the accountants' conference to share a bottle of red that Marcella had selected from their cellars.

Antonio was the curiosity here, and her sisters readily engaged him in conversation, peppering him with questions, even Marcella who normally preferred to listen rather than speak. For the moment, Lucia was the one to slip into that role.

She smiled lightly, content to watch him charm her siblings, to observe and soak him in as she might the subtle nuances in the changing colors of the sky during a particularly wonderful sunset.

Blinking, she glanced down at her wine. She had seen sunsets so beautiful they had halted her breath. She'd have frozen them in time if she could have because it was almost painful to watch them slip away, to know she might never see one just that gorgeous, just that perfect ever again once the night swallowed it up. She supposed that was why so many people took pictures of them, so they could remember, so they didn't feel like they were lost to them forever.

Lucia reached into the back pocket of her jeans for her cell phone and then held it out in front of her. Antonio looked at her from across the table where he sat flanked by two of her sisters. She zoomed in on his face and snapped a picture.

THE MOON WAS high, big and bright as it climbed into the sky and illuminated the rows of meticulously trained vines to Antonio's left, beside where he and Lucia were taking a walk after dinner.

"You were right. Caterina's a gifted chef. Whatever she did to that marinara sauce, it was one of the best I've ever tasted."

"That's high praise considering you live in the epicenter of the pasta world." The wind blew several strands of hair across her face. Antonio wanted to reach up and tuck them behind her ear, just to touch her in some way.

She beat him to it, gathering the dark mass together and with a couple of quick twists secured it into a knot on the back of her head without the aid of any pins or clips—one of those intriguing things all women seem to know how to do without even thinking about it. He found it fascinating, although he found most things about women fascinating...and with this woman, even more so.

"She is amazing," Lucia agreed. "And not because she's my sister."

"I get the impression you and your sisters are all talented at what you do."

"I think so." Lucia grinned over at him, the moonlight a soft wash of light bathing her face. "Our parents used to always say, pay attention to the times you feel the happiest and most content because within them are clues to help you choose which paths will lead you to the most fulfillment and satisfaction in your life. I didn't always realize how much sense that made at the time, but they were right. And if you enjoy what you do, you're probably going to be much better at it than someone who doesn't."

"Good advice. You're fortunate your parents didn't try to push you into a job they thought you should pursue versus one you wanted."

She searched his eyes a moment, her expression a pause between breaths waiting to be released. "Did that happen to you?"

"No." He shook his head and her face softened into a smile. "I've seen it often enough, though, even with loving parents who believe they're doing what's best for their kids. They push them in one direction or try to dissuade them from another."

"Yeah, I only hope if I ever have children I'm able to find the right balance between encouraging them to spread their wings and tethering them to me with one of those child leashes until they go off to college."

He laughed and she joined in.

"I'm sure I won't be that overprotective, but it can't be easy." She slipped her hands into her jeans' pockets. "So did you always want to be an architect?"

"Not until after I went to university. I've always had a fascination with buildings, their design and their history, and I realized I wasn't the type of person who could do the same thing day in and day out. I prefer projects that have a beginning, middle, and an end, and then am able to move on to something new. When the time came to make a decision about what I was going to do with my life, becoming an architect seemed like a good choice. I haven't regretted it, so I guess you could say I'm one of the lucky ones who enjoys my work."

She stopped and put a hand on his forearm. "That's nice, and it's also very nice of you to offer to do some drawings for us. I hope you didn't feel awkward about saying no to my sisters; they can be a convincing force when they want to be."

"Not at all. I meant it when I told you I was already considering staying another week to visit some of the museums in DC and tour a couple of the local wineries. Besides, I'll enjoy putting some ideas together for you. New projects are always exciting, and designing something from the ground up even more so."

"If we like what you come up with, maybe we can just use your drawings for the job."

He shook his head. "You wouldn't be able to do that. An architect will still have to do detailed spec drawings that your builder will work from. You can ask someone else to incorporate some of the ideas into their design, but whoever you hire is going to have their own ideas, which you might like better, and from a professional standpoint, they'd probably prefer to come up with their own design rather than finalize someone else's."

"Well, we won't tell them where the ideas came from, then. We'll just present them as things we'd like."

Antonio turned toward her and took a hold on her shoulders. "That would probably make for a better working relationship." He ran his hands up and down her arms. The connection felt natural to him, physically satisfying, yes, but oddly comforting as well, and it had been a challenge when they were with her sisters not to touch her.

"Since I'll be staying longer than originally planned, what are the chances I could convince you to spend a day or two playing tourist with me?"

She wrapped her arms around his neck and smiled up at him, a delicious curve of temptation. "Oh, I think they might be fairly high, but I should at least let you try to persuade me before I commit to anything."

"Okay, I don't know if this will help my cause, but I've wanted to do it all night." He tilted his head down, ran his tongue over her lips, tasted her smile, licked it up, and then molded his to hers. She kissed like the sun, warm and bright, heating his blood. He opened his mouth, angling it for a better fit, and groaned when he felt her fingers dig into his back.

When he broke the kiss to come up for air a couple of minutes later, she leaned into his chest. "All right." She sounded as breathless as he felt. "You convinced me."

"Are you sure?" He ran his fingers down her cheek, enchanted by the softness of her skin, and then lifted her chin so he could see her face. "I'm willing to put some more effort into it to reduce the possibility of you backing out at the last minute."

"Not necessary." She coughed on a laugh and held up a hand. "Any additional effort and you could probably persuade me to take part in more than a little sightseeing with you."

"Would that be a bad thing, Lucia?" He stared into her eyes, drawn even more to her when she didn't look away.

She studied him a few seconds before answering. "Not bad necessarily, but unwise perhaps."

"Ah, yes, wisdom, the great extinguisher of passion's flames."

"Who said that?"

"Me, I just made it up."

She smiled. "Maybe you should have been a poet instead of an architect."

"If I wrote you a poem, would you be less likely to intellectualize things and whisk me to your lair?"

She punched him in the shoulder and he laughed.

"Didn't think so."

"Alas, the door to my lair will remain barred to you. Passion is often feathered with promises meant in the moment but destined to be broken."

"And who said that?" he asked, already recognizing the wisdom of her choice but curious none the less.

"Me."

"I suspected you were more of a romantic than you let on; now you've confirmed it. So we have that in common."

"Yes, I suppose, but I'm a practical romantic."

"There's no such thing, *bellissima*. Romance by its very nature is impractical. It's too elusive to be practical; impossible to give a universal definition to, because the definition is in the mind of the one defining it. It has no limits and yet some find it in nothing more than a simple look."

She grinned at him, the moonlight highlighting the humor in her eyes.

"What," he asked, "do you find so amusing?"

She shook her head. "I'm just not used to a man giving so much thought, if any for that matter, to the concept of romance. Maybe you're right, maybe it's a cultural thing, but you're definitely different from most of the guys I know."

"Should I consider that a good thing or a bad thing?"

Lucia lifted up on her tiptoes and kissed him lightly on the lips. "In my mind, it's a very good thing."

He slid his hands around her waist and drew her closer. "*Sono contenta.*"

"I'm glad, too," she said as he covered her mouth again with his. He drew the kiss out, and couldn't help but wonder what she would think of him if she knew about his situation and how it impacted her. He needed to figure out what to do about that mess before it was too late, and if he could, without hurting her in the process.

Five

What contemptible scoundrel stole
the cork from my lunch?

W.C. Fields, *You Can't Cheat an Honest Man*

*S*aturday morning Lucia jolted awake, sat upright, and looked around. Something had startled her into awareness but she couldn't put a finger on what—a sense, a sound, something in a dream.

The soft, pale celery green sheers covering the two six-over-six windows on the side wall of her room wafted on the morning breeze, a reminder she'd left things open the night before for the fresh air.

She shivered as she slid out of bed. The temperature must have dropped more than predicted. It wasn't impossible to get a late frost this time of year, which would have Marcella fretting over crop loss, but frost now wasn't the norm. By mid-May the nighttime temperatures were usually solidly in the fifties. Definitely warm enough to sleep with the windows open, especially when snuggled under a down comforter.

Pulling the sheers apart, she reached up to lower the first window. The sun had already topped the mountains, and without the diffusing effect of the curtains it streamed into her room and across the polished floorboards. The air didn't feel as cool as she expected; in fact, she felt warmer now standing in front of the open window than when she'd been covered up in bed.

Deciding to leave them open after all, she turned back around to go into the bathroom to wash up. As she walked across the room in her bare feet, she caught a movement in her peripheral vision and spun to the right, startled that someone was there.

She turned in a circle, her eyes darting here and there, but landing on nothing beyond the familiar, beyond what belonged. There was no evidence of an intruder who may have somehow managed to scale the stone façade outside and steal into her room while she'd slept.

"Okay, that was strange," she mumbled, and shook her head. She might be standing up but clearly her mind wasn't fully awake yet, or more precisely her eyes, since they were seeing things that weren't there. Coffee would fix that.

She washed and dressed quickly, made up her bed, and then went downstairs to find all three of her sisters in the kitchen already having coffee and indulging in a quiche Caterina had made fresh that morning.

Eliana and Marcella were sitting at the old kitchen table in the corner of the room and Cat was fussing with something at the stove. Eliana eyed Lucia. "You're up late. You feel okay?"

"Ummm hmmm." Lucia stretched her arms above her head and then shook them out at her sides. "Nothing a cup of coffee won't cure."

"Or maybe getting Antonio to tuck you into bed before two in the morning." Eliana wiggled her brows.

"I didn't get to bed that late; it was only midnight. And he didn't tuck me in. We said goodnight on the second floor landing, and then I continued up to my bedroom and my lonely bed."

"Pity."

"Yes, it is, but in the long run the wisest choice. He's like the forbidden fruit, and if I allowed myself a taste, I might regret it the rest of my life." She dragged in a breath. "I don't know if giving in to the temptation would be worth it."

"Can't help you in the dessert department this early in the morning, but if you're hungry there's more quiche," Cat offered. She held up a pie dish to show her and then set it back down on the stovetop.

"Thanks, what's in it?"

"Leeks and bacon. I want to switch up the brunch menu at the restaurant and thought I'd include a couple of different quiches, so you all get to be my test group."

"No complaints here." Lucia got a plate and lifted some then joined Marcella and Eliana at the table. "I thought you were going to ask if you could start having Sundays off since you're working Friday and Saturday nights," she said, and then forked a piece of the quiche into her mouth.

"I did." Cat continued to busy herself at the counter without turning around. "Mitch said he needed one of us to be there because he doesn't trust leaving anyone else in charge."

Lucia traded glances with Eliana. Marcella looked between the two of them and frowned. "What?" she mouthed, taking note of the exchange.

Eliana strummed her fingers against her coffee mug. "Why doesn't he work brunches, or at least alternate weekends with you?"

"He needs that time to do all the back-office stuff: schedules, payroll, paying the bills, and everything else."

"Can't he do that on Monday or Tuesday when the restaurant is closed?" El suggested.

Cat stiffened. Even from across the room it was obvious she didn't like their questions, and Lucia wondered if the nerve they'd struck wasn't already a little raw. "He said he needs to do it on Sunday."

Lucia didn't want to upset Cat, but it seemed Mitch was taking advantage of her. Over the last two months she'd been spending more and more time at the restaurant and Mitch less. Something about that didn't add up.

Lucia couldn't imagine Mitch needed so much time to handle the administrative part of the business. He had an accountant handling the books, and payroll and scheduling couldn't take more than a few hours. Cat did all the food orders, so how much more could there be? No, things didn't add up, which made her wonder what Mitch *was* doing with his time.

Lucia worried her mouth around another bite of quiche. Should she let things drop or follow her gut that Cat was making excuses for Mitch? And if Cat was making excuses, did that mean she had her own doubts but was ignoring her instincts?

If pushing her sister to take off any blinders she might be wearing meant upsetting her in the short term, that was a risk Lucia considered worth taking.

"I thought your schedules were posted every two weeks and that most people worked the same shifts...and don't you get paid every other Friday?"

Cat turned around and crossed her arms, her expression tight. "What's your point, Luch?"

"I just don't understand why Mitch needs so much time to do the back-office stuff. And even if he does, can't he do some of it at the restaurant? I mean, it is *his* business. I'd think he'd want to be there more often to ensure things are running smoothly."

"You don't have any idea what it takes to run a restaurant," Cat blurted, clearly on the defensive. "And I don't know why you're all ganging up on me about it; it was my decision to work Sundays."

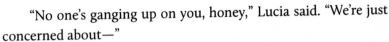

"No one's ganging up on you, honey," Lucia said. "We're just concerned about—"

"Don't be! I'm fine, work's fine, *everything* is fine." Cat pulled off her apron and threw it on the counter. "I've got stuff I need to do."

She turned and walked out of the kitchen, leaving the quiche sitting on the stove and all of them staring after her.

"Oookaay." Marcella looked back and forth from Lucia to Eliana. "Does anyone want to enlighten me as to what the hell that was all about?"

"Maybe we should have gone about that differently," Eliana suggested. "She seems really upset at us."

Lucia sighed. "Yeah, but it's not like we planned to talk to her about things this morning; it just came up. Our intentions were in the right place."

"I don't think Cat cares about our intentions right now."

"No, I'm sure she doesn't, which only confirms for me that our suspicions are right. She wouldn't be so upset unless we struck a nerve."

Eliana frowned. "Yeah. So what do we do now?"

Marcella waved her arms in the air. "Hell-lo! Remember me, the sister who obviously didn't get the *Trouble in Cat's World* memo?"

Lucia reached over and patted Marcella's hand. "Sorry. Eliana and I both have growing concerns about Mitch and what's going on with Cat." Between the two of them, Lucia and Eliana filled Marcella in about their worries.

"I never did get a good feeling for Mitch," Marcella admitted. "I guess I figured if Cat liked him, he must have some qualities I just didn't see."

"I think he had us all fooled at first." Eliana took a sip of coffee. "He knows how to turn on the charm, and he's got a pretty face, but once you get past his looks and start observing him in action there are definitely some red flags waving around the guy."

"Agree," Lucia said. "So do we back off like Cat asked, or do we try to find out more about Mitch on our own to see if we're right to be concerned?"

Marcella set her elbows on the table and propped her chin in her hands. "That's a stupid question. She's our sister."

"Okay, we're in agreement." Lucia leaned back in her chair and crossed her arms. "So where do we begin?"

"I'M NOT SURE, another week maybe and then I'll drive to New York."

Antonio narrowed his eyes, let them travel where the morning light wanted to lead them, to the places it highlighted, rested, and gave him guidance.

"No, Grandfather, Lucia has nothing to do with my reason for staying longer. I told you, she feels the same way I do. We met, spent time together, even kissed, and nothing. So I'm sorry to disappoint you, but I held up my end of the bargain by coming here. You and your old friend got it wrong. The coincidence of our births is nothing more than that, a coincidence, so I hope we can put an end to this nonsense."

He turned and faced the mountains that ran behind the property. Enshrouded under a cloak of misty blue haze, they invited the mind to consider adventure and the soul to muse over magic.

Antonio shook his head, rolled his eyes. "Because the Bonaveras are planning to do some new construction and when they found out I was an architect, they asked if I'd give them some ideas. Consider it a concession to your friendship with their grandfather, Nonno. I'll only be staying long enough to put together some rough drawings for them and possibly visit some of the area's museums."

Whoever drew up the final plans for the project would do so with the intent of maximizing the stunning view. If they didn't, they shouldn't be doing it.

"What's that? No, I'm not sure of the exact day. Look, I'm actually at the property they're hoping to buy getting some pictures. I'll give you a call in a couple of days when I have a better idea. We'll talk more then, and I sincerely hope you'll reconsider things now that you know Lucia has no more interest in getting married than I do. And do me a favor since I'm not there to make you. Promise you'll take care of yourself."

After saying goodbye, Antonio slid his phone into his pocket. His grandfather would turn eighty-eight this year. He didn't have any pressing health issues, unless one could count a stubborn streak unhealthy, but Antonio still worried he'd try to do something he shouldn't at his age and end up with a broken bone or two. There was no way to keep an eye on his grandfather from five thousand miles away, though, so he'd just have to trust the old man wouldn't do anything foolish while he was gone.

He lifted the camera strap from around his neck and began snapping pictures. About ten minutes later, he walked the half mile back to the winery and entered the main building.

Lucia had told him a little bit of history about the place. It had originally been built by her great-aunt's father as a home for himself, his wife, and their young daughter. The daughter had travelled to Italy as an adult, where she met and fell in love with Lucia's great-uncle. He returned with her to the States, where they married. Not long afterward, the daughter's parents died and she inherited the home. It wasn't until after that point in time, when Lucia's uncle decided to return to his roots as a winemaker, that the first vines were planted on the property and the seeds of what would become the present day Bonavera Winery were sown.

From what she'd told him, Lucia's parents came to this country to help her grandparents take care of settling her aunt and uncle's affairs after they were the victims of a double murder. Her parents fell in love with the land. They decided to stay in Virginia, begin a new life, and pursue her uncle's dream of establishing a vineyard.

He shook his head. "Grizzly beginning, but it seems they knew what they were about," he uttered aloud.

"Who are you talking to?"

Antonio turned to see Eliana sitting on one of the couches in the library where they'd all met the other night. She was leafing through a stack of mail.

"Just thinking out loud." He gave her a self-deprecating smile. "No need to worry, I don't have any invisible friends."

"Yeah well, you never know around here." She stood up and walked into the reception.

Eliana's remark intrigued him. He'd had a weird experience upon waking that morning that had made him question if he were actually awake or dreaming. He'd put it from his head, deciding he'd been in that crossover world between sleep and consciousness when the mind is still susceptible to fanciful imaginings; but now she aroused his curiosity. What if it hadn't been his mind playing tricks on him?

He cocked his head. "Really? Would you care to enlighten me?"

"I probably shouldn't. Like you, I was just thinking out loud. I doubt Cat and Lucia would be too happy with me if I were to scare you away before you got a chance to give them some of your ideas. They're both anxious to see what you come up with."

"Now I'm even more curious. Is this place haunted or something?"

Eliana's mouth dropped open and she stared at him a moment. "Why would you think that? You didn't...ummm...have anything strange happen, did you?"

"Like what?" he asked, thinking it best to see what she'd suggest rather than tell her about his experience right away.

"Oh, I don't know...the temperature in the room suddenly dropping, a door opening but no one being there, smelling a scent that wasn't there before." She shrugged. "You know, just something, anything that struck you as kind of odd."

"How about a woman standing over my bed watching me sleep and then disappearing a few seconds after I opened my eyes?"

"Shut up! You did not!"

Antonio chuckled at her expression. He didn't know if she thought he was joking or was worried he wasn't. Either way, he didn't want her or her sisters to think he'd go back on his word because of it.

"Honestly, I don't know if I saw anything. I was just waking up so I could have dreamed or imagined it. If you told me this place had a ghost, though, it wouldn't frighten me away. On the contrary, I'd think the possibility fascinating."

He glanced around the room and then lowered his voice. "So now that you know you can trust me with the family skeletons, what's the deal? Do the Bonaveras have a ghost roaming around the winery?"

"I don't know. Our mother believed so. She thought it was the ghost of our Aunt Rosa. She was murdered in this house, in this room actually...our uncle too."

"Yeah, Lucia told me a little bit about it. She said they caught the murderer, an old fiancé or something?"

"That's right. He never did admit to a motive. Most people thought he did it out of jealousy because he never got over her breaking off with him and marrying our uncle. I always found that a little hard to believe."

"Why? You don't believe in crimes of passion?"

"I do, but my aunt and uncle had been married for over five years when it happened. That seems like a long time for someone to wait to commit a crime of passion."

"Maybe. If he never told anyone why, though, I guess no one will ever know if there was more to it than that."

Eliana cleared her throat. "Anyway...my sisters and I have differing opinions. Marcella and I don't know what to believe. We're a little more open to the possibility Aunt Rosa, or someone's spirit, could be responsible for some of the unexplainable things that happen around here."

"What about the others?"

She gave a light snort. "Cat and Luch? Those two would need a lot of proof to even consider the possibility."

"Consider the possibility of what?"

Antonio and Eliana turned to face the hallway. Lucia stood in the opening with her hands on her hips. Her hair hung free. Her feet were bare. She had on a pair of slim jeans and a white tank top. Antonio felt a punch of desire, hard and fast, and completely forgot what he and Eliana were talking about.

THERE WERE FOUR other couples standing around one of 16 Oaks' three tasting stations waiting for their next pour. Each station had good-sized groups. Lucia wasn't surprised the wineries were busy. It was a gorgeous day, sunny and fair, and driving around northern Virginia's low rolling hills from winery to winery, past horse farms and well-manicured vineyards, was a pleasant way to while away a picturesque Saturday.

Bonavera's would be just as busy, especially since they included food pairings with their tastings. Not all the wineries did, but Marcella insisted on it. She was a firm believer wine and food brought out the best qualities in each other, and given Caterina's unique food samples and Eliana's gift for talking up the guests, Bonavera always received great tasting reviews.

Antonio reached past her for the water pitcher and poured some into two of the small plastic rinsing cups. "I'm glad you were able to join me," he said, sliding one of the cups toward her. "I had no idea there were so many wineries here. I wouldn't have known which ones would be best to visit on my own."

"I'm glad you asked." Lucia glanced up at him and smiled. "And I'm happy to be your tour guide for a day."

They were currently at stop number two of the four. The wine community was close knit, so she knew most of the people in the industry and a lot of their staff; as a result, pours had been on the generous side and she was beginning to get a slight buzz.

Lucia took a sip of water to clear her palate. They'd already finished with the whites and were working their way through the reds. Thus far, they had sampled a very nice Cabernet Sauvignon and Merlot. The next selection was a Cabernet Franc.

When they were given their last pour, she swirled her glass to release the wine's aroma and then lifted it to her nose and sniffed. She could scent hints of cherry and chocolate and knew before tasting it she would like it.

She took a sip, swished it around in her mouth, held it there a moment before swallowing, and then angled her head toward Antonio's. "What do you say we grab some lunch when we leave here and hit the last two wineries after we get some food in our bellies?"

"That's probably a good idea. Are you feeling all right?"

"I'm okay for now, but I think I need to counteract the alcohol with some food before doing another tasting. We can go to Twining Vines. My friend Jenna's the manager. She's on vacation this week so she won't be there, but I know all the staff so they'll take good care of us, and the food's good. I think you'll like it, and it just happens to be on the way to the next winery. "

Antonio reached out and tucked a strand of her hair behind her ear. Their eyes met and he held her gaze. Lucia found it impossible to look away. What was he thinking as he held her trapped in the space between this breath and her next? She longed to take his hand, touch his face, connect with him in a more meaningful way, and the desire to do so was almost painful—painful because it would go unfulfilled. A simple touch, but so intimate, too much a show of affection, a show of the heart—more so than a kiss of passion—and there was risk in that. As much as she liked him, opening her heart too much would be foolish considering their circumstances.

Antonio gave her a quick, almost tight, smile, and then picked up his glass and downed the rest of the cab franc.

ANTONIO HADN'T ANTICIPATED enjoying this area of the country so much. Not that he'd done a lot of research on it since the only reason he'd added it to his itinerary was to placate his grandfather in the hope of getting him to see reason. He'd only planned two days, enough time to honor his promise and be on his way, but he'd been here a week already and it had sped by.

He studied the woman sitting across from him as she studied her menu. She was part of the reason—a big part—he couldn't deny it. And that was an even bigger surprise. He'd never admit it to his grandfather, had in fact denied it when they'd spoken on the phone that morning. The old man would have latched onto it like a leech and started in on him all over again with the destiny nonsense. His desire to spend a little more time with Lucia before moving on had nothing to do with destiny; he was just enjoying her company, and as he had no time commitments, didn't feel compelled to cut it short. Why should he?

She put her menu down, caught him watching her, and smiled.

"What are you thinking of ordering?" She smoothed her napkin over her lap. The sun filtering through the wisteria-covered pergola picked up the highlights in her rich, chestnut hair. She wore a pair of large sunglasses with black frames and dark lenses so he couldn't see her eyes. But he didn't need to—they were imprinted on his memory.

"Can I have you?"

She laughed. He loved the sound of it, silk velvet, deep. It seduced him, as everything about her did.

"I'm not on the *carte du jour*, but the bluefish appetizer here is excellent."

He clucked his tongue. "I guess I'll go with that since my first choice isn't available."

She pushed the glasses up onto the top of her head, holding her hair back away from her face, and gave him a sidelong glance, humor dancing in her eyes. "At least not for lunch."

He wiggled his eyebrows and leaned in toward the table. "A late-night snack then, perhaps?"

"Perhaps, for both of us, and I can't believe I just said that." She picked up her fork and waved it at him. "You're a bad influence on me."

"I'm trying to be."

They continued that way for a couple of minutes, the way flirtations do, each enjoying it but keeping it light. They both knew nothing would really come of it—nothing more than a few heated kisses. As much as he might want to make love to her, she'd made it clear she wasn't interested in a brief affair, so that would have to be enough.

When their food came, they ate slowly. Sitting outside on the restaurant's wide patio, under a flowering arbor, they were in no rush to hurry through their meal. The day was too lovely, the food meant for savoring, and each was content to share the other's company.

Lucia picked up one of the pita crisps that came with her meal, spread a bit of bluefish and some horseradish cream on it. "So this morning, when I ran into you and El in the lobby, what was that all about?"

"What do you mean?"

"Ghost talk. I didn't have time to find out then because I was already running late, but when I asked what I'd need convincing about on my way out, she mentioned something about ghosts."

"She said you didn't believe in them."

"Of course I don't." She added a few pieces of slivered red onion to the crisp and then took a bite, chewed it as she looked at him. She swallowed and then cocked her head and said, "Don't tell me you do."

"Why not?"

"Because there's no such thing."

"How do you know?"

"Because. I've never seen any proof they exist, and unlike Eliana and Marcella, a drafty room, or the wind catching a door and blowing it open or shut aren't enough to convince me they do."

"Have you any proof they don't exist?"

She stared at him and he could tell by her expression that his own belief in the possibility surprised her.

"Antonio. Come on. Do you seriously believe there might be ghosts in our midst?"

"I don't disbelieve, and if there are, their existence would explain a lot of the unexplainable stuff most of us brush off as our imagination playing tricks on us...or coincidence. What happened in my room this morning is an example."

She reached for her water glass and regarded him. "Something happened?"

Wine is bottled poetry.

Robert Louis Stevenson

The following week saw everyone scattered in different directions. Most of the inn's rooms were booked, people checking in on the front end, some the back, and some for the entire week.

Antonio had barely seen any of the Bonaveras that one of them wasn't rushing here or there or off somewhere. Lucia had spent the majority of her time making sure guests enjoyed their stay—attending to them in one way or another, straightening up one of the common areas, helping Caterina with the inn's continental breakfast, or setting up afternoon cookies or biscuits, lemonade and tea. Almost every time he caught a glimpse of her she was fussing in one way or another to ensure everything met her high standards.

He'd hoped to get some time with her, to himself...selfish, but there it was. He understood, of course. She had her responsibilities, and he was...well...he didn't know what he was, what they were. Friends, he supposed. He did like her, a lot, but then there was the other. The burning attraction, purely physical, that found him lying awake several nights that week lusting for the feel of her body wrapped around his, the unquenchable desire to tap into the passion he knew flamed in her blood as hot as it did in his. She wouldn't be letting him into her bed, though, when there was almost no chance they'd see each other again after he'd gone.

Antonio frowned. He understood that as well, regardless of whether he liked it or not. He tapped his pencil against the drawings he'd been trying to finalize. Lucia had told him he could work at the large table in the library rather than the confines of his room, and he'd taken her up on it. It was easier to spread out his work there, and there was complimentary coffee just a few steps away. There was also the possibility he might see a little more of her if he worked downstairs than he had so far that week.

Tomorrow evening he'd be meeting with the four sisters again to share his ideas for their project. It was the only time they all had available to get together for more than fifteen or twenty minutes.

The drawings were taking longer than he thought they would... or should. His original intention had been to do a few rough sketches, throw in an original feature or two that would take advantage of the site, but they'd morphed into a lot more.

Their project was the kind most architects salivated over, and he was no exception. A lot of what he worked on was remodels and additions. He enjoyed the work but it could be limiting when you had to stay within the constraints of an existing structure. Yes, it was satisfying taking something ordinary and transforming it into something the client didn't think could be done. But to be able to design from the ground up without any limitations was always more exciting to him.

To see your vision come to life with each new phase, every board and nail, each peak and angle, the unique personality of your design as it revealed itself layer upon layer...that. That was the kind of project you dreamed would fall into your lap.

When it did, you clung to it, embraced it, celebrated it. You didn't walk away from it. Yet that's exactly what he'd be doing. Someone else would take his ideas, use some, discard some, incorporate them with his or her own...or throw them out entirely and work with Lucia and Cat to make their own vision a reality.

Someone else would be invited to the Grand Opening party when it was all done and be congratulated by the attending guests for creating such a jewel. Lucia would be handing him a glass of champagne, toasting him with everyone else, and perhaps leaning in to give him a kiss of gratitude for making her dreams come true.

Antonio pushed away from the table and stood up. He walked over to one of the windows and stared outside. There were several cars parked in the gravel lot off to the side of the main building. Another one pulled in as he watched and two couples got out and crossed over to the path that led to the front porch, probably coming to do a tasting.

Eliana had been busy doing tours and tastings all week. He'd even gone to one yesterday afternoon when she'd seen him working in the library as she was leading a group into the solarium, and invited him to join them. It had been an enjoyable break. Lucia's sister had a way with people, engaged them easily with her quick wit and outgoing personality. He'd been impressed with how deftly she'd drawn everyone out and made the tasting more fun as opposed to just pouring samples and describing the wine.

He reached up and rubbed the back of his neck, stretched it from side to side to work out the kink that had developed from leaning over his work. Why the hell was he putting so much into these drawings? It didn't matter how inspired his design might be, when whoever they hired would no doubt toss it and come up with one of their own to impress Lucia.

Was that it? Was that what he was feeling so frustrated about? If so, he'd better get over it. In the end, he wouldn't have any say over the final design. And he wouldn't have any say about how Lucia might decide to show her gratitude to whoever the lucky bastard was who did.

He went back to the desk and gathered his things. He needed to get out for a few hours and clear his head. Forget about the drawings. Forget about the project. Forget about the woman who'd gotten under his skin in a way he'd never imagined would happen.

"OKAY, I HAVE you scheduled to arrive on Monday of next week and checking out on Thursday morning. We look forward to seeing you then, Mr. Connelly, and thank you." Lucia hung up the phone just as the front door opened and Antonio walked inside.

"Hey there," she said, happy to see him after merely crossing paths with him most of the week, and walked out from behind the reception desk.

It had been an especially busy day, but most of the guests had gone out for the evening, off to get dinner at one of the area restaurants. After the last few days, she could think of nothing more pleasant than a quiet evening enjoying some down time—unless the evening included Antonio enjoying it with her. Yes, that would make it significantly more pleasant.

"Are you going out to eat this evening or will you be staying in?" she asked, hoping he hadn't already made plans.

"I'll probably run out to get something in about an hour. Or, since I was out most of the afternoon, I may pick something up, bring it back to my room, and spend the evening watching the television or reading. Why do you ask?"

"Most of the other guests are out and about, so it should be a quiet night around here. I'm thinking of opening a bottle of wine and seeing what I can forage from the kitchen. Would you be interested in joining me?"

"Yes."

"I like your decisiveness."

He sent her a sexy glance that made her want to groan. Good Lord but the man was dangerous to her libido! Did he have any idea what kind of effect he had on women when he gave them one of those looks?

"Well..." He raised his hand and held up an index finger. "I could spend the evening alone in my room eating lo mien out of a paper carton, or..." He raised a second finger. "I could spend it going on a scavenger hunt for my dinner, and then follow that up with a bottle of wine and a bit of lively conversation with a beautiful woman." He dropped his hand, a smile playing with his lips, teasing her. "It's not a difficult choice."

She grinned, impossible not to. He was flirtatious and charming, all in a good way, lighthearted and lacking the ulterior motives of some men who might use sweet words for the sole purpose of breaking down a woman's resistance. It was just a part of who he was, a natural, but playful, romantic side he wasn't afraid to show, and she liked that about him.

"You are so good for my ego, choosing me and potluck over Chinese take-out." She poked him in the chest. "I am really going to miss you when you leave here, mister."

He stared at her a moment, a look in his eyes that made her wonder what might have been if their circumstances were different: if they didn't live five thousand miles apart; if they didn't both have jobs, responsibilities, commitments; if they weren't both tied to something larger than the last ten days and this crazy, unexplainable, and unfortunately, to remain mostly platonic attraction. If she knew he was a more permanent fixture, would she be willing to take a chance on love again and risk a more intimate relationship with him?

"Okay, so..." He reached up, pushed a hand through his hair. "Do you want me to meet you back down here in the lobby in...what?"

"How about an hour?"

Antonio agreed and then left without saying anything else. Kind of abrupt, she thought, even odd given they'd been enjoying a pleasant bantering back and forth right up until then.

Lucia shook it off. Maybe he had to go to the bathroom. She couldn't think of why else he would have just bolted that way and left her standing in the middle of the lobby.

"FORAGING FOR FOOD is a lot easier in a chef's kitchen than the one in my apartment back home," Antonio told Lucia a short while later as they enjoyed the spoils of their hunt.

The evening was warm enough that Lucia thought it would be nice to eat on the stone terrace off of the solarium. She had covered one of the outdoor tables with a crisp white tablecloth and then added one of the vases of fresh roses and hydrangea blossoms from the library's mantle, as well as several white pillar candles in varying sizes.

The soft, flickering light, temperate weather, and a chorus of crickets serenading in the background combined to heighten the magic Lucia had always thought seemed intrinsic to the night. They would definitely have to include an outdoor dining area for the new restaurant where their guests could choose to eat alfresco when conditions allowed.

"Oh! I didn't get a chance to tell you; we put a bid on that property yesterday morning and Cat got a call back in the afternoon. The sellers accepted our offer."

"That's great. Congratulations." Antonio picked up his wine glass and raised it toward her in a toast. "To your success, may it become everything you hope it will be."

Lucia tapped the rim of her glass to his. "Thank you." She took a sip before going on. "I thought we had a good shot since it's been on the market so long, but I didn't want to get too excited until we had a deal. Now that we do I can't wait to see your ideas."

Antonio nodded and then looked down at his wine, turning his glass and staring at it as if it held a secret he wanted to discover. "I hope you find something in them you can use," he finally said, and then ran his tongue along the inside of his cheek.

Lucia drew her brows together. "Hey, are you okay?"

His eyes came back up slowly to rest on hers. "What's that?"

"I asked if you were okay. You look...I don't know...like something's bothering you."

"No, I'm fine."

She squinted at him, not so convinced.

"Really." He reached across the table and took her hand. "I'm very happy for you and Cat. Just promise me a couple of things."

"What?"

"Whomever you hire to take on the project, make sure it's someone who listens to you and you feel you can communicate with. This is your dream. You want to make sure they care enough to listen to you and understand it, and can then embrace your vision and give you what you want."

She gave a nod. "I promise we'll try." He had more on his mind, of that she felt sure, but if he wanted to share it with her, he would. She didn't feel she was in a position to push him.

An owl hooted from somewhere nearby; another answered its call from a different part of the woods. She and Antonio both glanced toward the tree line. They didn't see it, but Lucia recognized its call.

"A great horned owl." She cocked her ear when the sound came again. "I love hearing them. Sometimes a pair will get a duet going, calling back and forth to each other."

Antonio sat back, looked around. He rolled the stem of his glass between long fingers. Lucia swallowed. She could almost feel them caressing her skin. Maybe the scene she'd created held too much magic, or perhaps it was just the man who'd cast a spell over her. Whichever the case, desire stirred within her...a dangerous thing for a cautious heart.

"I can understand how this land captivated your parents, enticed them to start a new life here. It's nice that the city hasn't swallowed everything up and there are a few rural areas like this still around with the horse farms and vineyards. I think I expected it would all be one massive, never-ending DC suburb."

"A lot of people are surprised that way. You don't have to drive too far to find the urban sprawl, complete with the logjam traffic and everything else that goes with it. But you're right, we're lucky DC's tentacles haven't reached into every corner of the county. There are several local towns that have been able to hold on to their charm."

"Do you see yourself staying here then...growing old here?"

"I haven't thought much about it, but yes, I suppose so. I missed it when I was up north. I didn't realize how much until I came home again. Now that Cat and I are planning to open a new business less than a mile down the road, I suppose that means I've made a commitment to the area."

He only nodded, then stood, refilled his wine glass. "How would you like to go for a walk?"

"Sure." She wrapped a finger around the stem of her glass as she stood and came around the table.

Twilight deepened as they ambled side by side, their pace relaxed, unhurried. Lucia wondered again at Antonio's mood, the seemingly sudden changes she'd witnessed that afternoon...again this evening. Granted, she'd only known him a couple of weeks, but she'd developed a sense of him, at least enough of one to know something was off with him today. Maybe he was thinking about leaving. He'd only stayed the extra week as a favor to her and her sisters. Once he went over his drawings with them, there'd be no reason for him to hang around. Was he restless, looking forward to resuming his travels?

A wave of sorrow caught her off guard, washed over her, took a hold on her heart and gave it a good squeeze. She looked off toward the mountains, a rolling silhouette against the fading light, swallowed, and firmed herself against the emotion. His leaving was inevitable. She'd known all along he would go. She'd also known indulging her attraction to him would make his parting more difficult. She wouldn't dwell on that now, though, not yet.

What she wanted to do now was tuck away the sadness, just be with him—in whatever space of time they had left—and for both their sakes, she'd also tuck away the truth of how deeply she wished he could stay. The fact she wanted him to was proof he had the power to hurt her if he'd been anything but honest, but he'd been upfront with her about his plans since the night they met.

"So." Lucia swung her arms as they walked past a large swath of trellised vines whose grapes had produced an award-winning Chardonnay last year. She was determined to chase away solemn thoughts and to be in the moment. "I spotted some of Caterina's mini-cheesecakes in the freezer. Can I tempt you into pilfering a couple of them with me after our walk? I'll make some cappuccino to go with it."

Antonio flashed one of his heart-stopping smiles, and hers tripped and paused a moment before picking up the beat again. "Lead the way and I'll follow you into temptation."

"Tough to turn down Cat's cheesecake."

He continued to look at her, indigo eyes roaming over her face the way his fingers might if he put his hands there. And then he did, laid them against her cheeks, lowered his head, and she lost control of her thoughts again.

"Among other things, *bella donna.*

What though youth gave love and roses,
Age still leaves us friends and wine.

Thomas Moore

*H*e'd gone out for a jog, wanted the exercise, and hoped the fresh air might help dispel the funk that had hung over him for the last day or two like a dense fog he couldn't see his way clear of.

He was used to working out on a more regular basis and it felt good to get out and push his body, shake out his muscles. He wasn't sure the effort helped clear his mind, though.

Antonio sprinted up the short hill that ended where the road split. The right fork bent toward the property Lucia and Caterina would be purchasing if the deal went through. He slowed his pace as it came into view, taking in the landscape of it. When he reached the center point of the land, he stopped, faced it.

He grasped the hem of his grey tee shirt, wiped his face and the back of his neck with it. The fingers of a light afternoon breeze brushed across his stomach. He welcomed its cooling touch, breathed in the fresh, clean fragrance of the apple blossoms covering the copse of trees in the small orchard on the back of the property. Delicate, airy flowers covered the trees in a veil of pink and white, and as he studied them he imagined how they might be used as a landscape feature.

From where he stood, he could envision his design anchoring the property, the Blue Ridge Mountains as a backdrop. The setting sun would bathe the fieldstone façade he would suggest if it were his project in warm gold tones in the evening, inspiring the inn's guests to stroll the grounds, the restaurant's diners to order a café and dessert, an aperitif, some little thing to extend their meal and embrace the mood he imagined it all would inspire.

He expected they would do well. With Caterina's restaurant knowledge and flair in the kitchen, and Lucia's personal touch and high standards the cornerstones of the inn, once they got discovered, neither should lack for customers. And Eliana, he was certain, would take care of that.

He stood transfixed, a picture of what it could be clear in his mind's eye...his vision, crafted from theirs, brought to life. He struggled with a sense of vesting that had begun to take root from the first morning he'd walked the site, studied the angles of shadow from the mountains and how they played in the light. He'd asked the land to speak to him, to tell him what to make of it, for it, and when it did he'd listened. It whispered through his drawings, every line, every angle, every post and arch...all for someone else to silence his vision with one of their own.

Antonio pushed his hands through his sweat-dampened hair, shook it out. If he came back in five years, stood in this same spot looking at whatever that person designed, would he feel he'd betrayed it?

Several crows flew overhead, calling out. He looked up, watched them fly toward the vineyard, his thoughts taking flight with them, winging in and out of conflicting scenarios he couldn't believe he was even considering.

He'd planned on leaving Saturday morning, start working his way south, stop at a few different places along the way until he reached Key West. He hadn't decided whether he'd head west or north after that. And now, he didn't know, not after the crazy thoughts he had that could actually be a solution to his problems if Lucia would agree to play along with him.

He still hadn't worked out how he'd present his idea to her. If he told her the truth, would she understand his position and agree to help him out of it, or would she think the time they'd spent together had been nothing more than an attempt to win her over for his own selfish purposes?

His plan was a radical one, one he couldn't even believe he was considering. But his nonno had him by the balls, and he and Lucia's grandfather had arranged things so that it gave Antonio little choice but to play along or face the consequences. He didn't like deceiving Lucia, and not telling her about the financial stipulations he'd only just recently learned about himself felt like a deception...was a deception.

"Damn you, old man," he cursed under his breath. Right now he saw three possible scenarios: deceiving his grandfather, deceiving Lucia, or telling his grandfather to fuck the contract and deal with the fallout.

His mind circled back to the Bonavera project. What would Lucia think about the ideas he'd laid out for them? And how much would the answer to that question influence what he did next?

THURSDAY EVENING THE five of them gathered in the library. Caterina had whipped up a selection of hearty appetizers including miniature pastry tarts filled with crab imperial, some with Gorgonzola cheese and caramelized onions baked to a light, golden brown, skewers of broiled shrimp wrapped in bacon, chicken satay, fresh-baked bread, and a platter of assorted sliced meats, cheese, and grapes. And to drink, two bottles of the winery's award-winning Chardonnay.

They agreed it would be best to eat first while the food was still warm before getting down to the business and discussing Antonio's ideas.

"We've got a full house this weekend," Lucia said as she reached for a skewer with chicken satay and put it on her plate. "I got two more reservations this morning, so you'll probably be busy with tastings, El."

"I'll see if McKenzie can come in. She told me a couple of weeks ago she'd be willing to take any extra shifts she could get. We've got five pre-scheduled groups, but with three of us on hand we should be able to accommodate whatever guests and walk-ins we get."

"Does that mean I'm on tastings this weekend?" Marcella asked from behind them where she was already sitting on the couch attacking her food.

Eliana snagged a piece of still-warm bread. "That's right, and with things ramping up for the season, probably the next several unless we find someone to replace Carly soon."

Marcella snorted. "Damn Carly for getting married and moving to Boston."

"Yeah, how dare she fall in love and give up her part-time job here so she could go live with her new husband." Lucia got some bread, too, and exchanged amused looks with Eliana and Cat.

"It'll be good for you, Marcella," Cat said. "Look at it as an opportunity to practice your social skills."

"There's nothing wrong with my social skills. I just don't find talking to strangers all day particularly enjoyable, especially when they don't even seem to be trying to experience the wine properly. I mean, they're tastings, not mixers."

Eliana leaned forward and looked past Lucia to Antonio. "She'd rather talk to plants."

"I heard that. At least plants don't tell stupid jokes, spout meaningless flattery, or sit through three tastings trying to convince someone who has no interest whatsoever to go out to dinner with them."

The rest of them found a place to sit around the big, square coffee table, joining Marcella and Caterina who'd already gotten their food.

Cat reached for her wine and took a sip. She smiled mischievously at Marcella. "El told me you had an admirer. She said he was all big, puppy-in-love eyes, with drool running down his chin when he looked at you. Maybe you should have accepted his invitation."

Marcella grimaced. "If I decide to go out on a dinner date, it's not going to be with someone who creeps me out by staring at me all night and slobbering between courses."

When they finished eating, everyone helped clean away the food and dishes so Antonio could spread out his drawings on the coffee table. He took the rubber band off and unrolled them.

"Keep in mind these are just concept drawings, similar to the proposal drawings you'd get from someone after an initial meeting to discuss what you wanted to do. So—" He flattened them out over the table. "Based on my understanding of what you want, here's what I've come up with."

They spent the next forty-five minutes going over his ideas. He fielded their questions with a patience Lucia found admirable.

Everyone wanted him to expand on this or that aspect, tried to move ahead to lighting options, paint colors, what kind of material would work best on the dining room chairs, wouldn't a pergola be lovely over the outdoor eating area, and got so caught up in their excitement that he had to gently reel them back in.

"Most of those things won't come into play until the developmental drawings are done. Not that you can't think about what you'd like now," he allowed with a twitching grin, clearly amused by their enthusiasm, "but in the first phase of drawings that kind of detail isn't included."

"It's hard not to get ahead of ourselves." Lucia wrapped her hands around her arms as if trying to contain all the possibilities that started to take flight as soon as she'd seen what he presented. "Especially after what you've shown us. It's just so fabulous. I had a feeling whatever you did would be good, but it's beyond anything I envisioned."

"I second that," Cat said. "You're amazing! The way you took our mishmash of ideas and put them into such a clear vision, I mean, how were you able to decipher everything we said and give us exactly what we wanted when we weren't even sure what it was yet?"

Antonio chuckled. "That's part of my job, to try to understand what my clients want even if they have a hard time expressing it."

"Well!" Cat stood up and refilled her wine glass. "Based on what you came up with, I'd say you're very good at your job."

"Some more here too, please," Eliana held her glass in the air for Caterina to pour her some. "And in case anyone cares what Marcella or I think..." She looked at Antonio and smiled broadly. "It's simply fabulous, darling." She leaned into Marcella who sat beside her on the couch. "Right, sis?"

"You won't hear any argument from me." Marcella turned toward Lucia. "Are you planning on still living here when it's all done or moving over to the new inn?"

"I haven't thought that far in advance. But even if I do move, I'll only be a short walk away, little sister. We'll probably still see each other almost every day."

"Oh, I wasn't worried about that. I just wanted to put first dibs on your room in case El had designs on it. The bathroom's much bigger than the one in mine."

"So much for sisterly bonds." Lucia glanced at Antonio and realized they were straying off track again. "Sorry. We tend to take a lot of detours no matter what we're talking about."

He raised a hand and shook his head. "No, it's okay. I'm glad you all seem happy with what I've shown you, and I'm more than content to sit here, sipping my wine, in the company of four charming women. I'm in no hurry to rush the evening to a closure."

Lucia hiked a thumb toward him and looked at her sisters. "He's good, isn't he?" And he really was. Better than good. Almost too good to be true, which since he'd be leaving soon, he was...too good to be true. She sighed lightly, and tried to ignore the reminder that his time here was speeding away, no matter how dangerous it could be to her heart if he didn't leave soon.

"You really did manage to capture everything we wanted, Antonio. Do you think it would be possible for us to just hire a contractor and let them use your drawing to do the work?" Cat asked.

"No. You'll need someone to do full design drawings, and once you all agree on those, they'd need to do detailed ones that would include construction specs for the contractor."

Cat sat back down, frowned. "But what if they change things, like some of the stuff you talked about that you didn't put in yet?"

"We could insist they use Antonio's design and do the other drawings from that," Lucia suggested. "It is our project."

"We could, but would they feel the same level of commitment if we hired them to implement someone else's design?"

Lucia shrugged. "They might. Who knows?"

"Well, I don't really want to consider another design after seeing this one. It's exactly what we want and we shouldn't have to compromise."

Antonio looked from Caterina to Lucia and then sat forward and rested his elbows on his knees. "If you really want to use my design, and you're sure it will meet your needs, I know someone who'd be willing to take it on and not change anything."

All four sisters swung their gaze in his direction.

"Absolutely," Cat said without hesitation.

Lucia reached out and covered one of his hands with her own. "That would certainly make this easier for us, Antonio. I know I speak for Cat and me both...and Marcella and El, too," she added, glancing at her other two sisters and smiling. Even though they wouldn't be owners in the new venture, the change would have a major impact on all of them, and because they were a family, everyone's opinion was important.

"We've fallen in love with your ideas," Lucia went on. "If you know someone we could trust to implement them with the same kind of vision, we'd definitely be interested in talking to them."

He turned his hand up, wrapped his fingers around the back of hers, and looked at her, his expression serious.

"Me."

THE ROOM WENT dead silent for about five seconds and then exploded in a series of reactions with all four sisters talking and asking questions at the same time.

Lucia stood up and held her hands in the air. "Stop!"

The noise level began to abate, like a helium balloon losing air, gradually declining and then falling away. Not so the energy. Eliana twirled her foot with the fervor of a puppy wagging its tail at the sound of his mistress arriving home for the night. Cat paced behind the two club chairs in front of the fireplace. Marcella chewed on the side of her thumbnail as if it were a Belgian chocolate.

And Antonio. Gorgeous male, sculpted cheekbones, firm lips, cobalt blue eyes that had the power to make her start to salivate every time she looked into them. Antonio, the man she'd lusted after from the get-go but held it in check—not counting their steamy kisses—because she'd known he'd be leaving any day. And now...

He just sat there, leaning forward with his arms resting on his knees, his fingers laced together in front of them, watching her, watching and waiting for her response.

"By 'me' are you saying you'd be willing to work with us as the architect throughout the entire process? From beginning to end?"

"That's what I meant. If the four of you agree you want me to." He glanced around at them. "You don't have to decide this moment. You can talk amongst yourselves and let me know after you've had a chance to consider it more."

"No! I mean, yes! We don't need to think about it. You've got the job!" Caterina pumped her fist in the air.

"Hold on a minute, Cat," Lucia said. She'd be no less thrilled to have him work with them, but there were logistics to consider, and questions pushing into her head that needed to be asked. Not just for them, but for him...to make sure they weren't rushing into a decision on a whim.

Lucia sat back down. "Have you thought this through, Antonio? If you did this, it could take a year, maybe more depending on how it goes. Won't being away from your firm and home that long create issues?"

"Are you trying to talk me out of it, Lucia?"

"No, not at all," she hurried to assure him. "But it would be a huge commitment. What are the legal issues? Can you even stay here that long without getting some kind of work visa or something? What's going to happen with your job at home? And...why? Why would you want to do this when your life is in Italy?"

"You packed a lot in there." He gave her a crooked smile, one corner of his mouth hooking up higher than the other, and she lusted for the feel of it on her own. She was so weak where he was concerned...and that could create a whole bucket load of other issues.

"I'll have to make some arrangements with my team back home, but they're more than capable of running the office without me being there physically. If they want to consult with me on anything, we can do that by phone. I can also go back for a few days here and there. Once the construction begins I'll only be visiting the site to do routine progress checks and if any issues come up, so that's not as big a deal as you might think."

Lucia looked around the room; none of her sisters seemed to need or want any more convincing. They all appeared to be on board and ready to move full steam ahead. Someone needed to pause, be reasonable, understand the hows and whys.

"There aren't any real legal issues either." Antonio continued to address her questions. "We'll have the usual ones to deal with relating to the project but that's all standard stuff. I don't need a visa, just my passport to travel between countries."

"Are you sure about that?" Lucia furrowed her brow. She was no expert on the matter, but she didn't think a passport would be enough for him to come and go at will. "I didn't think you could stay in another country for an extended period without some kind of special documentation."

"Normally that's true, but I was born here...well, in Florida. My mother's family lived there and my parents would visit for a few months every year on holiday. I was born during one of those visits, which automatically made me a U.S. citizen."

"Oh my God, that's so cool," Eliana said. "So you have dual citizenship?"

Antonio chuckled. "Yes. A fortunate accident. And handy if I'm going to be here for a while. I'm also licensed to work in the States. The U.S. doesn't have a reciprocal arrangement with Italy, but I provided all the necessary documentation and went through the exam and licensing process several years ago when I was working on a project in upstate New York."

"It sounds like there shouldn't be any hurdles to your working with us, then," Cat said. "When will I get to see the kitchen design? I know the exact appliances I want, and how I want things to flow."

Lucia cleared her throat. "Before we get there—" She sent her sister a look that said *we're not done here yet.*

Cat threw her arms in the air, clearly of a different mind, but she acquiesced by sitting back down in one of the wing chairs.

"The fact you have dual citizenship would make things a lot easier, but there's still the question of whether you really want to commit to spending a year or more of your life here, and why."

"I guess the answer's the same to both of those things. Your project's the kind I get the most satisfaction from, and I don't want to see someone who doesn't have the same vision I shared with you come in and change it. The vision of what it can be, the possibilities, they're in my head. When I spent time walking the ground, it spoke to me. I don't know if you can understand that, but I know what it needs, what it wants. I already own it, in my mind it's mine, and I don't want to hand it over to someone else who doesn't see it the same way I do. It already has its hooks in me."

Antonio angled his head, looked into her eyes, and held her gaze. "I'm offering to take this on because I want to do it. The prospect is exciting to me and I know I'll get a lot of satisfaction from it. It's as simple as that."

Was it really? Lucia mused.

She drew in a slow breath as she considered all he'd said. She still had questions, or maybe they were concerns, but after seeing the thought he'd put into the design, she could understand how he might feel an ownership and not want to let it go.

Her sisters watched her with varying degrees of impatience. She was the only one dragging her feet on a final decision, and it wasn't because she didn't think he'd do an amazing job; she knew he would. They were friends, more really, but despite that, or maybe because of it, she wanted him to be sure about what he was getting himself into.

She tried to read what was in his eyes. He arched a brow, waiting for her response. "Well then," she said, hoping she wasn't making a mistake any of them would come to regret, "I guess we've got ourselves an architect."

They celebrated with a bottle of champagne. Cat surprised them all by going into the kitchen and returning with an exquisite lemon meringue pie she'd baked that afternoon.

"I had a craving," she said by way of explanation as she set it on the coffee table. "And now a good reason to celebrate."

Lucia caught her bottom lip between her teeth and grinned, let her excitement have its turn. "It's starting to feel real. We're going to have to start thinking of a name now."

"I've already thought of one," Marcella said, surprising everyone. "Serendipity. I like the sound of the word and it certainly seems to fit. Our decision to keep the winery after Mom and Dad died, getting the land just down the road so we can all stay close, Antonio showing up when he did and offering to work with us...it all feels very fortuitous."

"Well, I don't know about that, but I do like the name." Cat cut the pie and started lifting pieces onto plates for everyone.

"I like it too. Serendipity." Lucia rolled the name around her tongue and smiled. It was a good name.

"I'LL CHECK IN on you next week, Nonno. I just got to the car so I've got to go. Behave yourself, old man." Antonio slid his cell into his back pocket and got into the rental.

His grandfather could think whatever he wanted but the man was wrong. Dead wrong. His decision had nothing to do with fate. He'd decided to work with the Bonaveras because their project excited him, and he didn't want to see someone else come in and convince them to do something that would be totally wrong for the property, totally wrong for them. Try convincing the old man of that, though.

Antonio snorted. He didn't have that kind of patience.

No, he hadn't told him yet that he was considering honoring the contract. When he did, there was no reason to tell him the marriage would only be a temporary arrangement. But even if he did, his nonno probably wouldn't care. The man almost certainly would believe destiny was playing her hand, that he and Lucia were meant to fall in love and live happily ever after, and that the only person Antonio was fooling was himself.

What a fairy tale! The only reason he was even considering such a drastic action was to secure his financial independence and get out from under the restrictions of that damned contract once and for all. He had to figure the best way to present it to Lucia. He'd have to tell her about the trust so she understood why he'd suggest such a radical idea. But he thought he might have come up with something she could agree to, something that would be fair to everyone.

He put the car in reverse and backed out of the gravel parking lot. Now that he'd be staying indefinitely he'd have to look into getting his car shipped over to the States. It would be cheaper than renting one for a year or two.

The inn was booked for the weekend, tourists lured by the beautiful spring weather, the history, the wineries, the restaurants, and the pastoral countryside sheltered in these foothills of the Blue Ridge.

When he'd gone downstairs for coffee and one of Caterina's cranberry-orange muffins that morning, Lucia had been bustling about, refilling the brochure racks, straightening the magazines on the library tables, gathering cups and plates left behind by guests who'd decided to enjoy their breakfast in the library or at one of the seating areas on the large, wraparound porch rather than take it back to their room or eat in the solarium.

She had a greeting for any guests who were about, stopping whatever she was doing to take a moment to inquire about their comfort. *How were they enjoying their stay? Was their room to their liking? Yes, she'd be happy to make dinner reservations for them in town.*

She'd had a greeting for him, too. A good morning, how are you, topped off with an enchanting smile and a discreet pat to the backside he was pretty sure she hadn't given to any of the other guests.

Antonio smiled and clucked his tongue. She could handle his backside anytime she wanted. It might be his imagination but she'd seemed more open, more inviting since their meeting Thursday evening. And wasn't that an interesting development?

Maybe now that she knew he'd be staying for an extended period of time, she wasn't as opposed to a more intimate relationship. She'd definitely been a little friendlier than before with that little hand to butt maneuver this morning. Considering what he had in mind, he'd need to be very careful how he proceeded with her, though. The attraction between them was strong, and he'd fantasized about making love to her more than once, but at what cost? When the time came for him to go back to Italy, he didn't want to leave with regrets. He'd prefer if they could part friends.

With an inn full of guests, Antonio knew Lucia would be tied up most of the weekend, in full innkeeper mode, so he'd decided to head out on his own, get to know the area better, and while he was out he intended to pick up some things he needed.

After a morning of going from store to store, he'd had enough of shopping. He'd found most of what he needed to get started working on their job. He also had two new pair of jeans, one blue and one black, two grey tee shirts, navy running shorts, and some athletic socks to show for his effort.

Now, his stomach said it wanted food. He pulled out his phone and did a search for Caulfield's, the restaurant where Lucia told him Caterina worked, and keyed the address into the GPS. She was supposed to be working today. He didn't know what kind of menu they had, but based on what he'd tasted of her cooking, he suspected the food would be excellent.

Following the prompt on the GPS, he got on the Harry Byrd Highway. About fifteen minutes and a couple of turns later he found the restaurant. It was in Ashburn, which, like Leesburg where he'd done his shopping, appeared to be a bit more suburban and sophisticated than some of the other nearby towns.

Caulfield's was in a newer development that had been designed like a town center and included a number of other restaurants and retail stores. There were a lot of people out and about, and he had to hunt for a parking spot.

The restaurant was busy with a lunch crowd but he only had a short wait before being seated. After looking over the menu, he placed his order for a Croque-Monsieur and some specialty fries—parmesan and parsley.

The sandwich and fries were exceptional, and when his waiter brought the check, Antonio asked if it would be possible to give his compliments to the chef. Since he'd chosen the restaurant because of Caterina, he thought she might like to know he'd stopped in.

"Antonio! What are you doing here?" she asked when she walked up to his table, her surprise evident.

"I heard the chef was incomparable so I thought I'd give it a try."

Caterina laughed and wrapped one of her arms around her waist. "Oh, you did? And what's your opinion of the rumors?"

"They were absolutely correct. That was the best sandwich I've had in a very long time."

"What did you get?"

"The Croque-Monsieur. It's one of my favorites but not typically on a lot of menus." He had a small amount of wine left in his glass and finished it off.

"Would you like more wine?"

"You might be able to talk me into another glass if you can join me for a few minutes."

"For a couple, but not long." She signaled the waiter working his section and asked him to bring another glass of whatever Antonio was drinking.

"So you're out on your own? Taking advantage of this gorgeous day to do some sightseeing?" She pulled out a chair and sat down.

"That, and picking up a few things I needed. Everyone's busy at the winery. When I left, they already had two groups waiting to do tastings, and Lucia was restocking the breakfast selections for her guests."

"Spring's always busy with tourists. Fall's busier, more like try to find a moment to catch your breath busy, but this time of year we never lack for guests at the inn or coming for tastings."

The waiter returned with another glass of wine and set it on the table.

"That one's on the house, Drew," Caterina told him.

Antonio raised the glass. "Thank you."

"You're welcome." She crossed her legs and looked around the room, checking out the customers, gauging their pleasure with their meals, her eyes resting a moment on this one and that before moving on.

"I'm so happy we're going to be working with you. I *cannot* wait to see more detailed drawings." She leaned forward and grinned. "Not to be impatient, but when do you think you're going to have them ready?"

"I should have the next set ready soon. Those will have a defined layout of the spaces and construction materials. I'll make suggestions, but the final choices will be yours and Lucia's. Once we've all agreed on that we can move on to what will probably be the fun part for you and your sisters."

She laughed and started to say something but stopped when a man approached their table.

"Excuse me." He looked at Antonio. "I hope you enjoyed your lunch."

"I did, thank you. It was excellent."

"Good to hear." He gave a slight smile that looked more obligatory and practiced than sincere. "Would you mind if I steal Caterina from you? I need to speak with her in the kitchen."

The man turned toward Cat. Antonio thought he looked annoyed, or impatient. He could be wrong, but the guy seemed unhappy with her about something.

Caterina stood up stiffly and he saw her draw in a breath, as if trying to steady her emotions. The man took several steps to leave then turned back around and looked at her, as if to say, *are you coming?*

"Thanks for stopping by. If you come in again, let me know you're here before you pay for your meal." She patted him on the shoulder and the hard line of her mouth softened a bit. "See you later."

Antonio stopped her with a hand on her forearm. Lowering his voice, he asked, "Are you okay?"

"Fine," she said, but her expression was tight.

"Who the hell was that?" He heard the man mumble when Caterina reached his side. Antonio frowned after them. Whoever the guy was, his instincts told him she'd be happier if she didn't have to work with him.

Was he the owner, her boss? And although the possibility bothered him because he liked Caterina, he wondered if her relationship to the man might be something more—something more personal.

Eight

They gave each other a smile with a future in it.
Ring Lardner

A hike! What did she have to wear on a hike? Why had she agreed to go on a hike? And what the hell was she supposed to do when they were out there...on a hike?

Lucia combed her fingers through her hair, gathered it into a ponytail, and secured it with a hair band.

Okay, maybe it was just the word. It conjured images of slogging through woods, trudging up hills, sweating, and swatting away bugs.

She probably needed to wear something on her feet that had tread. She didn't have hiking shoes, but Eliana might have something in her vast shoe collection that she could borrow. She had some khaki shorts, and she'd wear a white tee so she could see any bugs, like ticks that might get on her.

"Oh God! I'm probably going to wind up with Lyme disease!"

Did she have bug spray? How she hated that stuff—the smell, the sticky greasy feel of it, the way every gnat, piece of grit, and dust in the universe clung to it like a magnet.

When Antonio asked if she'd go hiking with him, she'd said yes. Before giving it any thought—before remembering she didn't like snakes and berry brambles and lugging backpacks around—she'd said yes because she liked spending time with him. And they hadn't had much opportunity to spend much together this week.

She'd been busy taking care of guests and the dozen things that came up during the course of the day. She was happiest when guests were in residence, though, enjoyed doing little things to make their stay a memorable one.

She had a knack for decorating, creating pretty, inviting spaces, and making guests feel special. She'd already started several folders on Houzz and Pinterest with design ideas for Serendipity—premature, maybe, but she couldn't help herself.

Antonio would probably just smile if she showed him how much she'd already collected in the way of inspiration. Smile and then store it away, the things she liked, her design style, her visions, the same as he would when Cat specified what commercial range she wanted, what kind of shelving, work counters, and lighting. He would humor them their excitement but store it all away and remember their visions of the finished product. And he'd find ways to blend their dreams with his design. Just as he'd done in the initial drawings.

Yeah, he was a good listener, which appealed to her. So far, she hadn't discovered anything about him that didn't. And now that he'd be staying and she'd have a lot more time to get to know him, what would she do about the desire that had been growing between the two of them?

Part of her wanted to take a risk, experience everything they could be together, to enjoy being with a man she knew in her bones would be a lover like none she'd ever experienced before or ever would again. Could she do it, though? Embark on an affair with a man she also knew she had no real future with? Maybe she shouldn't worry so much about it and see what happened, let nature takes its course.

Ugh! Nature—the hike! They were supposed to meet downstairs in twenty minutes and if she didn't want Antonio to leave without her, she needed to get her butt moving.

She ruffled through her drawers and came up with some khakis and a tee, put them on, gathered things she might need—a hat, sunscreen, an extra hair band, Band-Aids, a long-sleeved white blouse—and stuffed everything into a backpack she found hanging in the back of her closet.

Before heading to Eliana's room, she searched the bathroom and found some bug spray. As she slid it into one of the pack's side pockets, she prayed, *Please Jesus, don't let me regret this outing.*

"I NEED HIKING boots," Lucia announced upon entering Eliana's room, her voice devoid of enthusiasm.

El rooted through her closet and came back out with three pair to choose from.

"What are you doing with so many pairs of these? Have you ever even gone hiking?" Lucia shook her head, although she shouldn't have been surprised. Shopping for something in Eliana's closet was as good as going into Macy's.

"No, but they look really cute with a pair of mid-calf socks. I've got some you can borrow." She pulled several pair from a drawer and laid them out on the dresser.

Eliana gave her a once-over. "Okay, these." She held up a pair of brown tweedy ones and tossed them to Lucia.

She sat on the bed and tugged them on, then put on the boots her sister chose for her outfit, a pair of brown leather ones that came about three inches above her ankles and laced up the front.

"Don't lace them all the way. Tie them off just under the top two eyelets, and fold the socks down so they come just over the tops."

Lucia glanced up. "Do you want to dress me?"

"Just saying. You want to look the part."

"What? Like a hiking fashionista?"

"Hey, no matter what you're doing there's no reason not to look good doing it."

Lucia took a last turn of the socks. "There. Do I meet your approval?"

"What's more important is whether you'll meet with Antonio's. Although from what I've observed, you seem to have that one covered."

Lucia grinned. "He might have a little thing for me."

"Ha! Little! The man wants to get biblical with you. And I don't mean read verses together. And I'll just bet he can perform some miracles between the sheets."

"We haven't gotten to that point yet, and I'm running late. Thanks for putting the finishing touches on my ensemble. Gotta go."

Eliana called from behind her, "I didn't miss the 'yet' part of that statement. Is my overly cautious sister actually considering letting her guard down with a man? I'll want details if it happens, you know."

Lucia smiled as she walked out the door. Surprisingly, she *was* considering it. And if she did give in to her desires, she wouldn't be surprised at all if Eliana was right.

127

MARCELLA STRETCHED OUT on one of the couches in the library. The last of the guests had checked out the morning before. Cat had gotten called in to work again on her night off. Eliana was out somewhere, Marcella didn't know where, and Lucia was traipsing around the foothills of the Appalachian Trail with Antonio.

Lucia hiking…she'd like to see that! Her sister never willingly ventured far from the paved path. She enjoyed tending the flower borders around the inn, but beyond that Luch preferred to look at nature, not commune with it.

Marcella settled back against the armrest, kicked off her sneakers, and opened her book, looking forward to enjoying a quiet evening and some uninterrupted reading.

She only made it through a couple of pages when the front door opened and Antonio strode in carrying Lucia in his arms. Marcella set her book down, got up and walked into reception.

"Is everything okay or are you two just…you know?"

"Your sister sprained her ankle," Antonio said, tightening his hold.

"It's nothing serious," Lucia assured her, "just a little sore, probably from the swelling. I could have made it in here on my own but Antonio insisted on carrying me."

Marcella grinned. She just bet he had. "Why don't you drop her on the couch and I'll get some ice from the kitchen."

Antonio carried Lucia into the library and set her down as if she were made of glass.

"Careful you don't break her," Marcella teased, and got the skunk eye from her sister.

She returned with an ice pack a few minutes later and handed it to Lucia. "So what happened? Did you lose your footing on some rocks?"

Antonio's lips twitched but he said nothing.

"It was these damn boots." Lucia smirked. "They've got all this tread, and it grips to tile. It wasn't my fault."

"They have tiled trails in the foothills these days?"

"Don't be a smartass, little sister. I did quite nicely hiking, thank you. It happened when we stopped to get dinner on the way home. The restaurant had a tiled entry and the toe on the boot caught and tripped me—then I turned my ankle."

Marcella cupped a hand to her mouth, laughed behind it. "Sorry, it's just ironic you waited until you were on a smooth, flat surface to trip yourself."

"Thanks for the sympathy."

"Hey, I got you some ice, didn't I?"

"You did. Thank you." Lucia rearranged the pack on her ankle. "It was embarrassing, though. I took a six-foot lobster down with me."

"What?" Marcella choked out another laugh and looked at Antonio. He shook his head, clearly trying to contain his own laughter.

"Yeah. When I started to go down, I grabbed out for something to hold on to and the closest thing was this giant plastic lobster in the entryway. I landed on top of it. Unfortunately, it lost a claw."

Antonio couldn't restrain himself any longer, and the three of them were wiping tears of laughter from their cheeks when Eliana walked in and found them that way.

AFTER FIFTEEN MINUTES with the ice pack and a rehashing for Eliana, Antonio carried Lucia up two flights of stairs to the third level where the family had their private rooms.

"The last door on the left," Lucia said when he turned into the hallway.

She reached down and opened the door and he carried her inside. "Bed or chair?" he asked.

"The bed. If you want to hang out, you can pile some throw pillows from the settee against the headboard and we can both prop ourselves up. I can text El to see if she'll bring up a bottle of wine. Interested?"

He dipped his head, pinned her with devilishly sexy eyes. "You invite me to join you on your bed and you think I might refuse?"

Lucia licked her lips. Maybe spraining her ankle wouldn't turn out to be such a bad thing after all. "I always believe in giving people a choice."

He chuckled low and deep. It vibrated along her nerves as if he were strumming his fingers over them. She cut off the flicker of apprehension that made her question if this was smart.

She was tired of denying herself because she might get hurt. Brad was one man, a man who happened years ago. He wasn't every man, just one bastard she'd believed when she shouldn't have and then let the hurt over his betrayal keep her from fully trusting anyone since.

It had to end. She had to move on. If she never let herself trust again, she'd end up a very lonely old lady. That wasn't what she wanted for herself.

Antonio helped Lucia get situated, propping her ankle on a large pillow. He took off her boots, and she could tell he was trying to be as gentle as possible.

"Are you okay?" he asked as he took off his own shoes and then swung his legs up to sit next to her.

"I think I'll live." She finished texting El, then turned her head and smiled at him. "You know I probably could have managed getting up the stairs on my own."

"Maybe, but I liked carrying you."

"Oh, you did?"

He leaned toward her and planted a kiss on her lips. "Yeah, I like getting my hands on you. Any excuse will do."

She nipped his lower lip. "Maybe you don't need an excuse."

"Good to know." He weaved his fingers into her hair and leaned in, kissed her again, hungry and deep.

It took no time for desire's flames to flare. His mouth was a potent accelerant, stoking the fire, and part of her wanted to welcome the burn. Despite her desire, another part cautioned they'd get there but shouldn't rush into the inferno just yet. It nagged and she grumped at it.

As much as she wanted to evict her more rational side, it wouldn't let go easily, so because she was trying to move forward, she negotiated with it. There was no reason not to enjoy some of the heat. That she would agree to. That she wanted to savor. A hearty snack until, and if, they both decided they were ready to bring on the full course.

There was a knock on the door. From the other side Eliana said, "Medicine's here."

Antonio pulled away, his eyes promised they'd continue where they left off.

Lucia smoothed her hair and then called to her sister. "Come on in, El."

Eliana walked in carrying a bottle of Petit Verdot and two glasses. She held them in the air. "Where do you want these?"

"The table on this side," Antonio suggested, and got up to take them from her.

She glanced at Lucia's foot, propped on the pillow. "How's the ankle?"

"S'okay. The ice took some of the swelling down and that helped."

"That's good. I'm going to make myself a snack plate for dinner. Since you two didn't get to eat after you did your jig with the lobster, do you want me to make one for you, too?"

"That would be nice. Thanks."

"No big. Nothing fancy, just some brie and crackers, and maybe some fruit. It depends on what I can find in the kitchen."

"I can help put together a plate for Lucia and me. That way you won't have to bring it back up," Antonio offered.

"That's fine." El spotted her boots at the foot of the bed and plucked them up. "Guess you won't be wanting to wear these again anytime soon."

"Doubt it. I think I'll stick to stilettos; they're much safer."

Her sister laughed and then made for the door.

Antonio walked around to Lucia's side of the bed and looked down at her. "Do you need anything before I go downstairs?"

"I'm good, but if I need to get up, I think I can manage. It's just a sprain."

"You still shouldn't be walking around on it. Promise me you'll stay put until I get back."

Lucia rolled her eyes. "Fine, I'll just sit here like an invalid. And if I need to get up to go to the bathroom or something, I'll hop."

She grinned when he scowled at her. "Just go. I'm not going to have to get up for anything."

"All right. I shouldn't be long." He turned when he got to the door. "Remember your promise."

She made the sign of an X over her heart. She leaned back against the pillows when he left and closed her eyes. Aside from the sprain, she'd had a great time today. She'd never have imagined she could enjoy trekking through woods, climbing hills, and spending almost five hours communing with nature. That was more Marcella's thing.

She had, though. Most of the trails were well maintained, so her vision of hacking through brambles, peeling vines off her skin, and picking twigs from her hair never came to pass. It had been a beautiful day, with plenty of sunshine and a light breeze that kept them from getting too warm.

There were many clearings along the trail, with scenic over-looks. They'd even come upon a pretty waterfall where she stopped to take some pictures, including a couple of selfies of her and Antonio, one in which they were smiling normally, and one with them making a face.

She sat forward and reached for her cell on the nightstand to look at the photos. She enlarged the first picture to see Antonio's features better. Good Lord, the man was handsome. His eyes were such a bright, clear blue. They reminded her of the water along the Nepali Coast in Kauai. She'd only been to Hawaii once, but she'd never forget how breathtakingly beautiful the water had been. And his eyes were no less so.

When she scrolled to the second one, she laughed. They both looked silly, and happy, like two kids goofing off.

He enjoyed life, and she enjoyed that about him. Too many of the men she'd dated were...not boring...but it was as if they couldn't let loose, as if they had some kind of playbook in their head about how men could or should act. She'd always just wanted them to be real. Maybe that was one of the reasons she had trust issues. She could never be sure if the man she thought them to be was the man they actually were. She'd never felt that way with Antonio.

She switched back to the first shot. He had his arm slung loosely over her shoulders. She was leaning into him, her free arm around his waist, and they were smiling. They looked like lovers. If things kept going the way they were, maybe soon they would be.

It warms the blood, adds luster to the eyes,
And wine and love have ever been allies.

Ovid, *The Art of Love*

June was barely two weeks old when Antonio went downstairs on a Wednesday morning to tell Lucia he'd made arrangements to take a short trip back to Italy and would be leaving Saturday morning.

"How long will you be gone?"

"A week, just enough time to meet with my associates, check in on my grandfather, and tie up some loose ends before I get too far into the job here. I'll be returning the following Saturday. Would there be an out-of-the-way place I could store some things if I return with a couple of extra cases?"

"There's plenty of room in the attic." Lucia tilted her head and he could see she had an idea brewing. "You know, you could probably put a makeshift office up there. It's fairly large and there's lighting and outlets so you'd have power. I haven't been up there since I was a kid, but I remember it being a decent space."

"If no one would mind me taking over a piece of it, I wouldn't mind having a dedicated workplace."

"No one will mind. It probably needs a good cleaning, so you'll need to ignore the dust and whatever clutter's up there."

"Thanks, I'll check it out when I go back upstairs." He leaned against the reception desk, saw the spark of amusement come into her eyes when he dipped his head and stared into them. "That wasn't the only reason I stopped down to see you."

"No?" Lucia rested her elbows on the desk and propped her chin in her hands. "What else can I do for you, Mr. DeLuca?"

"How about getting one of your sisters to cover for you and going out with me Friday night?"

"Caterina's working and El's got a date, but I don't think Marcella has plans. I'll check with her this afternoon and if she can, then I'd love to."

"Okay, let me know." He hesitated, wondering if he should say anything about the scene he witnessed at Caulfield's? He wasn't family, but he cared about Lucia and her sisters.

"Do you have something else on your mind?"

Antonio stuck his tongue in his cheek, debated, and then decided he'd want to know if it was his sister and someone had seen something concerning. "It might not be my place, and I won't be offended if you tell me to mind my own business, but does your sister have a problem with one of the guys she works with?"

Lucia narrowed her eyes. "Why do you ask?"

Both her look and tone told him he'd struck on something. He shrugged, not wanting to make too big a deal of it if he was off base, but wanting to make one of Caterina's sisters aware if he wasn't.

"Remember the day I told you I stopped there for lunch and Caterina came out to my table?"

"Yeah. You said she gave you a complimentary glass of wine. Did something else happen you didn't tell me about?"

"I observed a scene between her and a man who came over to my table and stood there until I finished whatever I was saying to your sister. He excused himself and then asked if he could steal her because he had something he needed to talk to her about in the kitchen."

"Was it Mitch?"

"He didn't introduce himself but my guess is he worked there. He acted like he was in a position of authority. I got the impression he was annoyed, and your sister didn't seem too happy with him either."

Lucia shook her head, a look of disgust on her face. "It had to be Mitch. I wish I knew what that guy's story is. Eliana and I are worried he's taking advantage of Cat and she's got blinders on or something."

"Is Mitch her boss?"

She frowned. "Yes, and unfortunately, he's her boyfriend as well. I've got a bad feeling about him, though."

"I didn't get a good one, either. I hope I haven't upset you by bringing it up."

"No. If you picked up negative vibes during such a brief encounter, it just convinces me more that Eliana and I are right about the guy."

"Have you talked to Caterina about your concerns?"

"Once or twice, but she gets defensive and makes excuses for him. Honestly, I don't think she's happy, but she either doesn't want to admit there's a problem or...I don't know, maybe she doesn't want to risk getting fired if she stood up to him."

"I don't get the impression she'd let any man push her around for long before she stood her ground, even if it meant losing her job."

"Let's hope so." Lucia reached out and took his hand. "I'm glad you said something. You wouldn't have brought it up if you didn't care, and that means a lot to me."

One of the inn's guests walked into the lobby, and Antonio gave her hand a squeeze before releasing it.

"I'll get out of here so you can get back to work. Since you offered, I'm going to go check out the attic to see if it might work as an office space."

LIGHT STREAMED INTO the room through two sets of double-hung windows on the front wall and another set on one of the long side walls, making the attic much brighter than Antonio had anticipated. The walls and ceilings were finished and would need nothing more than a coat of paint to freshen things up.

Pine planking covered the floors. It creaked when he walked across it. Old wood, but it seemed to be in good shape, and solid.

There were a few boxes scattered here and there, several old trunks, and some small furniture items, things no one had much use for but hadn't wanted to throw out. Forgotten items.

If he consolidated everything in the back corner, it would only take up about six square feet, leaving the majority of the room empty. There was enough space he could even pick up some inexpensive furniture and create a place to stretch out if he got tired of working at a desk.

He planned to reach out to some local builders when he got back from his trip, see if he could pick up a few more jobs, renovations, the like. He'd still be consulting with his team back home, but he'd need something else here to keep busy when he wasn't working on the Bonavera's job.

He turned around, took another look at the space. It would be more than adequate for his needs. Pleased, Antonio left the attic and went back down to the main level.

Lucia was on the phone taking a reservation. She looked up and smiled at him as he walked through the lobby. He gave her a wink and held his keys in the air.

"Be back in a couple of hours," he mouthed.

She nodded, holding the phone to her ear with her shoulder. She lifted her free hand in a wave as she jotted something in the registry book with the other. He found her efficiency a total turn-on. There was little about her that didn't turn him on. He wasn't sure what that said about his growing feelings for her, but he'd deal with them if and when the time came they needed to be dealt with.

They hadn't talked about their feelings, or what they might be involved in. Were they in a relationship now? Just friends? He shook his head as he climbed into the car. No, they'd become more than friends. He just wasn't sure what, or what it meant for his plans.

Antonio frowned. When had he ever spent time analyzing a relationship or where it was headed? He didn't want to do that now, but their situation was different. He enjoyed spending time with her, so he would. And when the time was right, he'd present her with his proposal and hope she'd be amenable to it.

Ten

The eye sees only what the mind is
prepared to comprehend.

Robertson Davies

*D*uring the week Antonio was away, Lucia and her sisters cleaned the attic and repainted everything with a fresh coat of crisp, white paint. They moved all the boxes and trunks, most of which they had no idea what they contained, to the back corner of the room. Lucia blocked them from view with two Chinese screens she'd bought for the purpose. One day they'd have to go through them to see what they contained and weed things out.

The glass panes in the windows, which probably hadn't been cleaned in decades, now sparkled and let even more light into the room.

It would be a nice surprise when Antonio returned and saw what they'd accomplished, and he could use the time he would have spent doing it himself to finish the next set of drawings instead. The sooner they could move on to the construction draw-ings, the sooner they could start interviewing contractors.

Next week they were going to settlement. Once they actually owned the property, Lucia knew both she and Cat would be even more anxious to move ahead.

It had been another full house that weekend, and Lucia had been glad to be busy. It surprised her how much she missed Anto-nio. She'd gotten used to seeing him every day, even if it was just to exchange a few words in passing. The first couple of days after he left she'd found herself looking up whenever the front door opened. Her heart would race at the possibility of seeing him walk through, and then she'd remember he was out of the country. It should frighten her, these emotions he stirred, and it did a little, but mostly he made her happy, and her heart kept telling her to trust him. Maybe it was time she listened to it.

With the last guest having checked out that morning, and no more scheduled to arrive until Friday, Lucia had the rest of the day, and most of Wednesday and Thursday, to herself.

Darcy would be in Thursday to give all the rooms a thorough going over, put fresh sheets and blankets on the beds, clean tow-els in the baths, and restock the necessary toiletries. She current-ly only came in two days a week, but when Serendipity opened as a boutique hotel and full-service restaurant, they might need to bring her on full time, and possibly someone else. At least that was Lucia's hope.

She ate a quick lunch of yogurt with fruit, went up to her room to change into a pair of jeans and an old, long-sleeved navy tee, and climbed the stairs to the attic.

The paint supplies and drop cloths they'd put down to protect the floorboards were still spread around the room. She wanted to get everything put away and give the floors a final cleaning before Antonio got back.

Gathering up all the empty cans first, she loaded them into one of the cardboard boxes she'd brought up earlier. She stacked those that still had paint in them by the door to return to the basement. Everything else—masking tape, caulk, the single-edge blades they'd used to scrape splatters from the window panes, trays, and the unused brushes and roller covers—went into another box.

Lastly, she folded the drop cloths and set them next to the boxes. Taking a final look around to make sure she hadn't missed anything, she picked up the box of empty cans. She could probably carry everything to the basement in three trips, and then she'd deal with the floor.

Balancing the box on one hip, Lucia reached for the doorknob and gave it a pull. The door stuck. She tried again but it didn't budge. She put the box down, grabbed the knob with both hands, and pulled. When it still didn't open, she put a foot against the frame and gave it all she had, as if she were in a tug-of-war.

"What the...?" *Maybe the little release thingy's catching.* She turned the handle again, as far as it would go—nothing.

"Are you freaking kidding me?"

Wrestling with the door was getting her nowhere. Lucia pounded on it. "Hello, can anyone hear me?"

No one heeded her summons.

Not sure what else to do, she sank to the floor with a groan. Good thing she'd eaten something before she came up here. There was no telling when one of her sisters would venture to their room and hear her up here banging about.

One of the Chinese screens she'd put up to block the boxes and trunks in the far corner fell onto the floor with a bang and she jumped.

Lucia slapped a hand over her heart. "Way to startle a girl." She blew out a relieved breath and stood up. *The windows.*

Hurrying across the room, she unlatched the lock on one of the ones that looked out over the front of the house and lifted up on it. "Really?"

She went to the next one, the next, the last. "You're all freaking stuck!"

They hadn't painted them shut. She knew it. They'd taken extra care to move them up and down while painting so that wouldn't happen, and they'd opened and closed easily enough then.

The second Chinese screen fell and she spun around, startled again by the sharp crack of wood smacking against wood when it hit the floor. She stared at the toppled screens. The foot braces were supposed to prevent them from falling over. Maybe the floor was uneven and they just hadn't noticed when they put them up.

She sighed in frustration. She had plans to get together with Jenna for happy hour at O'Dwyer's Pub, so if she didn't get out of here soon, the floors would have to wait until tomorrow.

She shivered and rubbed her hands up and down her arms. She hadn't noticed it being so cool when she'd been packing up the supplies. The temperature seemed to take another dip.

Lucia rolled her jaw, trailed her eyes around the room as a ridiculous possibility popped into her head.

No! She shook her head. There was a logical explanation for everything—the stuck door, the windows that refused to budge, the chill in the air, and...she turned toward the far corner, both of those screens spontaneously falling over by themselves.

She didn't believe in ghosts. *Yeah, but what about Antonio thinking he saw someone standing next to his bed on the same morning I thought I saw someone in my room? Well, he admitted he might have been dreaming. Still...*

"Okay, look, I don't believe in—I don't know—ghosts, spirits, whatever, but if by some..." She rolled her eyes toward the ceiling, staring at it a moment before going on. "I can't believe I'm even saying this, but if there is someone here, you know, like Rosa, or whoever, could you just cut the crap? I've got things to do."

The room remained awash in silence. Lucia reached up, massaged her temples. What would she do if no one found her for several hours?

"Please?" she whispered into the empty room.

She heard a click behind her and spun to see the door drift partially ajar.

Lucia bolted for it, yanked it all the way open and darted into the hallway. From the other side of the threshold she stood and looked around the room. The next time she came up here she was bringing something to wedge in the door.

"SO WHEN DO I get to meet this guy?" Jenna asked Lucia as they sat at one of the high-tops in O'Dwyer's for happy hour sharing a selection of appetizers and sipping three dollar glasses of wine.

"He's out of town until the weekend, gone back to Italy to take care of some things, but now that he's going to be working with us I'm sure you'll meet him when you come by the winery."

"Have you slept with him yet?"

"Jesus, Jenna, I told you I've only known him a month."

"So? You want to, and don't try to deny it. You've got this *bill's long overdue and the creditor's knocking at the door* written all over you when you talk about him."

"Maybe I don't want to rush things." Lucia swirled her glass on the top of the table, making small circles with the foot, and then took a sip.

"Why? You like him. You said you think he likes you."

"Because I'm still not sure it's worth the risk. Even though he's going to be here a while now, he *will be* returning to Italy when everything's done. I could fall in love with him with no effort at all. I mean the real thing—the want to spend every spare minute with, share food from your own fork with, offer to give barefoot massages to and not get grossed out by it—kind of thing."

Jenna laughed. "I've never liked a guy enough to offer to rub down his smelly feet."

"Me neither. That's just the point. If I think about massaging Antonio's bare feet, it doesn't make me cringe. It should make me cringe, but it doesn't. Don't you think that's dangerous? Maybe I'm already half in love with him, and if I start sleeping with him, I might not be able to slow down the train. We'll just keep barreling down the track until we come to the last stop and it's time for him to get off and go back to Italy."

Lucia leaned toward the table and propped her chin in her hand. "And where would that leave me? Standing on a platform waving goodbye as I watch him walk away, trying to keep the pieces of my breaking heart from scattering all over the tracks to get crushed even more."

"You know you're doing it again, right?"

"Doing what exactly?"

"Talking yourself out of what could be a very satisfying relationship because of Brad."

"Oh, here we go. Don't start with that, Jen. That was over three years ago. I'm over it. Wanting to take a little time to get to know someone better before getting sweaty and naked with them isn't the result of any long-harbored psychological repression over someone I should have never gotten involved with in the first place."

"Yeah, it is. He charmed you, swept you off your feet, you lost your head over him, wanted to marry him and make babies together, and then you found out you weren't the only one who wanted to spend your life with him and make babies together. He broke your heart, you felt like a fool, and although you say you've scrubbed the last of the grimy dregs from that experience from your subconscious, you still keep a foot on the brake pedal, and whenever you start feeling something for a guy, that foot starts twitching."

Jenna picked up a piece of the shrimp appetizer. "Remember who you're talking to, honey. This is me, your best friend, so I know better. You're not willing to risk your heart again, so to avoid any possible pain you deny yourself the joy."

"Are you gonna send me a bill for that diagnosis, or should I just pay your part of the tab?"

"No charge. That's what friends are for." Jenna dipped her shrimp into some cocktail sauce and, holding it by the tail, wagged it in the air at her. "And friends are also for telling you when you should take a chance on something that you might regret *not* taking a chance on when you had the opportunity. Take your foot off the brake, Luch. If you're not ready to push the accelerator to the floor and fly into paradise with the man, try coasting."

Lucia flipped her hair back behind her shoulders, smiled across the table at her friend.

Jenna popped the shrimp into her mouth, chewed, and then swallowed. "You're thinking about it, aren't you?"

"Kind of."

"Go for it, honey. Trust me, you'll regret it if you don't, and if it doesn't work out and he breaks your heart, I'll apologize for steering you wrong and let you have my Donatella."

"The strapless, powder blue satin dress with the full-length back zipper?"

"Yeah. The one I wore New Year's Eve."

Lucia tilted her head, thought a moment, and then reached her glass across the table to tap it to Jenna's. "Okay, deal."

"Wow. You must really love that dress."

"Who wouldn't? It's gorgeous, but the truth is, I don't know if I can resist him much longer even if I wanted to. The attraction is just too strong, and you're right, I let what happened with Brad make me overly cautious. It's time I stop denying myself because there's a chance I might get hurt. There's just as much a chance I could be missing out on something wonderful."

Jenna stared at her with an open mouth. "Then what the hell was that *I don't know if it's worth the risk,* and *I might have to rub his feet* shit all about?"

Lucia shrugged. "I wanted to get your perspective, give you a chance to talk me out of it in case you came up with a compelling reason I should reconsider."

"You just snookered me out of my Donatella."

"I'll let you borrow it."

"Maybe he won't break your heart and it stays in my closet."

"In this particular case, I hope you're right. All joking aside, Antonio's a good man and I care about him a lot. When the time comes for him to leave, it would be nice if we can remain friends and remember each other with a smile rather than sadness."

"Sounds like you're ready for another glass of wine."

"Yeah...you?"

Jenna signaled their waiter. Lucia had begun to wax poetic, but she meant what she'd said. Regardless of what happened between them, she hoped she would always look back on their time together as a special chapter in her life...without regrets.

"WHERE ARE YOU going?" Eliana asked when Lucia passed her on the stairs carrying a WetJet and a three-foot-long two-by-four.

"The attic. I just finished clearing everything out of there, and now I want to clean the floor so it'll be ready for Antonio to set up his office next week."

Eliana hitched her head toward the two-by-four. "What are you going to do with that?"

Lucia grimaced, not sure if she wanted to say anything about what had happened the day before. The door and window might just have been sticking because they'd swelled from the heat... although that rationale didn't hold water since the temperature had dropped to the point she'd started shivering.

"I want to wedge the door open so I don't have to keep opening and closing it when I'm going in and out—you know, like if I've got my arms full or something."

"I thought you said you just finished clearing everything out." Eliana narrowed her eyes, looked suspicious.

"Yeah, well—" Lucia had told her that, and although it might be a plausible reason if she actually was planning to take things in and out, the explanation rang hollow at the moment, and El was a master at reading subtleties. It was one of the things that made her so good at her job.

"What's the deal, Luch? You've got that look you get when you're trying to hide something."

"I don't get a look."

"Yes, you do. Like the time you borrowed my white jeans to wear to Billy Wilson's graduation party, and you spilled a plate of meatballs all over them and then couldn't get the stains out. That look."

"You're asking me what's up because of *a look* you remember from when we were in high school."

"No, not just then. You get it whenever you're trying to cover something up."

"There's no cover-up going on, El. It's no big deal. The door got jammed when I was up there yesterday, and I don't want to take a chance of it happening again today and I end up stuck in there for hours before I can get it open or one of you comes looking for me."

"So why do you need to wedge it? Why don't you just leave the door open?"

"Because it might not stay open. It might get blown shut by a draft...or something."

Eliana stared at her a few seconds. "Okay, suit yourself, but just so you know, you're being weird about it. Makes a person wonder why." She turned and started jogging up the stairs.

"Where are you going?"

"To the attic. I had to cut out early the other day and never got to see what it looked like after you guys finished. I'm curious to see how it came out."

Lucia tucked the WetJet handle under one arm and the board under the other and followed her sister up.

The door to the attic stood open and El was inside looking around. Lucia propped the board between the door and the frame and closed it just enough to make sure it held fast so it wouldn't fall out before committing to going inside.

"The light in here's fabulous," Eliana said, turning in a circle. "It's a shame none of us realized what a great space this was until now."

"Maybe when Antonio's done using it, you and Marcella can turn it into a retreat. Paint the floorboards white to make it even brighter, bring in some sparkle, loads of cheerful pillows, glass tables..."

"I hope that doesn't mean you and Cat are planning on spending all of your time at Serendipity. This is still the family home, you know. We'd want you guys to be a part of anything we might do up here. And you're the one with the most talent for decorating, so you'd have to be involved in that part of it."

"Of course, this will always be home, and we'll still spend lots of time here. There's no reason for Cat to move. She's not going to be running the inn, just the restaurant, and I haven't decided what I'm going to do. I may keep a room there just in case I need to stay for some reason, but I might keep living here and have a pager so guests can reach me at night if they need to."

"Okay, well that makes me feel better. Don't get me wrong, I'm excited about the project. I just don't want to go for weeks without seeing you guys."

"Yeah, that's not going to happen, so stop worrying." Lucia put an arm around her sister and gave her brief hug. "So, I think Antonio's going to be pretty comfortable in here."

She turned, took in the rest of the room, admired how nice it had come out, and then stopped short.

"What the hell's the problem with those screens? I just stood them back up before I carried down the last load of stuff to put in the basement." She shook her head and went to put them up again. "We're going to need to brace these things. They fell over when I was up here by myself yesterday and startled the bejeebies out of me they made such a racket."

"I thought that's what the cross feet were for," Eliana said, "to stabilize them."

"Yeah, me too, but they don't do a very good job. This is the second time they toppled."

Her sister walked over and gave them a jiggle. "They seem sturdy. Are you sure you didn't bump up against them and knock them over when you were doing something?"

Lucia looked at her and skewed her eyes. "No, El, I didn't accidentally bump them over, *twice*! I wasn't anywhere near them when they fell."

"Gee, I don't know, Luch. You get locked in here and can't get the door open, things start falling over on their own. Maybe it was Rosa trying to tell you something."

"So you think I should blame it on the family ghost? You think *that's* the most logical explanation?"

"Hey, just saying. Did anything else happen? Like the lights flickering off and on, the room suddenly getting cold?"

Lucia hesitated a moment too long and Eliana jumped on it.

"Ha! Something else did happen. What?" Her eyes danced with excitement, but then, like Marcella, El was more open to and, Lucia thought, might even think it would be cool if their aunt's spirit haunted the family home.

"So give it up, Luch. Tell me."

Lucia dropped her head back and moaned. "Okay, so a couple of things might have happened that I can't explain yet." She hooked her thumbs through the belt loops on her jeans. "The windows are stuck now, too. We had them open when we were painting, but now they won't budge."

Eliana darted across the room and unlatched one of the front windows. She gave it a push and it slid up with no effort. She turned and arched a brow. "Stuck, huh?"

Lucia sputtered. "Well, it was, they all were!"

"Umm hmm. What else?"

"That's all. That and the room..." Lucia waggled her head. "It did sort of get cooler after the door jammed."

"Sounds like some pretty convincing stuff to me, sis. So what'd you do to get out?"

Lucia cleared her throat. Of everything that happened, that was the thing that had freaked her out the most, and how did she explain that without adding more fodder to her sister's already racing imagination?

Oh, what the hell? Eliana already believed Rosa was behind everything.

"The door opened. I sort of...and look, I'm not saying I believe anything, but I was feeling kind of desperate to get out. So, I said I was tired of the crap and if someone was there to cut it out because I had things to do. And nothing happened. And then I said *please*, and...well...the door just kind of opened by itself."

"Oh my God! And you still have doubts? That's what that board's all about, isn't it? Insurance in case Rosa thought to shut you in here again. I can't wait to tell Cat and Marcella; they're going to die when they hear about this."

"I hope not. In the event I'm wrong, one ghost haunting our family home is enough."

One of the Chinese screens fell over. Lucia and Eliana both let out a little scream at the sudden clatter.

"Holy crap!" Eliana twirled around and laughed. "Hey, Rosa, if that's you, I hope you like what we've done up here. It looks good, doesn't it?"

There was no response. When Lucia realized she was holding her breath, she let it out slowly. Just great! Was she going to start questioning her own logic and reason now, or was it possible they could still come up with a rational explanation for the growing number of odd happenings?

Eleven

I can certainly see that you know your wine.
Most of the guests who stay here wouldn't know
the difference between Bordeaux and Claret.

Basil Fawlty, *Fawlty Towers*

ucia was clearing away the Saturday afternoon setup when Antonio walked into the inn, back from his trip to Italy. When she saw him, her heart leaped, hopping around like a child who'd just been set free in a toy store.

She set the cups she'd been about to carry into the kitchen back down on the guest bar and faced him.

"Hey, you. How'd it go?"

"Hey yourself," he returned her greeting with a grin that made her leaping heart pound even faster. "The trip went well. A day and a half travelling each way was a bit rough, but I accomplished what I wanted and got to spend some time with my grandfather, so I'm glad I went."

He rolled the two suitcases he'd come in with to the side of the door and walked over to where she stood. Lucia got a whiff of his cologne, clean, slightly spicy—him. He slid a hand around her waist, eyes smiling into hers, and pulled her hard against him for a kiss.

Yeah, she'd missed him, missed that, and now that he was back she wouldn't have to cram her days with things to do when they didn't have guests to keep from thinking about just how much.

"I'm glad you're back," she said when he broke for air.

"Me too. I've got a few more things to bring in from the car. If it's not a problem, I'll put the stuff for work right in the attic. I'll probably spend most of tomorrow up there cleaning, maybe buy some paint and splash it on the walls and ceiling if you and your sisters don't mind."

"Already done. We had a bunch of paint in the basement from prior projects, so we had a pizza and painting party. It came out nice. I think you'll be amazed how bright and airy it feels."

"That was generous of all of you. Thanks, and I'll thank your sisters when I see them. I guess that means I'll go shopping for office furniture tomorrow instead now."

"You're welcome, but we weren't being completely altruistic. The sooner you get your office set up the sooner you can get down to work and the sooner we can move forward with our plans."

"Ahh, I begin to understand. I'm just a cog you're trying to keep oiled so everything runs as efficiently as possible."

"Well, not just, although you are an important cog. And the most important one to help us get things off the ground. Off the ground, get it?"

He smirked and she waved a hand in the air. "Okay, dumb joke; you've probably heard a version of the same one a hundred times."

"A couple, but no one ever looked as cute saying it as you did."

Lucia punched him in the shoulder. "Flatterer."

Antonio chuckled. "I'd better get the rest of my stuff unpacked. I parked in front of the walkway to unload and should bring it in so I can move the car in case any of your guests are about."

He went in and out three more times, putting his haul on the side of the lobby, and then went back out again to move his rental. When he returned, he spent the next fifteen minutes carrying everything upstairs, either to deposit in his room or the attic.

Lucia busied herself by finishing up the task she'd started before he'd gotten back from his trip. After clearing away the last of the afternoon setup, she wiped down the refreshment bar and put the large floral arrangement she'd temporarily tucked underneath back on top of the sideboard.

"I'll unpack later," Antonio announced as he strolled back into the lobby. "I don't really feel like getting back in the car, but I've got to go get something to eat. They ran out of sandwiches on the last leg of my flight, and the only options left didn't appeal to me. All I've had since breakfast during my layover was something called a scramblewich, basically some liquid eggs wrapped up in a tortilla shell with two overcooked turkey sausage patties."

"Poor baby."

"Is that false empathy?"

"No, I mean it. You must be starving." She ran a finger down his muscular chest, wanting do more but limiting her affection in case a guest walked in on them.

"Would you be interested in another option?" she asked, grinning up at him.

"If it's as tempting as you are right now, I'm all ears."

"I can't leave. We've got a full house, so I need to be here in case something comes up, but if you'd rather not go out again, we could order something and eat it together in the solarium. I can leave the doors open and put a note on the front desk that I'm in the adjoining room if any guests come looking for me."

"I like your idea much better. What are you in the mood for?"

She was going to say *you*, but stopped short of the word popping out of her mouth and instead said, "How about lasagna? The pizza shop we order from makes pretty good pasta. We can get an order of garlic knots, too. They're to die for."

"No arguments here. I'd much rather spend my first night back sharing a meal with you than eating alone."

"Great." Lucia beamed at him. He just made her feel so good.

SHE'D ADDED TWO cannoli to the order that they were currently enjoying with a glass of Marcella's latest dessert wine experimentation. It was a sweet white she'd dubbed *Final Moments*, with hints of honeysuckle and apricot. Sweeter wines weren't typically Lucia's cup of tea, but this one was light and crisp and went well with the dessert.

A piece of the shell broke off when he bit into it, and Antonio caught it with his tongue before it could fall. "Umm, these are very good."

"Aren't they wonderful? I could easily become addicted to them. The shop's owner told me they use a blend of ricotta and mascarpone for the filling. Most places just use one or the other, and I think the combination makes the difference."

By the time they finished their pastries it was after nine. Lucia didn't expect any guests to come looking for her this late, but when they decided to take the rest of the wine outside to enjoy on the back patio, she left the solarium's French doors open just in case.

The night was warm but dry. A heavenly aroma from the night-blooming jasmine growing on the side of the house perfumed the air with its heady scent. Lucia breathed it in. "Do you smell that?"

Antonio sniffed the air. "Something sweet. It's nice." He held a chair out from one of the wrought iron café tables for her, and then pulled another beside it and sat down. He draped an arm around her shoulders, as if touching in some way had become a natural thing between them. "What is it we're smelling?"

"Night jasmine. It grows on the side of the house, but the blossoms don't fully open to release their scent until after dark, so you only smell it at night."

Lucia turned her face toward his. "Thus the name." She smiled. "I think it's one of the most delicious-smelling flowers there is, but because of its nature it isn't something you're likely to enjoy unless you happen to be out on a night like this when it's in bloom. Makes it special."

He leaned in, brushed his lips across hers, soft and light, tempting. "You're special," he whispered into her mouth, and instead of sounding trite or clichéd if someone else had said it, he'd made it sound sexy and charming at the same time.

Lucia reached up and held his head to hers, her hands cradling his face, demanding another, more thorough kiss. She knew what was happening...and wasn't it time? Didn't she want this? The thrill of it all, the heart-pounding excitement, the hot desire roaring in her blood, the chance to satisfy it all in his arms, and when it flamed to do it all over again—yes, she wanted it, craved it, and after more than a month of imagining what it would be like to experience loving him, she didn't want to only imagine.

Now that they'd be working so closely together for an extended period, to go on the way they were, denying their mutual desire, would be a cruel torture. She knew he planned to go back to Italy at the end of their project, but what if he changed his mind? Things changed, people changed, and if she refused to give them a chance, see where things went, she might be closing the door on one of the best things that might ever happen to her. Antonio wasn't like Brad. He'd never deceive her.

She angled her head back and caught her bottom lip between her teeth, gazed up at him, and leaped out of her comfort zone. "How would you like to have a pajama party tonight?"

Antonio's eyes roamed over her face, met her gaze. They looked black in the shadow of the night, serious, questioning, and with a definite gleam of interest. "A pajama party?"

"Yeah, you know. I go up to my room and get into my pajamas. You go to your room and get into your pajamas, and then you come up to my room and spend the night."

He rubbed a hand over his mouth, dragged it up over his forehead and pushed it through the black silk her fingers itched to tousle. "Are you asking what I think you're asking?"

"I'm asking if you want to spend the night with me."

He took hold of her hand, stood up, pulling her with him as he did. "Is it too early to go change?"

Lucia laughed and wrapped her arms around his waist. "Can I take that as a yes?"

"*Tesoro mio*, I've wanted to wrap myself around you and fall asleep with you in my arms since the night we met." He pulled her against him, crushing his mouth to hers.

If he doused her in gasoline and set it on fire, it couldn't match the inferno his lips working their magic on hers ignited in her blood.

"Antonio." She laid her hands against his chest, caught her breath. "I don't think I need to stay downstairs any longer. None of the guests should need me for anything this late. If they do, they can reach me on the after-hours number listed on their room phone."

"So it's pajama party time?"

Lucia stuck her tongue in the side of her mouth and bit back a laugh of pure exhilaration. Yeah, it was party time, and she couldn't wait to see what he showed up in.

WHEN LUCIA OPENED her bedroom door twenty minutes later, Antonio stood on the other side in the same black jeans and light grey oxford shirt he'd had on when he returned from his trip.

He looked at her sheepishly. "I don't have any pajamas." He stepped into the room and pulled a toothbrush out of his shirt pocket. "I brought this, though."

"You were supposed to wear what you sleep in." She spun around and showed off her satin jammies. They were the color of freshly churned cream with sprays of blushing apricot roses sprinkled all over them. She had plenty of flannels, and some comfy cotton nightgowns too, but these pretty satin ones had said *wear ME tonight*.

"I didn't think you'd want to deal with the complaints tomorrow if any of your other guests saw me in the hallway wearing what I sleep in."

"Why, what do you wear?"

He pushed the door shut and pulled her to him. "Nothing."

"I should have known. And I doubt the guests would have been grumbling, at least not the women. They probably would have booked an extra week if they thought they'd get another peek."

"Then I'm still invited to stay?"

She rose on her toes, ran her tongue along the seam between his lips. "Pajamas can be overrated. I don't always sleep in them either."

Antonio lifted her up and she wrapped her legs around his waist. He covered her mouth with his and Lucia tasted his desire as he slanted the kiss one way then the other. Neither seemed able to get enough, as if their lives depended on deepening the kiss. They feasted, ravenous with a passion to experience what each had craved for weeks.

He held her tighter, carried her over to the bed, and then turned and sat down with her legs still cradling him. He reached for the hem of her satin camisole. His fingers brushed her bare midriff as he skimmed the material up. Delicious little shivers danced along her nerves like a flock of giddy ballerinas flitting across the stage that was her skin.

Antonio whisked the thin barrier off and tossed it aside to land where it would. His lips found her neck, lingered there, tasting, nuzzling, and stoking her desire with each nip, every lick and glide, turning the little shivers into trembling quakes of need.

Lucia didn't think she'd ever wanted to make love to a man more than she did in that moment. She yanked the tails of his shirt out of his jeans and pulled it higher, running her hands up the sides of his torso. Firm, smooth, bunching with lean muscle, she knew he was going to be even more gorgeous with his clothes off. Could a woman stand that much beauty in a man?

Yeah. She thought she could handle it. She drank him in with her eyes, as he did her, as if they were desert dwellers whose thirst might never again be quenched.

He was, indeed, a fabulous specimen of a man.

SHE SEDUCED HIM. A siren he couldn't, didn't want to resist. Antonio trailed his mouth over her beautiful body, wanting to memorize every dip, curve, and swell, every inch of this woman who'd enchanted him.

The feel of her, the scent of her, the touch of her hands caressing his back and shoulders, destroyed him. He moved against her, restless with need but wanting to take his time, to savor what he'd only fantasized about until tonight.

He slid his hand up her ribcage, over her breast, felt the strong beat of her heart there, steady but fast, and he knew she wanted him as much as he wanted her. The muscles in his shoulders bunched, tension building as he tried to hold back, wanting to stretch the seconds into minutes, the minutes into moments he'd never forget.

She wasn't having it. Lucia took hold of his head and pulled him up, captured his mouth. Lips clung to lips as she clung to him. Beneath him, she burned, sexy, silken, and seductive as hell as she took the wheel and drove him out of control.

Something inside him burst and he lost the battle. His fingers sought out the root of her pleasure. A gasp rushed past her lips, into his, and he lapped it up, his senses on overload.

He molded his mouth to hers for another searing kiss before trailing it across her cheek, down her neck and then lavished her breast. She moaned, let herself go, writhing as he licked and tugged, and he thought he'd go mad.

She arched, a plea for him to take more, give her more, snapping his will. They were both frantic with desire as she gave, he took, and tried to give back to her, to answer her demands as the thin threads holding his sanity together began to unravel one by one.

Neither seemed capable of speech, too caught up in the frenzy to be able to form words. He dipped a finger inside her heat and she let out a groan that seared his soul. He inserted another and she began to ride them, hot and hungry, slick with readiness. He could stand no more.

He buried himself in her pleading warmth and she cried out. Antonio struggled to hold on, to give her more pleasure than she'd ever experienced, to drive her as crazy with need as she was driving him before she found her release.

They rode each other, hot, flaming higher and higher still as he took her beyond the bounds of anything he imagined possible. And then he felt her tighten, shudder, and fall apart in his arms. Her cry of release snapped the final tether of his will and he drove into her, his own release ripping away the last vestiges of strength he'd managed to hang on to before he poured himself into her.

They lay depleted, skin against skin, pounding heart against pounding heart, their breathing labored, mingling together so he wasn't sure which was his, which was hers. When enough time passed he could speak, he rose up on one elbow and looked down at her.

Her eyes were closed, but a satisfied smile began to lift the corners of her mouth. He leaned down and kissed it lightly. "Glad to see we both survived that."

The smile broadened and her lids fluttered open. "Me too. I wasn't sure we were going to, but if we did, I was certain the bed and everything within fifteen feet on all sides of it would be charred beyond recognition."

Antonio lay back down beside her and pulled her into his arms. "You're beautiful. Every inch of you is a work of art." He drew his hand up her arm. "I've never lost control like that before. Next time I'll try to take my time so I can draw out your pleasure."

Lucia gave him a grin that would have stirred him into action again if he had an ounce of energy left to stir.

"I've got an inn full of guests so I have to be downstairs by seven tomorrow, but if you're an early riser maybe you can show me what you mean by taking your time."

"And drawing out your pleasure."

"Yes, that too."

"Which you should know is selfish on my part since driving you to the point of no return, watching you in the throes of pleasure, and knowing you'd do anything in that moment for your release only fuels my own."

"Then by all means, take as much time as you want next time. Maybe we can set the alarm for three o'clock. That would give us a little more than three hours to drive each other mad."

Antonio let out a bark of laughter. "You, Lucia Bonavera, might possibly be the death of me."

"And you, Antonio DeLuca, have stirred to life something in me I suspect could become insatiable after tonight."

"Perfect! I'm going to be bedding a smart, funny, beautiful woman with a demanding and insatiable desire." He kissed her forehead and then whispered into her ear, "Which I'll do my very best to try and satisfy."

Lord, make me chaste – but not yet.

St. Augustine

*L*ucia snapped up her head when a cup of coffee plunked down in front of her on the reception desk.

"Thought you might need this." Her sister Caterina stood on the other side eyeing her with the attention of a bird zeroing in on a plump worm.

Picking up the cup, Lucia downed a much-needed gulp of the aromatic brew. "Thanks, I didn't have time to get any this morning."

"No wonder." Cat continued her intense study.

"*What* are you looking at? Is my lipstick smeared or something?" She rubbed a finger around her lips and looked at it to see if there was anything there, and then took another, smaller sip of coffee.

"No, I was just trying to see if you looked different after a night of hot, mind-blowing sex."

163

Lucia coughed, spitting half of the coffee back out and spraying the stack of receipts she needed to go through. "How do you know I had a night of—" She looked around and lowered her voice. "Hot, mind-blowing sex?"

"Have you forgotten my bedroom is right next to yours? You and your Italian stud weren't as quiet as you might have thought. I figured you were either practicing your wrestling moves together or you were doing some pretty heavy sweating between the sheets." Cat waggled her brows. "So how amazing was it?"

Lucia grinned. "Think the grand finale on the fourth, the perfect storm, or a fifteen on the Richter Scale."

"I think the seismic measurement only goes up to ten."

"Yeah, I know."

"I'm jealous."

"I don't know why. You're the only one who's been enjoying any action on a regular basis around here for months. Marcella hasn't been on a date in over a year. None of the guys El's gone out with lately has made it to the second date, and the last one I dated long enough to even consider going to bed with destroyed any chance when he picked me up two hours late because he didn't want to miss the end of a baseball game—and that was at least eight months ago."

She cradled the coffee cup and lifted it to her lips. "I think you'd have to agree I was overdue."

"You were, and I'm glad it happened, especially since we all placed bets on how long it would take, and I think I might have won. That doesn't mean I still can't feel a little bit jealous."

Lucia stared up at Caterina with an open mouth. "You did what!"

"Placed bets. It wasn't like there was any great mystery whether you and Antonio were going to do the deed; it was just a matter of how long you could hold out before one of you started to lose it."

Lucia shook her head and then asked, "What did you bet?"

"The losers have to pay for a pedi-mani for the winner."

"Nice. Well, happy to oblige whichever of you turns out to be the lucky benefactor of my night of pleasure." Despite learning about the bet, Lucia couldn't help but smile at the memories that sprang into her head. "My delicious, decadent, sensually perfect night of pleasure," she drawled.

"Okay, now that's just cruel. You don't have to rub it in."

"How is it cruel for me to relish one night when you've been sleeping with Mitch for who knows how many months? Don't you think the rest of us could use a satisfying romp with a man who can get the job done once in a while?"

Caterina shrugged. "Just because you get a steady diet of something doesn't always mean it's satisfying."

Lucia took in her sister's expression. It revealed more than Cat probably realized. The fact she'd even hinted there might be a problem between her and Mitch gave Lucia some hope Cat might be looking at the relationship more honestly and questioning it.

"Look, honey," Lucia began, intending only to let her sister know she had an ear if she wanted one. She didn't get the chance because the front door swung open and one of the couples staying at the inn walked inside.

"Good morning," they called, waving from across the lobby.

Lucia stood up and put on her best innkeeper's smile. "Good morning, Mr. and Mrs. Decker. You're out and about early. Are you enjoying your morning?"

"Oh, it's been lovely!" Mrs. Decker looked up at her husband. "Hasn't it been lovely, George?"

George nodded. "Lovely."

"We went to that little restaurant you recommended for breakfast. I ordered the stuffed French toast and it was so big I had to take a picture of it. George had creamed, chipped beef on toast. He always orders the same thing. I tried to get him to try something different—the restaurant had so many wonderful looking

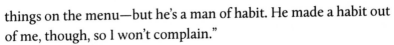
things on the menu—but he's a man of habit. He made a habit out of me, though, so I won't complain."

George smiled.

"I'm glad you enjoyed it," Lucia said, endeared by the easy, comfortable way they seemed to have with each other.

They were just rounding the entrance to the hallway from the lobby when Lucia heard Antonio's voice, exchanging good mornings with the Deckers.

She leaned sideways, peered past Caterina, and saw him saunter into the lobby. He looked like a man well pleased with himself and his world. Her spirits soared, renewing some of the energy their night before and early morning lovemaking had drained.

Cat cleared her throat. "Well, well, if he doesn't look like the cat that just lapped up the last of the cream."

"Stop it," Lucia warned under her breath.

"Good morning, ladies." Antonio's eyes took on a distinct gleam when they shifted from Caterina to Lucia.

"Good morning," Cat returned with an amused lilt to her tone. "And isn't it a beautiful one at that?"

Antonio must have picked up on her sister's teasing intent and arched a brow at Lucia. She rolled her eyes but found she couldn't hold back a smile at their expense. She was a satisfied woman this morning. Happy, content, and saw no reason not to let it show.

"I couldn't agree more." He walked up to the reception desk and came around behind where Lucia was standing. "I'm guessing our secret's out?"

Lucia nodded. "Caterina's bedroom shares a wall with mine."

"In that case..." Antonio wrapped a hand around Lucia's waist. "I guess there's no need for sneaking around, is there?" He swooped in and gave her a blistering kiss, short but deadly, hot and inciting.

"Holy crap, where's the fire extinguisher?" Cat burst out.

Antonio chuckled. "I just thought I'd give your sister something to think about while I'm out running errands today."

Lucia stretched her neck. "Like what, how uncomfortable I'm going to be all day?"

"No." He leaned in close to her ear and whispered, "How good I'm going to make you feel tonight."

Lucia closed her eyes. She couldn't help it. She managed not to groan. She looked at him again. He licked his lips and then ran his tongue over them. "*Stasera la mia bella.*"

When he walked out the door a minute later, Caterina dropped her jaw and stared at Lucia. "Are you kidding me? Is he for real? Does he have a twin brother? Jesus, Luch. Jesus!"

Lucia laughed. "I know, right?"

"Damn. We better make sure the insurance is paid up on this place because I'm seriously thinking the heat you two put off could send it up in flames."

"Oh, that was nothing, sis."

"You know what, I'm out of here. I've got to get to the restaurant." Cat slung her purse over her shoulder and made for the door. Just before she walked out she turned and said, "And just so you know, no one likes a braggart, Luch."

Lucia hugged herself and chuckled under her breath. Probably not, but wow, he was a whole lot of magnificent to brag about.

THE FURNITURE HE picked out on Sunday arrived by one thirty the next afternoon, and when the two delivery men carried everything up to the attic, Antonio was glad he'd paid the extra fifty dollars to have it delivered.

He tipped them something extra for their efforts when they were done and then got to work arranging things the way he wanted them. He turned and looked at the boxes leaning against the side wall. They contained a desk, two small file cabinets, and a printer stand, all unassembled. If he was lucky, it wouldn't take more than a couple of hours to put them together. He hadn't thought to pick up any power tools, not even a screwdriver, but he hoped Lucia and her sisters had some he could borrow to get the job done.

Before dealing with those, he arranged all the furniture into an L-shaped seating area on the area rug. In addition to having a comfortable lounging area, it could double as a meeting space if he ever needed one.

Glancing back at the boxes, he frowned. No time like the present to find out what he was up against. He opened them up and read through the instructions. It turned out the only thing he needed that wasn't included was a Phillips head screwdriver. Antonio laid out each box with the pieces for that item on top and arranged them into an assembly line of sorts.

Optimistic he'd be able to knock it all out in two hours max, he went in search of a Phillips head.

The good news was the Bonaveras had every tool he could have possibly needed and then some. Marcella, who'd taken him to the basement and told him to use whatever he wanted, said they had belonged to their father. She told him the man had liked tools.

Antonio grinned as he took the stairs back up to the attic. What she'd actually said was *my dad would drool over a new tool the way Eliana drools over a pair of Christian Louboutins.* When he'd frowned, she gave him an amused look and said, *shoes.*

He'd begun getting to know each of the sisters a little better, and it amazed him how four people with the same parents could have grown up together and turned out to be so different. They had their similarities, yes, in the way they moved, their gestures, speech patterns and the like, and their looks, of course, but their personalities were more dissimilar than not.

The job turned out to take twice as long as it should have. When he checked the time, he was surprised to see it was after six. He decided to call it a day and see if Lucia might be able to get some dinner with him.

He was worried he might have complicated matters by making love to her before telling her about his idea to nullify the betrothal contract. She knew nothing about the trust their grandfathers had established or the terms associated with it.

Although his grandfather had told him a trust had been set up for him a number of years ago, and that he could receive distribution when he turned thirty, he'd withheld a very important stipulation that, if Antonio had known upfront, he would have made different choices about how he'd managed his life up until this point.

He should have told Lucia everything before going to bed with her, but he hadn't. The moment was wrong, he didn't want to spoil the mood, she was too busy—he could list several reasons, and they might have seemed legitimate at the time, but none of them sounded very good now, not after last night.

When he'd gone to see his grandfather last week, he'd admitted that he and Lucia had gone out together a few times. It seemed like a good way to lay the groundwork for his idea in the event she agreed to go along with it. Now, he wished he'd held off because he might have made matters worse if she didn't.

His grandfather would probably push him even harder to honor the agreement. That wasn't what bothered him most about his current situation, though. What did was what Lucia would think of him when she learned the truth. He couldn't tell her now, not yet, not when she looked at him with so much trust and affection. He'd have to wait until she knew him well enough to believe his motivations had nothing to do with making love to her before trying to enlist her help with his plan.

THE GRAHAM THOMAS roses were a riot of blush-ing gold; the taller branches grew through the rails on the side of the front porch and bloomed in total abandon. Lucia snipped off enough stems to make an arrangement in the antique milk pitcher that her mother would always fill with whatever was blooming in the garden and put on the dining table.

When she was alive, her mother insisted on always having fresh flowers in the house, no matter what the season, even if it meant driving into town to buy them during winter when the gar-dens were dormant.

Lucia had inherited her mother's love for flowers. She carried on the tradition in part because she enjoyed them so much, and in part because they were a special connection she and her mom had when she was still alive. Having them in the house made Lucia feel like they were still connected.

Satisfied she had enough for a nice bouquet, she went back inside.

"Good morning, Lucia."

Lucia glanced around. "Oh, good morning, Mrs. Farrell." She walked over to the reception desk. "Can I help you with anything?"

"No. We're going to visit some of the other wineries today. I thought I'd come down and wait for my husband on the porch. I love sitting there. The gardens around the inn are so pretty, and yesterday morning when we took our breakfast out there we saw some hummingbirds. We had a lot of fun watching them. There was one that would sit on the shepherd's hook you have by the steps and guard the feeders. Whenever any other birds tried to get something to eat, it would zip in and chase them away."

"Yeah, we call that little guy Greedy McSweedy. He's got a small white patch on the shoulder of his right wing. They tend to be territorial by nature, which is why we hang several feeders, but he seems to think every one of them is for his dining plea-sure alone."

They chatted another minute or two until the inn's phone started ringing. Mrs. Farrell gave her a wave and went out to the porch. Lucia answered the call, someone wanting to make a reservation for the second week in July.

She took down the necessary information, and after confirming it and hanging up from the call, she restocked the breakfast bar with pastries, made fresh coffee, and checked to make sure there was still a nice selection of teas for guests to choose from.

She hummed as she worked—a tune she'd had stuck in her head for weeks—an earworm. She didn't know if it had a name. If it did she didn't know what it was. She vaguely recalled her mother humming something similar whenever she'd be working around the house.

Lucia smiled...another connection perhaps that she hadn't even been aware of.

She tended to be upbeat as a rule, but her mood had been even more cheerful than normal the last few days. She had Antonio to thank for that.

And now, just the thought of him was enough to warm her blood. They'd spent the night together again last night. She hadn't been able to go out to dinner with him because she'd been too busy, but she told him he could come up and spend the night without his pajamas again if he wanted to.

And he had, showing up with a pint of Chunky Monkey ice cream. They'd gotten into a conversation shortly after they met about favorite foods, and she'd told him she'd once eaten an entire pint of it by herself.

When he joined her for their no-pajama party, he brought it and two spoons with him, and they sat on her bed and fed it to each other. It was silly, and probably a little gluttonous, but it had also been one of the most romantic things any guy had ever done for her.

If she wasn't careful, she was going to fall hopelessly, no turning back, guaranteed to fall apart when he finished their project and moved back home, in love with him. Maybe she already had.

Lucia sighed, pushed away the warning to pull back now so she could avert the heartache. Anything could happen between now and then, though. She could die next week, get hit by a car crossing the street, choke to death on an olive, and she would have missed out on all the good times, the wonderful times, the incomparable times she could enjoy while he was here.

She wasn't going to deny herself in the now. She'd already jumped into the fire with both feet. If she walked out of it in a year with a few blisters, she'd deal with it.

Determined to keep all grey thoughts at bay on such a beautiful day, she busied herself around the common areas, and when there was nothing left to busy herself with inside, she went out to water the plants.

A short while later Eliana got back from her meeting with one of the vendors for the fall festival and said she could take over in reception for a couple of hours if Lucia needed a break.

She'd been dying to go up to the attic to see what Antonio had done. She hadn't been up since he returned from Italy.

"I'd love a break, thanks." Lucia gave her sister a quick hug. "I think I'll make some lunch, and while I'm at it, I'll make some for Antonio, too, and take it up to him. He's been in the attic all morning working on his office. He's probably getting hungry."

"I'll bet he is." Eliana shot her a sinful grin.

Lucia rolled her eyes. "I swear you and Cat make it sound like all Antonio and I are interested in is sex. At least Marcella can appreciate that we might be attracted to each other's personality and intellect as well."

"Oh, I know you're attracted to those things, too, but right now it's mostly about the sex. It always is in the beginning."

Lucia waved a hand in the air and headed toward the kitchen. "Fine. I'm going to go make us both a sandwich and head up to see if he has time for a quickie."

Eliana burst out laughing behind her. Lucia smiled. Of course, they'd probably indulge in no such thing in the middle of the day, but it was a delicious little thought.

"THIS IS GREAT, thanks." Antonio leaned sideways and gave Lucia a quick kiss. "I didn't realize how hungry I was."

"You're very welcome. Try some of these olives."

She'd put together a platter of cheese, sliced apples, olives stuffed with almonds, and then taken half a baguette and made a sandwich with tomato, prosciutto, provolone, salami, some oil and oregano, and cut it into six hand-sized pieces. She'd packed it all in a picnic basket with a half bottle of Petite Sirah, and they were enjoying it now on his new coffee table.

"Umm, good. You didn't have to go to all this trouble, though; a simple sandwich would have been fine." He glanced at her and smiled. "But I'm glad you did. It's all delicious, and," he added, wiggling his brows and flashing her another toe-curling smile, "I might get a chance to cop a few feels before you have to go back downstairs."

Lucia punched him in the shoulder. "You're as bad as my sisters."

"Why, do they want to cop feels too?"

She hit him again. "Eat another sandwich."

When they finished, Lucia packed the remnants of their meal back into the picnic basket.

"By the way, I talked to my grandfather this morning and he wants to come for a visit. He's thinking the first two weeks of August. He's only visited the States once, about twenty years ago.

He said since I'd be here for a while, he might as well come again to see if he likes it any better than the last time."

"What does he have against it here?"

Antonio smirked. "It's not Cortona."

"Boy, does that sound like my grandfather. I don't remember him—my grandparents both died when I was young—but based on what my parents told us, they acted like Cortona was akin to nirvana, and they would never have even considered living anyplace else. The one time they came here, when he had to come to handle his brother's estate, they couldn't wait to get home. When my mom and dad told them they wanted to stay and start a new life here, my grandparents thought they were crazy."

Antonio got a strange look in his eyes and she wondered at his thoughts. Her curiosity got the best of her.

"What were you just thinking?"

"It was nothing."

"It looked like something."

He gave her a half grin, amused more, she guessed, by her comment than anything on his mind.

"I was just wondering what would have happened if your parents had stayed in Cortona. What our relationship would have been. We would have grown up together; I think our grandfathers would have seen to that, but if you'd known me growing up, you might not be too fond of me today."

"Why, were you the kind of boy who teased little girls? Pulled their hair and called them names?"

"I never pulled their hair or called them names, but I might have stuck a frog or two down their shirts or doused them with water balloons."

"I assume you've outgrown all that."

"About the time I turned fifteen and discovered I didn't find girls nearly as repulsive as I'd once thought them to be. Everything changed after that."

"You might not have liked me too much, either." She grinned over at him. "When I was in eighth grade, I beat up Billy Molton, gave him a black eye and a bloody lip. I got suspended for three days. My parents were mortified and on top of the suspension they grounded me for two weeks."

"Good Lord. What did poor Billy do to deserve such a brutal lashing?"

"He called me fat."

Antonio almost choked on his laughter. When he regained his composure, he looked her up and down. "You used to be fat?"

Lucia hiked her nose in the air. "Chubby. It was during my *Charmed* days in the nineties. I was obsessed with it and didn't want to do anything but watch it and write my own episodes, which were awful of course. I got zero exercise, which was compounded by the fact it was also my Oreo and Big Mac and fries phase."

He wrinkled his brow. "What do you mean your charmed days?"

"Not charmed days, *Charmed* days. It was a television show about these three sisters who were witches. Good witches. There were called the *charmed ones*. I'd wait all week for the show, and in my free time I'd write my own episodes. Sometimes I wrote myself into them. Well...I often wrote myself into them." She looked at him and gave him a self-deprecating smile.

"So I guess in addition to being a big girl, I was a bit of a nerd as well."

His eyes sparked amusement, little shots of light dancing in their blue depths. "Maybe it's a good thing we didn't know each other growing up. If I'd put a frog down your shirt, you probably would have knocked my lights out and destroyed my male ego."

Lucia laughed. "We never would have ended up in bed together."

Antonio chuckled. "I never would have discovered how sensitive your ear lobes are."

"Yeah, and I'd never have known you have that really sexy mole on your ass."

He draped an arm over her shoulder. "I think I'm glad your parents fell in love with Virginia."

"Me too." Lucia leaned against him a moment. "Now, I've got to get back downstairs."

WHEN HE WALKED her to the door, Antonio saw her looking at the pile of boxes and trunks in the corner with a frown on her face and wondered if she thought he'd been looking through them. He hadn't, but when he found the screens lying on the floor again this morning, he'd propped them against the wall with the intention of wiring them together so they wouldn't keep falling over.

"I hope you don't mind I moved those screens," he said in explanation. "They kept falling over for some reason, and I thought if it kept happening they might crack. They seem stable enough, so I'm not sure what the problem is, but I leaned them against the wall until I could secure them better. I could wire them together if you're okay with that."

"That's fine." She ran a hand over her hair and looked askance. "You, umm...haven't had any problems with the door or...the windows, or...anything else up here, have you?"

"Problems? No, not that I've noticed."

"Nothing sticking, or...any problems with, I don't know, temperature control?" She looked up at him through hooded eyes. "Anything?"

He shook his head. "No." He hadn't known her long, but long enough to tell when something was up. And something was definitely up.

"Okay...well...good then. If you do have problems with anything, just let me know."

She turned as if to leave and he caught her by the elbow.

"Not so fast, *amore*."

He heard her tongue cluck.

Antonio twirled her back around to face him. "What don't you want to tell me?"

Lucia blew out a breath. "Eliana thinks it's Aunt Rosa. I don't know what I think. Marcella agrees with El. They're both convinced there's no other explanation. Cat's not so convinced. Like me, she thinks there's probably a very logical explanation to everything...we just can't figure out what it is yet."

He angled his head, tried to follow the flow. "Okay, wait a minute, back up. Aunt Rosa's your aunt who was murdered, the ghost."

"For the sake of this discussion, yes, the ghost. Some odd things happened when I was up here cleaning last week. Eliana and Marcella don't have any question it was Rosa messing with me. I have to admit I considered the possibility, but it's hard to accept one of my dead relatives could actually be inhabiting the house with us."

Antonio rubbed his chin. "I wonder if that's who I saw standing over my bed that morning in my room."

Lucia rolled her eyes.

"So that's what all the odd questions were about. Nothing bad happened, did it? You weren't hurt in any way?"

Lucia gave her head a quick shake. "Yes to the first and no to the second, unless you consider being stuck in the attic for about twenty minutes because I couldn't get the door open a bad thing. If Rosa's real, I don't think she had any bad intentions. My sisters think she was just trying to get my attention."

"I wonder why?"

"I have no idea, or, if she's been hanging around all these years, why she's waited until now to start acting out."

Lucia wrapped her arms around his neck and lifted up on her toes. "I don't have time to wonder about it now; I've got to get back

down to reception." She kissed him goodbye. "Oh, by the way, tell your grandfather that if he comes for a visit that my sisters and I insist he stay here at the inn. I'd love to meet him, and I know they will as well."

"I'm sure he'd like that." He lingered on her lips a moment more. "Do you want me to come by your room tonight?"

"I would, but wait until after ten. We've got a sisters' meeting at nine thirty. Marcella came up with a new red blend she wants us to try and give our opinion on. If it's good and there's any left, I'll bring the rest of the bottle up so you can try it."

After she'd gone, Antonio went back to his desk and sat down. He swiveled his chair to face the room, trailed his eyes around the space slowly, saw nothing out of the ordinary, sensed nothing unusual, yet still wondered.

"Are you here, Rosa?" He cocked his ear for any whispered response, turned his head degree by degree, looking for any sign he might not be alone.

When no rejoinder came after a few minutes, he turned back to the computer to get some work done. He fingered his mouse, dragged it closer, and looked at the screen.

At the bottom of the checklist he'd been compiling were two words, highlighted in yellow.

I'm here.

Thirteen

Magic lives in curves, not angles.
Mason Cooley

The wind was up, whipping down the mountains, rapping against the inn's window panes like an unwelcome squatter, in a mood to whistle and moan—a good day to talk to a ghost.

There were no guests in residence, no reason she had to stay downstairs, and nothing to keep Lucia from giving Rosa a piece of her mind. She marched up the stairs toward the attic, as much as it was possible to march in stilettos.

Antonio had been back for a week and a half. This morning he was out, meeting with a contractor he'd contacted to establish a relationship, see if the man would be willing to refer him to any of his clients in the hope of picking up some additional architectural work.

With Antonio gone for a few hours, Lucia could confront her prankster of a relative without interrupting him. She threw open the attic door, a woman on a mission. She didn't wedge it. If Rosa wanted the two of them to be on good terms, she'd need to understand locking her in the attic wasn't any way to win her over.

She walked to the middle of the room, her heels clicking against the exposed floor boards, and set her hands on her hips.

"Okay, Rosa, let's get a few things straight. First, if we're going to be living in this house together, then we need to establish some boundaries."

One of the Chinese screens fell onto the floor.

Lucia rolled her eyes. "Yeah, I know. That trick's getting old. I'm up here talking to you, right? So I give in, you got my attention, I believe you must exist. Especially after that little note you left on Antonio's computer last week."

The wind rattled the attic windows, making itself known again, as it had been doing since the wee hours of the night. Outside, something banged against the side of the house and Lucia jumped.

"I'm going to give you the benefit of the doubt and not blame whatever that was on you." She pulled in a long breath. "So look, I don't know what you want, or why you've started making your presence more obvious, but whatever it is, if you want me to work with my sisters to try to figure it out, then you're going to have to work with me, too."

This would be a lot easier if she could see the woman. At least then she'd know in which direction to look. She screwed up her mouth as she turned and scanned the attic for any indication Rosa might be hovering nearby. A shimmer, a glow, a flicker of light, whatever it was a spirit did to show itself.

"For starters, no more locking me in a room. I'm a busy woman, I've got guests to take care of and things to do, and you're going to have to respect my time more than that. And those Chinese screens weren't cheap, so stop throwing them around when you want attention; they might break. You want to drop the temperature a few degrees to let me know you're there, fine, but the other crap's got to end starting right now."

Another crack sounded outside making Lucia jump again. She huffed. Wasn't trying to talk to a ghost enough to put a woman on edge?

She was going to go out there when she went back down to see if she could locate the problem. She hoped it was nothing worse than a tree branch banging against the side of the house and not a loose gutter or something worse.

Lucia glanced to her left, to the right, looked up toward the ceiling.

"So, that's all I've got for now. If you've got anything you want to let me know, maybe some clue about what you want, feel free to speak up or whatever."

Rosa remained silent. Maybe her relative was hanging out in another part of the house.

"Okay, since I don't even know if you're here, I'm going back downstairs. I hope we've got an understanding now. You respect me and I'll respect you, and if we figure out what you want from us we can...well, I'm not sure what we can do, but we'll try to work with you."

Lucia wasn't sure what she expected. After all, this was the first time she'd ever tried to talk to a ghost. Maybe it took a lot more energy for the spirit world to communicate with the living and Rosa had used up whatever ectoplasm or power source needed to materialize or make her presence known at the moment. It was also possible she was just being difficult.

Whatever, she'd done her bit, said her piece. It was up to her aunt now to decide if she'd accept Lucia's olive branch.

She walked out of the room and closed the door behind her. As she rounded the landing to take the stairs, she heard a soft humming. Her earworm. The same tune she'd had stuck in her head for the last month.

"HOW'D YOUR MEETING go?" Lucia asked when Antonio got back to the inn a few hours later.

"Even better than I'd hoped. Liam, the man I met with, owns a construction business with his two brothers, whom I got to meet as well. They started the business about eight years ago, and from the research I did before contacting them, they've got a good reputation."

The lock of hair that tended to fall across his forehead did its thing and Antonio pushed it back, his long fingers used to the habit. Lucia swallowed.

"Liam's meeting with some potential clients Friday afternoon. He doesn't think they've hired an architect yet, so he's going to see if they'd be interested in meeting me at the same time."

"Wow, that's great. You two must have hit it off pretty quickly for him to make that offer."

"We did, and..." He gave her a sheepish look. "I told him I'd put in a good word for him with you and Cat to see if you'd reciprocate by interviewing him for your job."

"If you think we should talk to him, then we will. I trust your opinion, and you've already done some vetting, so sounds like a no-brainer."

"Thanks. I got a good feel for him. The final decision is yours and Caterina's, of course, but I wouldn't have recommended someone I didn't think would do a good job. Especially since I'll have to work with whomever you hire."

"Did you tell me you're meeting with another contractor on Friday?"

"A guy in Silver Springs."

"That's a bit of a hike."

"Yeah. I didn't realize it when I made the appointment, one of the problems with not being familiar with the area yet. I don't mind driving an hour to a job, but I'd prefer to stay more local. That meeting's at ten, so I'll go straight from there to the one with Liam."

"Well, if you meet anyone else you think we should talk to, let me know. Cat got a referral from one of the regulars at Caulfield's. We thought we'd talk to him since it came from someone she knows."

"You should probably talk to at least three builders."

Lucia grinned. "That's what we told ourselves about architects."

"Having regrets?"

"No. When you know you've found the right person, why waste time looking any further?"

Caterina came walking into reception on her way to the kitchen.

"Hey, you two, what's up?"

"Antonio just got back from a meeting with a contractor he thinks we should talk to."

"Okay." Cat looked at Antonio. "When can you arrange it? I'm anxious to get a team in place."

"I'll call him this afternoon to let him know you want to set up a meeting."

"Sounds good." Caterina pulled out her cell phone and checked her calendar. "I've got Monday, Tuesday, and Wednesday evenings open next week. What's your schedule look like, Luch?"

Lucia smiled over at Antonio as she picked up her own cell from the desk. In addition to being a perfectionist, Cat was a taskmaster. Give her a box of junk and she'd organize it. Give her a to-do list and she'd prioritize it. Give her an open-ended plan and she'd hand you back an itinerary.

"I can't do Monday because we'll still have guests, but I'm good for Tuesday or Wednesday evening."

Her sister pointed to Antonio. "Do it, handsome. You're planning on being there, aren't you?"

"As I told your sister, I've got a vested interest since I've got to work with them, too, so I'll be there."

"Marcella and Eliana will want to come too," Lucia said. "Whatever we do impacts them so they should be in on the decision."

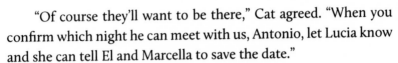

"Of course they'll want to be there," Cat agreed. "When you confirm which night he can meet with us, Antonio, let Lucia know and she can tell El and Marcella to save the date."

Antonio saluted her and Lucia laughed.

"Hey, someone around here needs to keep this family on track, and unless we want to leave everything to chance, that means me." Cat slid her phone back into her pocket. "I've got some chocolate chip cookies in the oven and they need to come out now or they're going to get too crisp."

"Who are the cookies for?" Lucia called after her, hopeful there might be some extras. "You know we don't need to do a set-up this afternoon; the guests have all checked out."

"I know. I was just hungry for chocolate chip cookies," Caterina answered as she left the room through the solarium doors.

"Oh...that's not good." Lucia nibbled her bottom lip. "Whenever Cat gets sugar cravings, it means there's a storm blowing in. Oh, speaking of which..." She wrapped her hair into a long tail and pulled it over her shoulder. "Any chance you've got experience reattaching gutters?"

"You mean like the one I saw in the grass on the side of the house when I got back?"

"That's the one. I don't know if it was already coming unfastened, but the wind ripped it loose and was playing lift and drop with it all morning. I went out about an hour ago and attempted to secure it with some line, but when I tried to pull it over to tie it to the downspout, it came all the way off."

"I could try, but I'd need someone to hold it while I try to reattach it, and a very tall ladder to get up onto that roof."

"Never mind. I'll call someone who does that for a living to come take care of it. I wasn't thinking you'd have to get up on the roof. I'd probably be a nervous wreck if you went up there." She pulled the local business directory out from the top drawer.

Antonio leaned a hip against the desk. "I was thinking since you're guest free, I might be able to convince you to get dinner out with me tonight."

Lucia smiled up at him. "I'd like that. Would you be interested in making it a foursome? If my friend Jenna can get a date, we could meet them somewhere. She's been bugging me about meeting you."

"That's fine with me. Anything I need to know so I don't embarrass you?"

"You won't embarrass me. I just hope Jenna doesn't embarrass you."

He leaned over the desk, brushed his lips over hers. "Don't worry, I don't embarrass very easily."

Lucia watched him walk away, enjoying the view. When he rounded the reception doorway into the hall, she stood up and headed for the kitchen to talk to Cat, the smell of warm cookies filling her nostrils as she walked into the solarium.

"I'M SORRY!" CAT said the following Wednesday afternoon. "I have to go in. Jerry's wife went into labor and Mitch is in Philadelphia. There's no one else to take the shift."

"Okay, fine. What do you want us to do? Should we try to reschedule?" Lucia looked at her watch. "I mean...the guy's supposed to be here in two hours."

"Just go ahead without me. I don't want to drag things out now that Antonio finished the second set of drawings. If we reschedule, I could end up having to work at the last minute again."

Cat sighed heavily, her frustration evident. "Look, I trust you guys, so if you think he'll do a good job, tell him to give us a proposal."

Lucia preferred to have her sister at the meeting, but she was right. They might reschedule only to have her called in again, something that had been happening more and more. She could understand Jerry needing to take his wife to the hospital, but what the hell was Mitch doing in Philadelphia when he was supposed to be Jerry's backup tonight and knew the guy's wife was about to pop? Her sister had to be furious.

"If you're sure," she said, not wanting to upset Cat any more than she already was.

"I'm sure."

"Just go get ready and don't worry about it. I'm sorry I got bent out of shape earlier."

Caterina waved Lucia's apology off. "It's okay. I'm just as frustrated about it as you are." She ground her teeth, and Lucia could see her sister was boiling beneath the surface. "I'll be so glad when we open Serendipity and I don't have to—"

After her sister was gone, Lucia wondered what had been going through Cat's mind that she didn't finish saying. If she were a betting woman, she'd put money down it had something to do with Mitch.

Fourteen

Why not go out on a limb?
That's where the fruit is.

Mark Twain

*L*iam Dougherty showed up in a pair of blue jeans, a tear in one knee and a rip in the thigh of the other. His black tee shirt stretched over well-formed, hard muscle that would make most women salivate. He stooped down to untie his work boots and then stood up and toed them off.

"I apologize for showing up like this for our first meeting," he said, making eye contact with each one of them. "I got held up on a job and didn't have time to go home to get cleaned up and changed before coming over."

"No problem," Antonio assured him.

"Yeah, no problem," Lucia chimed in, and glanced over at Marcella and Eliana.

Her two sisters looked as if they might start drooling any second. She wasn't surprised with El, but it usually took a lot more

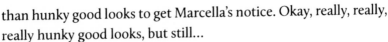
than hunky good looks to get Marcella's notice. Okay, really, really, really hunky good looks, but still...

Lucia didn't think he was as gorgeous as Antonio, but he was pretty damn close. Antonio's looks were more sophisticated, cultured, and debonair, mixed in with a healthy dose of elegant sex appeal she found irresistible.

Liam's were rougher, brooding, and more rugged, but she certainly understood their appeal. She looked at her sisters again and nudged Eliana with her elbow.

"No problem, right El?"

"Uh, yeah, you're fine," El said, coming out of her lust-induced haze.

"Why don't we go in and sit down?" Antonio suggested, shooting Lucia an amused glance.

Once they were situated in the library, Liam gave them a brief history of Dougherty Construction, the company he'd formed with his brothers, and talked about a couple of projects they'd done that showcased their work. When he finished, he asked them to tell him what they were looking to do.

Lucia took the lead. "We want to build a boutique hotel with fifteen to twenty guest rooms, and a full-service restaurant. I'll be running the hotel, and my sister Caterina will manage the restaurant. I'm sorry she couldn't be here; she got called into work at the last minute."

"Should I set up another meeting with her?"

Lucia shook her head. "No, that's not necessary. She said she trusts us to make a decision without her. Antonio's done an amazing job of capturing what we want to do. It might be easiest to look at what he's done and go from there."

As Antonio went over the design, he and Liam got into more of the specifics. Liam asked a lot of questions, many of them technical that Lucia and her sisters didn't understand, so most of the discussion was between him and Antonio. Lucia appreciated that both of them paused here and there to explain what they were talking about, or to ask if she or her sisters had any questions.

When they were finished reviewing the plans, Antonio sat back and looked at Lucia. She interpreted the move as a silent handing of the meeting back over to her.

"Thanks for meeting with us, Liam. I think we all feel comfortable you'd do a good job on our project." She glanced at her sisters to make sure they were in agreement and got two head nods. "I wish Caterina could have been here as well, but I feel confident if she were, she'd agree. So if you're interested, we'd like you to give us a proposal."

"I'm interested, and after seeing what Antonio's done, it would be refreshing to work with someone who understands how to design something that isn't going to be an engineering nightmare. I've worked with one or two architects in the past whose designs were so fffu—" He shifted and backpedaled. "I mean so—"

"So futilely unworkable as to be laughable," Lucia suggested with a grin.

Liam's lips twitched. "Yes, ma'am. That's what I was going to say."

She laughed. "Okay, so you'll write us up a proposal. How long do you think that will take?"

"I can get it to you within a few days." He turned to Antonio. "Can I get a copy of these drawings?"

"I printed this one for you. I've got other copies." Antonio rolled up the plans and put the rubber band back around them. "I haven't finished the spec drawings yet, but I should have them done in another week."

Liam took the plans. "These are detailed enough that I should be able to put together a realistic estimate."

"We'd like to get a couple of other bids," Lucia said, thinking she should clarify that they hadn't made their final decision.

"I figured as much." Liam stood and shook everyone's hand. "It was nice to meet all of you, and thanks for giving me an opportunity to bid on the job."

Lucia and Antonio walked Liam to the door. He put his boots back on and before walking out leaned past Lucia and gave an abbreviated hand wave to her sisters. When he was gone, she turned around and looked at them.

"I would have offered him the job on the spot," Eliana declared. "Imagine getting to look at that butt every day." She jockeyed against Marcella. "Right, sis?"

Marcella grinned. "It wasn't bad."

Lucia tilted her head to face Antonio. "You know if we hire him he might have his hands full with a lot more than a hammer and some wall studs."

"I doubt you'll get any complaints from him if that happens," he said, amusement clear in his tone.

THEY INTERVIEWED TWO other builders the following Monday. Fortunately, Caulfield's was closed and Caterina made both meetings. By Thursday they'd received all three bids.

Lucia wanted to hire Liam, hands down. Antonio, Marcella, and El all agreed they thought he'd be the best choice. Cat conceded to the majority, even though she hadn't met him yet.

His bid came in right between the other two. Antonio thought the price seemed fair for the scope of work, and they trusted his experience.

Friday morning Lucia called Liam to tell him they wanted to hire him. He came by the winery Saturday afternoon to leave a contract for her and Caterina to review and sign off on. Lucia was tied up with a guest and didn't have time to talk, so she motioned for him to put it on the reception desk and mouthed a *thank you*.

After reviewing the contract with Caterina and Antonio, Lucia scanned it Monday morning, and since Serendipity would be a new business, sent it to her friend Laura Taskins, who also happened to be the family's lawyer, to go over it as well. Laura called just before noon to say she had no problems with it, and satisfied everything was fair and in order, Lucia and Cat both signed off on it.

"I can drop it off with Liam if you want me to," Antonio offered later Monday afternoon when Lucia told him they'd gotten a thumbs-up from their lawyer. "Now that you've got a signed contract, and I get Liam the construction documents, he can apply for a work permit to get the process rolling."

"That would be great. You don't mind making a special trip?" Lucia asked.

"I'm not. Liam's brother Shawn invited me to visit another potential client of theirs. You'll get to meet him and their brother Burke at some point. Liam's going to be your lead contractor, but they all spend a little time on every job so they're familiar with them in case they need to fill in for some reason."

"Oh, that's good. I hope it goes well and you get some more work out of it." Lucia put the contract back into the envelope it came in and handed it to Antonio.

"If we're done here, I'm going to take advantage of the rest of my day off and run some errands," Cat said.

Eliana got back from wherever she'd been as Cat was leaving.

"We just signed the contract to hire Liam," Lucia told her. "It looks like things are going to start happening very soon."

Eliana bumped fists with Lucia. "I can't believe you and Cat are finally going to be able to do this. The new inn and restaurant are going to be so fabulous. It's going to be hard to wait until it's all done."

"I know, I feel the same." Lucia glanced back to Antonio. "When's your meeting?"

"This evening at six thirty. Shawn called this morning. Liam told him I was looking to pick up a couple of projects, and I guess he put in a good word for me with his brothers."

"Well, I'm not surprised. The way he talked about your drawings it was obvious he liked your work," Eliana said.

"I'm surprised," Lucia said. "Surprised you heard anything the man said. Every time I looked at you, you were staring at him like you were in some dazed trance."

"I wasn't that bad. I'll admit he's got some extremely nice *assets*." She grinned at her own joke. "As much as I might have enjoyed the view, though, he's not my type. All that raw sexuality—it's terribly appealing, but frightening at the same time. And I didn't get the impression he'd be very malleable. We'd probably have some issues over that."

Antonio cleared his throat. "If you don't mind, ladies, I think I'll go up to my office and get in a few hours of work. When a man finds himself in the company of two beautiful women and all they want to do is discuss the attributes of some other man, he realizes his presence has lost its appeal."

He tucked the envelope into his shirt pocket and gave them a nod as he walked away.

"You've got more than your fair share of pretty amazing attributes, too," Lucia called after him.

"Yeah," Eliana piped in agreement. "You're hunky, too, big guy."

Antonio waved a hand over his head as he rounded the doorway into the hall.

Eliana leaned her hip against the desk. "He does know he's hot, doesn't he?"

"I doubt he thinks about it. I'm guessing he was just looking for an excuse to escape."

"Okay, good. Well then—" Her sister pushed away from the desk. "I'm off again, lots to do, catch up with you later." She blew out of the room as quickly as she'd blown in, leaving Lucia to sit and ponder some of the amazing attributes Antonio had that she'd alluded to a few minutes earlier.

LUCIA LAY IN bed staring at the ceiling. She and Antonio hadn't spent the night together in more than a week. He'd been here for over two months, and as they grew closer, it became harder to lie in her bed alone at night knowing he was just a flight of stairs away. It wouldn't do for her to go down to his room, not when one of their guests might see her entering another guest's room at night and not coming out until the morning. They might get the wrong idea.

She pushed her head back into the pillow and closed her eyes, and lasted about ten seconds before grabbing the phone off the nightstand and dashing him off a text.

Can't sleep. Want to come up?

He knocked on her door five minutes later and she let him in. He kicked it shut and pulled her hard against him, covering her mouth as if he'd been feeling just as starved for her as she'd been for him, and sent her spiraling with a blistering kiss.

"Stay the night," she managed between gasps for air.

He swung her up into his arms and carried her to the bed. When he set her down, they undressed each other feverishly. Her blood rushed through her veins fast and hot, her heart pounded in her ears, and when he took her down onto the mattress with him, it was clear neither one of them was in the mood to take things slow.

Their hunger drove them on, both feeding off of the other's need. When he drove into her, Lucia thought she'd fly off the bed. They were so good together. She'd never experienced anything close to what she had with Antonio, on any level. He satisfied her in every way—physically, intellectually, emotionally.

She wrapped her arms around his back and held on for the ride. He buried his face into her neck, kissed her, whispered in her ear, words in Italian. She didn't understand most of what he said, was too wrapped up in the feelings to translate in her head, but she felt them against her skin, the slide of them across her soul, and they only drove her higher.

They flew together, soaring through the sublime, skin against skin, lips against lips, entwined, two melded into one. They found their release in tandem, a faultless moment that defined perfection. She clung to him, he clung to her, and they held on, feeling nothing but that perfect flash in time—one she knew she'd never forget.

In silence, they drifted down in concert, and when their bodies stopped drifting and came to rest, each sighed, content, at peace.

"I think I'm falling in love with you," she said, her voice no louder than a whisper.

"Then we've got something in common." He rolled onto his back and pulled her into his arms.

"You think you're falling in love with you too?"

She felt him smile and grinned against his skin. He pulled her up so they were face to face.

"I'm not sure how it happened." He lifted his head a couple of inches so he could kiss her. "The night we met my plan was to say hello, give you my grandfather's regards, and be on my way. And here I am, two and a half months later, in your bed, more than happy to be here, and unconcerned that nothing is happening the way I planned it."

"I'm more than happy you're here too. Let's not try to analyze any of it, though. Let's just enjoy it. I don't want to think about what it means, or where it's going, or what's going to happen when—"

"When what?"

"Nothing. I was starting to ramble. I just want to lie here with you right now and run my hands over these gorgeous pecs."

"You think my pecs are gorgeous?"

She gave him a look like *seriously?* "Every part of you is gorgeous, Antonio. I don't think I've ever seen a man who's as perfectly gorgeous as you."

"Have you ever taken a good look at my feet?"

Lucia laughed, shook her head, and then dropped it to his chest and snuggled against him. Antonio combed his fingers through her hair, dragging them all the way down to the ends and then over again. It wasn't long before they both found the sleep that had eluded them earlier.

As night darkened and sped toward morning, they slept on— sound, deep, uninterrupted. Neither heard the soft humming that floated over the bed just before the dawn.

Fifteen

Love rarely overtakes;
It merely comes to meet us.

Wilhelm Stekel

Antonio found Lucia on the side of the house. She was on her hands and knees, tending the flower bed that curved around from the front porch steps and ran all the way back to the stone terrace behind the solarium.

There was a square metal tub on the ground next to her that she dragged along as she inched her way down the bed, pulling weeds, deadheading flowers, leaning in to smell an occasional blossom.

She was wearing flip-flops, a navy cap, a pair of blue jean shorts, and a light grey tee shirt. She hadn't noticed him standing near the corner of the house yet, so he took advantage of the opportunity to watch her, to absorb everything about her.

She reached up and rubbed a gloved hand over her jaw, leaving behind a small trail of dirt on her chin. She swatted at something. "Leave me alone, you bothersome flies," she grumbled loud enough for him to hear.

196

Even with a smudged cheek and swatting at flies she appealed to him. He had it bad. Yeah, he had it bad all right, something he'd never anticipated, and it changed everything.

She must have sensed a presence and swung her head to the right, spied him.

"Hey," she said, her expression lighting up, and gave him a sunny smile.

"Hey yourself." He strolled over to where she knelt. She spun around and then sat on the grass, wrapped her arms around her knees and looked up at him from beneath the rim of her hat.

"Did you come out here looking for me, or are you just taking that coffee mug for a walk?"

"Guilty on both accounts. I needed a break, and I wanted to remind you in case you forgot, my grandfather will be arriving in four days."

"Didn't forget. I reserved a room for him when you first told me he was coming. He's going to be in Petit Verdot, right next to you."

"I should have known you had it under control. Thanks."

"No big." She stood up, slid her gardening gloves off, and dropped them into the metal tub. "It's good he's not arriving until Monday." She brushed her hands against the sides of her shorts and then stuck them into the back pockets of her shorts. "We have a full house this weekend, but the last of the guests check out Monday, so we're good."

"He could have bunked in the room with me for a night or two, but I'm glad that won't be necessary. The old man snores horribly."

"Then I'm happy for your sake you won't have to share. By the way, I got an email from Liam this morning. He's applying for the permits today."

"Good. He said they've been coming through a lot quicker the last couple of months because they hired a new administrator who made streamlining the process a priority. I don't anticipate we'll have any issues, so it's possible we could have the necessary approvals in as early as two weeks."

"Does that mean we'd be able to start construction then?"

"Once we've got the permit that gives us the go-ahead, but Liam's contractors will need to clear the land, the utility companies will have to do their thing...it could be several weeks before you actually see any activity."

"That's okay; I'm just so excited everything's actually going to happen I can hardly contain it."

Antonio grinned. Her enthusiasm was infectious. He might not be as eager as Lucia and Caterina, but he felt more excited about their project than most.

He could no longer deny the biggest reason was because he wanted to make Lucia happy. When he first realized he was considering offering to take on their job, he tried to convince himself it was because it had gotten its teeth into him, because he already felt an ownership after coming up with a design.

That was part of it, but the bigger reality was he'd thrown his entire life into limbo so he could spend more time with her.

He'd put his life on hold for Lucia because she fascinated him, drew him like no other woman ever had before, made him laugh, and lust, and feel good...and because he'd been falling in love with her since the first night he'd met her. She'd turned his whole life upside down over a piece of cheesecake and a couple of glasses of Seyval Blanc...just like that.

He'd even been fooling himself when he'd come up with the idea to ask her to marry him on a temporary basis so he could fulfill the terms of their grandfather's betrothal contract and receive the trust they'd established. He realized he didn't even care about the trust anymore. It was Lucia he wanted. It had been Lucia from the start.

She stepped back and looked up at him. Antonio pulled a clean tissue from his pocket and rubbed it over her chin then held it up for her to see the dirt.

"I must look a mess." She reached up and brushed her hands over her face, as if there might still be something there.

"I think you look kind of cute. In fact, I was getting really turned on watching you play in the dirt."

She smirked at him. "You're not hiding some fetish I should know about, are you, like secretly wanting to mud wrestle with me or something? Because I'd hate to disappoint you but I'm pretty sure I wouldn't enjoy being covered in sludge."

Antonio chuckled. "No need to worry. As much as I enjoy rolling around with you, I'd also prefer not to do it in a pool of muck."

"Well, that's a relief. And speaking of rolling around together—" She sent him an inviting look. "Would you like to stay with me tonight?"

"I would, but on one condition."

"What's that?"

"When I met with Liam's brother Shawn, he told me about a restaurant he went to a couple of weeks ago. He recommended it highly. Since you don't have guests right now, let me take you there for dinner tonight."

"Okay," she agreed. "With your grandfather arriving Monday, we probably won't get to see as much of each other over the next couple of weeks. And since we'll have to put any no-pajama, rolling-around-together parties on hold while he's here, this will probably be the last time we can spend a night together for a while."

Antonio frowned. "Why should that prevent us from being together?"

"Antonio. We can't be sleeping together while your grandfather's staying here. He might think—" She closed her mouth and shook her head, but he had an idea what she'd been about to say.

He'd told her early on that his nonno was hell-bent on getting Antonio to honor their grandfathers' archaic betrothal contract, and she was probably worried that if he knew they'd been intimate, he'd press him even harder.

He needed to tell her about the trust, and also that he didn't give a damn about it. Somewhere between trying to find a way around the stipulations and hold on to his independence, she'd stolen his heart. He had fallen in love with Lucia, and wasn't that a kicker. He didn't believe it had anything to do with destiny. *He* was choosing her, but it looked like their grandfathers were going to get what they wanted after all.

Antonio slid his fingers under her chin and lifted her face to his. "Let me worry about my grandfather," he said, and lowered his head for a kiss.

Tonight, after they made love and she lay wrapped in his arms, he'd tell her about everything, and then he'd ask her to marry him.

LUCIA AND ANTONIO didn't get back to the inn until after eleven. They had a wonderful evening, dinner at Au Lapin Agile, a delightful French restaurant that recently opened in Leesburg. They'd dined alfresco. Their meals were excellent, the atmosphere romantic. She had enjoyed just sitting and chatting, content in his company, the easy, natural way they were together. It was—she didn't really know what it was about him, or them together, that was different. It just was. She'd never felt so comfortable with any man, or known one who could make her laugh one moment and want to climb into his lap and kiss him crazy the next.

"I had a great time tonight," she said as they walked up onto the inn's front porch.

"Me too." He squeezed her hand. "And the night's far from over, or did you forget you invited me to come to your room for dessert?"

"Another one? You mean that massive Grand Marnier soufflé wasn't enough?"

He spun her into his arms, grinned down at her. "That was pretty amazing, but not as good as the one I've got in mind."

"Glutton," she teased, even as a shiver of anticipation raced along her nerves, inciting her desire.

"When it comes to you, *mia bella*, I never get my fill."

A car turned into the driveway, its headlights sweeping across the porch, and they both turned to look.

"It's Cat," Lucia said, recognizing it immediately, and glanced at her watch. "She's late getting home. They must have been really busy tonight."

The car pulled into the lot and after it shut off, they heard a door slam shut. A few moments later Cat walked into view. Lucia could tell by the way she moved that her sister was in a mood, and when she saw the expression on Cat's face, knew something bad had happened.

"Hey," Lucia ventured as Cat stomped up the front steps.

Her sister stopped suddenly and jerked her head up. When she looked at them, it was clear she hadn't known they were there.

"Hey," Cat said, and then brushed past them. She went inside, closing the front door behind her without another word.

Antonio rubbed a hand over his jaw. He looked at Lucia like a man who knew troubled waters when he saw them.

Caterina was normally even tempered. The last couple of months, though, she'd had more than her share of moods. Lucia wondered if she should go after her to see if she wanted to talk about whatever had her upset. She was pretty sure she knew and the question was more like, what had Mitch done now?

Antonio and Lucia went inside and up to the third floor. When they got to her room, Antonio hesitated outside the door.

"Do you want to go talk to your sister?"

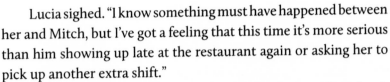

Lucia sighed. "I know something must have happened between her and Mitch, but I've got a feeling that this time it's more serious than him showing up late at the restaurant again or asking her to pick up another extra shift."

He rubbed his hands up her arms, rested them on her shoulders, and then leaned down and kissed her on the forehead.

"Go ahead." He hitched his head toward Cat's bedroom door.

She looked up at him. "You don't mind? If she wants to talk, I might need to back out of our sleepover."

"I'll expect a rain check."

"You've got one." Lucia rose up on her toes and kissed him lightly. "Thank you."

"You don't have to thank me. She's your sister, and I think she might need you even more than I do right now."

He stepped away and started walking backwards down the hall, his beautiful blue eyes never leaving her face. "*Buonanotte amore.* Good luck."

He left with a longing smile, one that hinted at his disappointment they wouldn't be spending the night together, and Lucia swallowed. The fact that he would put her sister's needs before his own desires touched her deeply.

He disappeared down the stairs. Lucia closed her eyes a moment and listened to the words whispering across her heart. She was in love with Antonio.

"I CAN'T BELIEVE I allowed him to play me for such a fool!"

Caterina paced at the foot of her bed, which she'd been doing for the last ten minutes, her temper high, and, Lucia thought from where she sat watching her spin around again, with good reason.

"And the audacity of the man!" Cat stopped and faced Lucia. She put her hands on her hips and gave a good snort. "After confronting him about everything Darla told me, he had the nerve to tell me it would be unprofessional for me to quit before the weekend because I'd be leaving the restaurant in the lurch."

Lucia caught the corner of her bottom lip between her teeth, worried it. "You didn't agree to that, did you?"

"Ha! I told him if he was worried about that, then he better get his own sorry ass in there for a change and work it because in case he'd forgotten, it was *his* damn restaurant, not mine!"

"Good for you."

"Yeah, right. I should have told him that when he started with all the excuses a couple of months ago about why he couldn't be there as much as he was when I started working for him."

Cat looked up toward the ceiling, shook her head. "I knew something wasn't right. And you and El tried to get me to see it, but I didn't want to believe Mitch would lie to me. And—" She sighed, held her hands to her head. "As oblivious as it might make me sound, I never suspected he was cheating on me. I just thought... He told me he didn't feel like he had to be there as much because he had so much confidence in me, that it gave him time to pursue other opportunities, look into opening another restaurant or two. It was a line and I fell for it."

She picked up her pacing again. "What an idiot! All the extra shifts, covering for him at the last minute because he had a chance to meet with someone about a new opportunity—opportunities bullshit! While I was covering his ass, he was out screwing around with other women!"

Cat squeezed her eyes shut. "How could I have been so—?"

Lucia got up and went to her, wrapped her in a hug, held her. "Don't. Don't beat yourself up. He's not worth it. You're not the only one he fooled. Eliana and I didn't start worrying something was up until recently, and it's easier to see a situation more clearly when you're not the one caught up in it."

She stepped back and looked into her sister's eyes, as deep and dark as her own, rubbed her shoulders, felt the tight, hard knots bunched there.

"Mitch took advantage of your relationship, and he took advantage of your honest nature by deceiving you about what he was doing. Most people want to believe the best in others, and when you're honest with people, like you are, you want to believe they're honest back. It hurts if you discover they aren't, especially when they're someone you're in a personal relationship with, someone you trusted. It hurts."

Cat swallowed. "It hurts, yes, to find out I meant so little to him, but mostly...I'm angry—at him, at myself for being so quick to dismiss the doubts. And I had them. I made excuses for him because I didn't want to face the possibility I'd been so wrong about him. I didn't want to think all I might be was someone to run his restaurant so he didn't have to, and someone to warm his bed when he was in the mood."

She groaned. "God, Luch, he was sleeping with other women at the same time he was sleeping with me. I'd already started to suspect he was using me, to admit things weren't right between us, but not like that. If he was bored with our relationship, with me, he should have ended it, or told me so I could—not sleep around behind my back while I was busting my butt at the restaurant providing him with the time to do it. He made a fool of me, and what's worse, by agreeing to work all those extra shifts I was freeing him up so he could."

"I know. I know how it feels to invest your time in a relationship, to trust someone with your heart, and to have them break it. As hard as it might be right now, though, I'm glad Darla considers you enough of a friend that she risked telling you about Mitch's carousing. And I'm glad you ended it."

Cat nodded. "Me too. I knew deep down we weren't going to make it. I wasn't happy, but I tried to make it work because I loved what I was doing, not all the extra shifts when they got so out of hand, but I had all the autonomy I could have wanted. And a part of me hoped I was wrong about Mitch, that he wasn't taking advantage of me, that he did care about me."

Lucia put an arm around Cat's waist and walked her over to the side of the bed, sat down beside her on it. "You've still got your catering business. You can do more of that now, and Liam applied for the permits for Serendipity today. Think of all the time you'll have to plan for your own restaurant now."

Her sister smiled. "Yeah, I'll probably drive Antonio and our new contractor crazy with all the time I'll have on my hands. I've got very specific ideas of what I want. They're probably going to groan every time they see me coming because of it. I know I'm going to be over there every spare minute checking things out to make sure I get what I want."

"Nothing wrong with that. I'll probably be over there with you, so we can drive them crazy together."

"Teamwork's a wonderful thing. I'm betting they come up with some not-so-flattering nickname for the two of us that they call us behind our backs." Caterina leaned her head on Lucia's shoulder. "Thanks, for tonight, for being here."

"Always."

"Maybe now that I'm unemployed I'll finally get a chance to meet our contractor and see if I approve of everyone's choice."

"I have no doubt you will. Of the three we interviewed I thought he showed the most attention to detail. And he and Antonio hit it off from the start, which should make everything run more smoothly."

"El says he's a hunk." Cat glanced at her and smiled. Lucia was happy to see a spark of humor in her sister's eyes. She got her heart and her pride stomped on tonight, but she was going to be all right. She was strong, and she was good, and she deserved so much more than a man like Mitch could ever be.

"He is, in a rugged kind of way. The first time he came to meet with us, even Marcella had a stunned moment when she first saw him."

"No!"

"Yes. And you know how hard it is to make an impression on her when it comes to men. She's never been one to be awed by someone's looks, but her jaw was definitely on the verge of dropping when he walked through the front door."

"Do I need to watch out for my baby sister? Make sure she doesn't get seduced by a pretty face into something she'll regret?"

Lucia chuckled. "His face is more rugged than pretty, but no worries. She might have had a brief flash of appreciation for the man's physique—he's a whole lot of hard, lean muscle—but she recovered quickly, and I'm pretty sure the initial zing was nothing more than a passing lapse." She curled her lips. "So, I don't think your baby sister is in any danger of being led astray by our hunky builder."

"I'm relieved to know it. I may only be five minutes older than she is, but I take those five minutes very seriously. I consider it my job to look out for her. "

Lucia tightened her hand on Caterina's waist. "As we all do for one another, and always will."

FRIDAY MORNING LUCIA stopped by Marcella and Eliana's rooms before going downstairs to inform them that Cat had broken off with Mitch, and that their sister might need a little extra support in the coming weeks.

They were as relieved and happy as she'd been that it was over, as none of them had cared too much for the man. They would watch out for their sister now, for her spirit, find ways to boost it when it needed boosting, be a salve, an ear, an open arm, and a bridge to help her cross over and leave it all behind her where it belonged now.

When she made it downstairs, Lucia found Cat in the kitchen, cooking up a storm—quiche, muffins, scones, chocolate-chunk cookies already baked and lined up in neat rows on the counters. Bacon was sizzling on the grill, potatoes frying next to it, two different omelets sat on the family dining table ready and waiting for whoever wanted breakfast.

She was dealing, Lucia thought, with her emotions, the hurt, the anger, the determination to move forward, and this was how she'd work through it. Cooking, baking, doing what she did so well, and finding comfort there.

"Your guests will eat well this weekend," Cat said, holding a spatula in the air and nodding toward the counters. "I'm in a mood to cook, so there'll be more than the usual fare for them to choose from."

"So I see." Lucia walked up behind her and dropped a kiss on her cheek. "Looks like you've been at it for hours."

"Since four thirty. I woke up and couldn't get back to sleep." She glanced over her shoulder, met Lucia's gaze. "Not to worry, it wasn't because I was all broken and upset, just restless. I didn't expect to, but in some ways I'm feeling relieved to be free of Mitch. It all still smarts, but I'd begun to lose sight of me toward the end, and what I wanted. I missed me. I won't ever subordinate who I am for a man again. That's not love."

"Glad to hear it. I missed you too."

"Omelets are on the table, and the bacon and potatoes soon will be," Cat said, signaling she was done wasting time with talk of Mitch. "There's fresh coffee, and I think I just heard our sisters, so get out plates and silverware and we'll all have a nice breakfast."

She did, and they did. They talked, they laughed, and they ate. Marcella predicted a promising harvest, Eliana updated them on plans for the fall festival, Cat and Lucia dreamed big plans for the

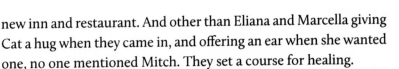

new inn and restaurant. And other than Eliana and Marcella giving Cat a hug when they came in, and offering an ear when she wanted one, no one mentioned Mitch. They set a course for healing.

The weekend came and went in a blur of guests, day visitors, wine tastings, tours. They were all kept hopping, with little time for the four of them to catch up after their shared breakfast Friday.

With summer easing toward autumn, Marcella was busier in the fields, tending the vines, coddling the grapes, keeping a vigilant eye out for anything that might compromise the harvest at this point.

Because Marcella had less time now to help with the tastings and Caterina had more since leaving Caulfield's, she jumped in to fill the void. Eliana ran tours, and Lucia made sure no guest wanted for anything that was within her power to accommodate.

Monday they all breathed a sigh, looked forward to a more relaxing pace until the next weekend when odds were they'd be just as busy as the one past.

Antonio stopped by the reception desk around noon, on his way out to go to the airport to pick up his grandfather. They'd had no time together since their dinner date Thursday night, bar a few minutes here and there, nothing long enough except for a quick kiss and an *everything okay?*

"You must be eager to see him," Lucia said when he came around behind the desk and leaned down to give her a kiss.

"I am. I'm used to seeing him often, so even though he can be stubborn and tiring, I've missed him."

"I'm looking forward to meeting him. I'm guessing he's a real charmer and that I'm going to fall in love with him instantly."

Antonio hiked a brow. "What makes you think so?"

She grinned, her lips curling up at the corners under their own volition. "He raised you, didn't he? And I fell for you in nothing flat."

He pulled her up out of her chair and gave her a proper kiss—lips, tongue, breath stopping—not at all what she needed knowing they had two weeks of abstinence staring them down.

"You know we're both going to suffer for that until you put your nonno back on a plane to Italy," Lucia told him when they finally broke the kiss.

"I told you to not to worry about that; I'll deal with my grandfather. Besides, I couldn't help myself. You're the one temptation I'm an utter failure at resisting."

"You better get going before we both throw our resistance out the window, and your poor grandfather is left to roam the baggage claim at Dulles looking for you."

Lucia watched him go, clucked her tongue when he walked out the door and it clicked shut behind him. It would be a difficult, almost impossible, challenge to stay away from him. Even harder to mask all the feelings he stirred in her so his grandfather didn't discover how close they'd become. Despite Antonio's assurance she didn't need to worry about what his grandfather thought, she didn't think they should flaunt their relationship and give the man false hopes.

Would they be able to last two weeks without giving anything away? Or were their feelings for each other too strong, too obvious, that they were only fooling themselves to think he wouldn't see?

Sixteen

It's odd to think we might have been
Sun, moon and stars unto each other;
Only I turned down one little street
As you went up another.

Fanny Heaship Lea

Caterina made dinner. Bruschetta, buffalo mozzarella, assorted hard cheeses, and stuffed zucchini flowers for appetizers, with wine from their cellars. For the main course, linguini and shrimp in a delicate saffron cream sauce, warm olive bread, a simple salad made of lettuce and tomatoes from her kitchen garden, some herbs, and fresh-grated Grana Padano. And for dessert, tiramisu, made with biscuits instead of cake, served in individual glass bowls the color of sparkling champagne, and tasting like heaven.

They dined on the terrace, the sun setting the sky on fire as it dipped behind the gentle swells of the Blue Ridge Mountains. Then they lit candles, opened more wine, embraced the fine summer night as the crickets began their evening serenade—a warm welcome for the elder DeLuca, in any country.

"You honor me with this meal," Antonio's grandfather said to Caterina. "For I suspect you chose the menu with me in mind. I believe you may be as fine a cook as my grandmother was, and she was one of the finest Cortona ever knew."

"I'm glad you enjoyed it, Mr. DeLuca," Cat said with a smile just for him. "And I'm sure that's a high compliment you give, so thank you for it."

"Please, call me Vincenzo." He looked around the table. "All of you. I'm an old man, I know, but I prefer not to be reminded of it when in the company of four such young and beautiful women. So I give you leave to indulge me, and dispel with the decorum of respect."

He angled his head toward Antonio, who wore an amused smirk at his grandfather's remark. "Except for you, lad, who I expect to continue regarding me as your elder, older and wiser, and as such, in your case, deserving of your deference."

"And have I not always respected you, Nonno?"

"You have, even though you don't always listen to the wisdom of my advice."

Antonio chuckled, but didn't counter. Lucia fought the impulse to keep her eyes on his beautiful face, to share a smile that hinted at anything beyond amusement over his grandfather's jibes. It wasn't easy but she managed to pull them away, to give her attention to their newest guest.

"You must have some wonderful stories about our grandfather, Vincenzo." She hooked a finger around her wine glass and slid it toward her. "Would you share some of them with us?"

"Oh, I could tell you some tales for sure. We grew up together, you know. As thick as thieves, as they say, from the time we were young boys. So we had our share of adventures."

"We'd love to hear a few." Marcella sat forward, put her elbows on the table. She'd always been a lover of stories, real or fictional, and as a child was constantly begging their parents to tell one.

211

"None of us ever got to meet him, except for Lucia, and she was too young to remember him or our grandmother."

"And the stories our parents told us," Eliana chimed in, "they were from their later years, when they were already adults. It would be fun to hear about some of the escapades of your youth."

He sat up straighter. Even though his face was lined with age, his eyes were still as bright and blue as his grandson's, and they glinted with pleasure. He took a sip of wine, cleared his throat. "I could probably tell you a few things about your grandmother that you don't know, as well. I knew her when she was just a girl, too. A fine, fine woman she was, and a beauty, just like the four of you; but we can save those for another day."

He scratched his head, looked thoughtful, and then gave a nod. "Okay, let me begin with how we almost burned down the church. We were six years old. It was the day Rodrigo and I first met..."

Lucia leaned back in her chair, a smile playing over her lips. She lifted her glass, watched the myriad of expressions that flitted across Vincenzo's face over the rim of the bowl as she took a sip, and he began his tale.

What a charmer he was. She'd been right to think he would be. He had a way with a smile, with a word, and she imagined in his earlier days, with the ladies as well.

Not so different from his grandson, she guessed. She stole a look at Antonio, caught him stealing one at her. She dipped her head, took another drink from her glass, and then tipped it ever so slightly in his direction.

HIS NONNO HAD only been there three days but Antonio was getting punchy. He didn't know how much longer he'd be able to hold out, spending time in the same room with Lucia, at the same table, within touching distance, but not being able to touch, to taste, to satisfy his desire for her. She'd insisted on it and it was driving him mad. It was going to end, though, just as soon as he could get her off to himself and clear the air.

I'm a man bewitched, he thought, in every way, helpless to break the spell. Not that he had any desire to. He was perfectly content, enjoyed the magic she lent to his life...and he'd be damn glad when she agreed to marry him and realized they didn't need to pretend about anything. And she would—he knew in his heart she loved him—and although he'd need to make some major changes in his life, they'd all be worth it.

He yanked on a pair of black jeans, buttoned his shirt and tucked it into the waistband. Liam hadn't walked the site yet, so they were meeting in the parking lot and walking down to the plot from there so he could check it out.

The builder wanted to do some preplanning in anticipation of the permits coming through quickly so he could start lining up his contractors. He'd also told Antonio he wanted to discuss some questions he had on the newest set of drawings Antonio had given him to make sure they were on the same page.

Antonio liked that Liam was a forward planner and wanted to get all their ducks in a row up front so they could avoid potential problems down the road. He'd worked his fair share of jobs where the project suffered from time lags because the contractor hadn't planned properly, or something had to be ripped out and redone because it wasn't done to his specifications. He didn't want that to happen on this one.

He got his sunglasses and cell off the bureau and left the room. At least he had things to keep him busy this morning, to keep his mind occupied on something other than Lucia.

When Antonio walked out of the inn a few minutes later, he saw Caterina coming up the walk. He stopped to chat with her for a couple of minutes. He thought she looked tired, and was more sub-dued than usual, but overall she seemed to be managing okay.

Her sisters had rallied around her, making sure she had things to do, that she was never alone for too long that one of them didn't suggest they go for a walk, have a glass of wine, or play a board game. She was one of their own and they would care for her, boost her up, and find ways to help her move on.

He wasn't family yet, but he was a friend, and he would do what he could to try and aide them in their efforts.

LIAM LEANED AGAINST the tailgate of his truck chewing on a mint-flavored toothpick while he waited for Antonio so they could walk the property together. He'd seen him come out of the winery's inn and stop to talk to the woman who'd pulled in several cars down from his truck a few minutes earlier.

He hadn't gotten a look at her face, but the rest of her was mighty fine. She had great legs, long and toned, and although he admired the way they looked in those fancy shoes she was wearing, it boggled his mind how women managed to walk around in such spiky high heels—especially across a gravel parking lot. It had to be uncomfortable as hell. Still, he wasn't one to complain when the view was so enjoyable.

He wondered if she might be Caterina Bonavera, the one sister he hadn't met. The first time he met with the Bonaveras, he couldn't believe how attractive they all were. Drop-dead...all three of them, and he guessed the fourth would be as well. The family had definitely gotten more than their fair share of *stop 'em in their tracks gorgeous* genes.

He frowned. If the woman Antonio was talking to was their other sister, and if she turned out to be another stunner like the others, he hoped she and the other one, Lucia, weren't going to be coming over to check on things all the time.

Some clients had a need to be involved every step of the way, down to the smallest detail. They had a right if that's how they wanted it, but he hated working with the control freaks. It slowed everything down, and half the time they didn't understand why things had to be done in one way over another.

He would be happy to give them weekly updates, even to do a weekly walk-through to show them what was happening. If his newest clients decided to pop in all the time, though, they were going to be a distraction. The way they looked, his men would spend all their time checking out the sights, and any work would screech to a halt whenever one of them was on-site.

The woman his gut told him was Caterina patted Antonio on the shoulder and then turned and ran up the steps to the porch, taking them as lightly as a gazelle leaping through the air. Liam shook his head. How the hell did they move so gracefully in those things?

Antonio spotted him a moment later and raised a hand in a wave, started walking over to meet him.

"I hope I didn't keep you waiting long," he said as he approached the truck and extended a hand.

Liam pushed away from the back of the bed and clasped his hand, gave it a firm shake. "Just got here a few minutes ago."

He glanced toward the inn. "The woman I saw you talking to, is that the sister I haven't met yet? The one who'll be opening the restaurant?"

"Caterina. Yes, that was she. I told her I was meeting you to check out the site, and she asked if you had time when we were done if I could bring you back to the inn so she could meet you."

Liam nodded as they walked through the parking lot, the gravel crunching under his heavy work boots. "Probably a good idea since she's one of the bosses."

"She was disappointed she couldn't be at the initial meeting, but I don't doubt she'll agree her sisters made the right choice when she meets you. She and Lucia should be easy to work with. They're both smart. In my experience, Caterina's more structured, more into planning and organizing, but normally easy to get along with. She's had a bit of a rough week. So if she seems a little off when you meet her, it's probably because her head's not in the best place right now."

Antonio tossed him another glance. "Just thought I should mention it so you don't get the wrong impression out of the gate."

Liam gave a nod. "Thanks, I'll keep it in mind. Nothing too serious, I hope."

"Relationship issues," Antonio said with a frown. "And she just quit her job at the restaurant where she worked. Unfortunately, the guy she's been seeing was also her boss, so—"

"Yeah, that can cause problems if things sour."

"It's too bad, too. She loved what she was doing. She's a chef." Antonio looked over at him as they turned onto the road and continued walking. "Which you've probably already guessed since you'll be building her a restaurant," he added with a self-deprecating grin.

"Where'd she work?"

"A place in Ashburn. Caulfield's. I stopped in for lunch once when she was working and the food was excellent. I'm not sure if they'll be as good after losing her." Antonio gave him an inquiring glance. "Have you heard of it?"

The muscle in Liam's jaw twitched. He ran his tongue along the inside of his cheek, clamped down on the blade that tested his anger, a prick, a jab, one he'd spent the better part of two years battling to control.

"Yeah, I know it. Was her boss Mitch Gregory?"

"I never got a last name, but you got the first one correct. You know him?"

Liam sniffed, looked out over the back side of the property toward the mountains. "Yeah, unfortunately, I do."

He felt Antonio looking at him but didn't feel like getting into any kind of discussion about a bastard like Mitch Gregory. If Caterina Bonavera was mixed up with him, though, he doubted she was anywhere close to being as smart as Antonio seemed to think she was. Some women knew how to fool a man, though—he knew that well enough—which was why he'd never give one an opportunity to sink her hooks into him again. If he ever settled down with a woman again, it would be because he wanted to, not because he had to.

When they reached the property about ten minutes later, Liam reached into his back pocket and jerked out the list of questions he wanted to go over. His mood had taken a downward turn.

They walked the area where the structure would be, planning, troubleshooting, clarifying. When they were done working their way through everything, he and Antonio started back to the winery.

Liam took out his cell phone and pulled up his messages, made a show of checking for anything important. "I'm going to have to hold off on that meeting until another time," Liam said, and then stuffed his phone back into his pocket. "Something's come up at one of my other job sites, and I need to swing by there and assess the situation."

"Not a problem. Caterina might be disappointed, but I'm sure she'll understand. Let me know as soon as you hear anything about the permits."

"I will."

Liam pulled out of the drive onto the road a few minutes later. It was just his goddamn luck he was going to have to spend the next year or more working with a woman who was involved with Gregory. There weren't too many people he didn't like, but if he had to name two or three, that bastard would probably be first on the list.

There was no reason he had to rush off. The issue at the other job wasn't urgent. He'd used it as an excuse because he didn't feel like playing nice with Caterina Bonavera after what he'd just found out. She might not be anything like Sylvie, but the fact she was hooked up with someone as slimy as Gregory meant she already had one strike against her, and they hadn't even met.

She was a client, though, so he'd have to find a way to work with her that didn't make him want to punch a hole through one of the walls he'd just put up.

THE FOLLOWING AFTERNOON Antonio took his grandfather to the Spy Museum in Washington, DC. It was a welcome diversion, and they both enjoyed the outing. Afterward, they went to an early dinner at a nearby tapas bar.

"I'm enjoying my visit. Rodrigo's granddaughters are delightful, and they are all so beautiful it makes an old man wish for a bit more youth. Not only are they striking to look at, they all seem very smart and kind. I'm happy I was able to come here, to meet them. They are good people. My old friend would be proud of them—good people, good hearts."

"They're all that," Antonio agreed.

"I think they like spoiling me."

"And I think you like their spoiling. For someone who's always telling me you don't need me looking after you, that you're perfectly capable of taking care of and doing for yourself, I find it interesting you don't seem to mind being fussed over by them."

His grandfather took his cap off and set it on the table, amusement crinkling his eyes. "A man never gets too old to enjoy the attentions of women, my boy. And if the day ever came that he stopped, it would be a sad one indeed."

Antonio imagined there was a fair amount of truth in that. Not unlike his grandfather, he loved women. He loved all things about them—the way they looked, moved, the softness of their skin, their scent. He loved talking to them, the sound of their laughter, and making love to them. He loved making love to a woman.

His mind conjured an image of Lucia, the woman he most wanted to make love to, the only woman he'd had any desire to make love to since he'd met her almost three months ago.

"From that look on your face right now, I'd say it's a woman filling your head with pleasant thoughts."

Antonio picked up his menu and glanced down at it, evading his grandfather's probing stare. "More like thoughts of filling my stomach with some food and perhaps sharing a pitcher of sangria."

Vincenzo chuckled. "Have it your way for now, lad."

Antonio glanced up at him from behind the menu, right into a familiar, amused blue gaze. It was the same look he gave him every time Antonio concocted a story to cover up one of his youthful antics, only to discover at some future date his grandfather wasn't as gullible as he'd thought. Apparently, that hadn't changed.

He intended to have it his way, though, and as soon as he proposed to Lucia he'd tell his grandfather they were getting married. He'd already met with an attorney and drawn up papers to transfer his distribution from the trust to Lucia as soon as it was made. She could decide what to do with the money. If she wanted to put it into Serendipity, or the family's winery, or donate the whole damn thing to charity, he didn't care. He didn't want there to be any doubt in her mind about his motivations to marry her. And a quarter of a mil could foster a few doubts if there was any question.

With the matter settled in his mind, Antonio relaxed. They enjoyed a pleasant dinner, his nonno flirting with their server, an attractive young woman named Audrey who had a great sense of humor and, he guessed, a keen understanding of increasing one's tips.

When they got back to the winery, his grandfather was in a mood for a walk, so they walked, skirting the vineyard, past the well-manicured rows of vines hanging heavy with clusters of grapes almost ready for harvest.

He'd seen less and less of Marcella the last two weeks. Lucia told him her sister would be like one possessed until October now, testing the Brix, the sugar level of the grapes, on a daily basis to ensure they were picked at the optimal time, not a day too soon nor one too late. Her youngest sister would fuss and fret, Lucia said, worry if the rains came, too long or too heavy, and threw everything off schedule.

The chardonnay would be the first to get picked, and viognier, the pinot noir, then the other whites, with most of the other reds following in September and October. It was Marcella's busiest time of year, and Antonio had noticed there had been a significant increase in workers brought in over the last week.

After their walk, his grandfather went up to his room to retire for the night. Antonio searched out the common areas looking for Lucia and not finding her in any of them, poked his head into the kitchen. And found his heart's desire.

LUCIA SPUN AROUND with a surprised gasp, clutched the container of Chunky Monkey to her chest, and slipped the spoon she'd just put in her mouth with a rather large bite of ice cream, back out again.

"Hey," she said around the healthy dose of deliciousness and leaned her hips against the counter where she was standing next to the freezer. She feigned a look of innocence as she tried to tuck the evidence of her guilty pleasure behind her back. "What brings you to the kitchen at this hour?"

Antonio stalked toward her, a wicked grin tugging the corners of his sensuous mouth. A mouth, she was suddenly reminded, she hadn't tasted in much too long a time for her liking.

"I could ask you the same question, but—" He stepped up to her, slipped his hands around behind her and brought one back out holding the pint of Chunky Monkey. "I believe this speaks for itself."

Lucia caught her lower lip between her teeth. "Guilty." She slid her hands up his chest and around his neck. "Your turn, what brings you in here?"

"I searched everywhere I could think, and when I couldn't find what I was looking for thought I'd check in here."

"And have you found it?"

His eyes sparked amusement and the flickering flames of desire. "Yes." He dipped his head, his blue gaze never leaving hers, and covered her mouth with the heat of his own.

Lucia moaned. Lord, how she'd missed these lips, this heat... this man. At no other time, with no other, had she felt the things he stirred within her. Body and heart, he touched them both, and she knew that forever more, they would belong to him. It wouldn't matter what happened next year, or the next, they were his.

"I've missed you, *amore mio*." He whispered on a kiss, the words, drenched with desire, like a thousand, and a thousand, and ten thousand more raindrops washing over her senses in yearning, calling out to her, a plea, and she knew his need...knew because it was her need too.

"I've missed you, too, missed talking to you, laughing with you, and this." She traced her tongue along his lips then slid it into his mouth to taste him fully.

"There's a very good chance I might start punching things if I have to go another day surrounded by you but not being able to touch, taste, to feel. Let me come to your room tonight. We can talk." He kissed her forehead. "We can laugh." He kissed the tip of her nose. "And we can make love." He angled his mouth over hers and moved against her, giving her a delicious taste of what he had in mind.

Lucia slid her hands down and took hold of his hard, perfect butt, wrapped a leg around his thighs, and returned the favor.

"Oh, God," Antonio said with a groan. "Say yes."

"Yes. You can come. We can't have you destroying things." She pulled back and gave him a satisfied grin. "And if you hadn't suggested it, I would have. It's either that or I keep sneaking in here every night to try to soothe my craving for you with ice cream or whatever Cat made during her latest baking marathon. I've probably gained four pounds since your grandfather got here...a pound a day. At that rate I'd need a new wardrobe by the time he left."

He bit back a chuckle. "Ahhh. So you've replaced me with ice cream and baked goods."

"A poor substitute. And it's the truth when I tell you although I may enjoy the taste of them in the moment, the pleasure is fleeting, and afterward, I regret the indulgence."

"Mmmm. And what of me, *mia bella?*"

Lucia touched the tip of her tongue to her upper lip. "You." She dragged the nail of her index finger down the front of his shirt. "Are an indulgence I can savor all night long and never feel disappointed, never regret."

"There's another benefit my lovemaking has over your other indulgences."

"There are many, but tell me what you're thinking."

"I'm not fattening. You can have as much of me as you want and not gain an ounce."

She laughed, and then wove her fingers through the beautiful black silk of his hair. "Come up in an hour?"

"If I have to wait that long, I want another taste to hold me over. I didn't have the benefit of a pint of ice cream to sate my desires."

"I didn't eat an entire pint." Lucia gave him a poke. "It was just a few bites. Big ones, I admit, but still... They did nothing to satisfy my craving for the real thing." She gave him another, more inviting grin. "So go ahead, give me another kiss, and a good one—one that will hold us both over."

And he did. He kissed her breath away. His lips possessed, his hands caressed, and the fire inside her flamed. Tonight, at last, she would know the magic of his touch once more. They would love, and she would soar to the stars and back again. He would take her there, with him, as he always did each time they made love.

Lucia dropped her head against his chest and gasped to catch her breath.

"You inflame me, Lucia." Antonio's arms tightened around her.

"And you me."

"Should I be looking for a fire extinguisher then?"

Lucia froze. Antonio groaned. He dropped his arms and she squeezed her eyes shut a moment before peeking around his broad chest to see his grandfather standing in the doorway.

He lifted his hand, gave her a wave, and smiled. She made an odd little noise in the back of her throat, returned the wave, and ducked back behind Antonio.

So much for discretion...

"I DON'T THINK I've felt that mortified since my dad caught me making out with Shane Riley in the backseat of his car my junior year of high school."

"An Irish boy?" Antonio dipped his brows at her. "You know Irish boys can't be trusted, Lucia. They'll all try to charm the pants off a girl with little intention of helping her pull them back up after they've succeeded."

Lucia put her hands on her hips and smirked. "And you never tried to charm the pants off any of the girls you dated?"

"Well, of course I did, but I'd never leave them bare assed in the end."

She stared at him for a full five seconds through narrowed eyes before responding. "Right," she finally said. "I know what you're doing, and I appreciate your attempt to inject a bit of levity into the situation, but I'm serious, Antonio. What's your grandfather going to think of me after walking in to find us eating face in the kitchen?"

He took her shoulders in his hands and sighed. "My guess is nothing could have pleased him more." He drew her against his chest. "For the wrong reason, but pleased him none the less."

She echoed his sigh. "That old marriage contract."

"Yep. He probably fell asleep thinking that despite my resistance, despite all the times I told him I'd make my own choices in life, that you and I were never going to meet, fall in love, get married, and that finding us kissing in the kitchen was proof I'd been wrong."

Lucia stood quietly in his arms, swallowed. His words, although she was certain he didn't intend them to, dripped into her thoughts like tears, and she felt them in her heart, a sadness, a silent weeping. She loved him. Perhaps, even though she'd never before believed in such a thing herself, he was her destiny.

Antonio cared for her; he cared for her a lot. She knew it. She believed it. She felt it in her heart even though at the moment, it wept silently at the prospect he might not love her, not the way she did him.

Antonio slid a finger under her chin and lifted her face toward his. "Don't look so serious, love. There's no need to worry about my grandfather. He adores you, you know, and all your sisters as well. You'd have to do something a lot worse than kiss his grandson to change that."

He brushed his lips lightly over hers. "And don't be embarrassed. We're both adults, not two teenagers who were caught making out in the backseat of a car by their parent. I don't think my grandfather's going to try to ground either of us."

"Let's hope not. I'm going to have an inn full of guests again this weekend so it won't do if he tries to confine me to my room."

"If you're going to be tied up with guests again for the next few days, let's not waste anymore time talking about my grandfather. I'd rather spend whatever time we have right now focusing on you and trying to help you satisfy those cravings we were talking about earlier. And after we've both had our fill, there's something we need to talk about."

"Is it a good thing or a bad thing?"

"I'm hoping you'll think it's a good thing."

She took his hand, led him over to the bed, and slowly started to undress him.

"Make love to me then, Antonio."

He brought her into the circle of his arms. "Whatever your heart desires."

"Lucia!" Eliana pounded on her bedroom door and called again. "Luch, you need to come downstairs, quick!"

"What the—?" Lucia scrambled for her clothes.

Antonio did the same. He yanked on his pants and made for the door. "What's wrong?" he asked, when he pulled it open and Eliana spilled into the room.

She threw her arms in the air. "It's Mitch. He showed up about ten minutes ago demanding to see Cat. She told him to leave, but he's drunk and he's giving her a hard time. I think she's going to need all of our help to get rid of him."

Antonio didn't wait to hear more. He took off, jogging down the hall. Lucia pulled her tee shirt on and she and Eliana followed close on his heels.

WHEN LUCIA AND Eliana got downstairs, Cat and Marcella were standing behind Antonio who'd positioned himself between them and Mitch.

"This is between me and her," Mitch said, and sneered at Antonio as he tried to push him to the side.

Antonio took hold of the other man's wrist and held his arm in the air. "She told you to leave. She doesn't want to see you, doesn't want to talk to you, and if you don't do as she says and go now, you can spend the rest of the night sleeping off your drunk in the local jail cell."

Mitch jerked his arm in an attempt to break Antonio's hold but failed. He tried to throw a punch but Antonio blocked it and then pushed him up against the front wall.

"You don't want to go there, Gregory," Antonio said, his words laced with a threat Mitch would be wise to heed. Antonio had at least three inches over Mitch, and Lucia knew firsthand he was all lean muscle and sinewy strength.

Mitch's face contorted as he glared at Antonio through narrowed eyes, but he must have realized his disadvantage. He shook off Antonio's hands and backed toward the door.

"I'll leave, but this isn't over." He shot an angry look at Cat and raised his finger, pointing at her. "You don't just walk out on me and get away with it. You owe me, Cat."

"I don't owe you anything, Mitch," Cat said, her head high. "Now go."

Marcella slipped in front of her twin. "Yeah, she owes you nothing, and contrary to what you might think, this isn't between you and her, it's between you and us. And between you and us, you don't stand a chance."

Before Mitch could retort, Antonio helped him the rest of the way out the door and then closed it in his face.

Marcella wrapped her arms around Cat. Lucia and Eliana rushed to their sides and made it a foursome.

"What a bastard," Eliana said.

"A total loser," Marcella chimed in.

"The worst," Lucia agreed.

"Okay, you can all let go now; I'm starting to sweat," Cat said.

They gave her some room and Lucia took one of her hands. "You all right?"

Cat nodded. "I'm fine, and thanks." She glanced around at everyone. "Thanks for having my back. I probably could have handled him, but it might have taken a lot longer and gotten much nastier."

She looked at Antonio. "I'm sorry you got dragged into this, Antonio, but I'm glad you were here. I don't think Mitch wanted to risk what you might have done to his pretty face if he didn't take your advice and leave."

"No need to apologize. It was my pleasure to push the scum out the door."

"What's all the commotion?"

Everyone turned toward the hallway to see Antonio's grandfather standing in the opening.

"Nothing to worry about," Cat said, walking over to where he stood. "I'm sorry if we woke you. It was just someone who needed directions. Antonio took care of him."

Vincenzo nodded and let Cat steer him back down the hall.

"Well, I guess the excitement's over for now," Antonio said.

"Yeah." Marcella sniffed. "But just to be on the safe side we might want to start locking the front door when we don't have guests in case Mitch gets the stupid idea he wants to talk to Cat again."

After Eliana and Marcella went back upstairs, Lucia wrapped her arms around Antonio's waist and laid her head against his chest. He held her close, kissed the top of her head.

"You okay?" he asked.

"Umm hmm. I'm not the one with a drunken jerk of an ex-boyfriend showing up on my doorstep and ranting at me."

"Do you think Cat's all right?"

"She will be. She's strong, and we'll all make sure Mitch doesn't get near her again."

She leaned back and looked up at him. "Would you be upset if we didn't finish what we started before Mitch showed up?"

"You want to go see your sister?"

"Yeah. I know she's going to be fine, but I don't want her to be alone right now."

Antonio hugged her tight and then turned her around and gave her a gentle push. "Go. Go be a sister."

"Thanks."

"No problem, I'll just go finish that pint of Chunky Monkey and catch up with you tomorrow."

Lucia smiled softly, grateful for his understanding. When she got upstairs, she tapped lightly on Cat's door, and getting no answer, opened it quietly and poked her head inside.

Caterina was in the middle of the bed. Eliana lay next to her on one side and Marcella on the other.

Lucia slipped into the room, shut the door with a gentle click, and walked across the floor. Pulling back the comforter, she slid in next to Marcella and draped her arm over her side, adding her hand to the pile of three resting on Cat's stomach, and closed her eyes.

Seventeen

*All architecture is shelter, all great
architecture is the design of space that
contains, cuddles, exalts, or stimulates
the persons in that space.*

Philip Johnson

Lucia had just finished checking in a couple who got their dates wrong and arrived a day early, when Marcella blew in through the front door and rushed over to the reception desk.

Marcella looked anxious, but the harvest was upon them, her sister's most frenetic time of year.

"I need a huge favor. El's off somewhere and I don't want to bother Cat, so you're it."

"What's up?" Lucia asked. Marcella was usually the quiet sister, low key, the even-keeled, not given to histrionics. Until the harvest hit—then look out anyone or anything that threatened it in any way.

"I need more pickers, tomorrow. I need them. The Brix is at 23 percent, right where I want it, but we have to pick tomorrow! I've got them all lined up, but I need to let them know tomorrow's the day, not next week. With this week's heat we're a couple of days earlier than I thought we'd be, but it's time.

"Okay, calm down, honey. I can get the calls out to let them know. Where's your contact list?"

"Oh thank you! Thank you, thank you. I know you're busy today, so I owe you." She ran around behind the desk and started punching keys on the computer, brought up a file. "Okay, just go down the list here. We're going to need whoever can make it, which should be most of them as they knew we'd be picking soon." She gave Lucia a quick hug. "You're the best."

"It's just a few phone calls, Marcella. And by the way, you were already out there when I came down this morning, and this is the first time I've seen you all day. I hope you took time to eat something. We don't want a repeat of last year when you passed out during harvest because you hadn't eaten for two days."

"I'm fine. I had a banana this morning."

Lucia shook her head. "At what, six o'clock? It's almost two now. You need more than a banana to hold you over, especially out there in that heat all day."

"I've got to get back to work. I'll get something later, promise."

"Not good enough. Cat's upstairs. I'm going to text her before I start making these calls and have her fix a sandwich to bring out to you."

"I told you, I don't want to bother Cat."

"You know Cat wouldn't like it if she thought we were coddling her. She'd want to be bothered, so I'll bother her and know she'll be happy to make you a sandwich."

Marcella huffed and rolled her eyes. "Okay, fine, but I have to get out there now." She darted for the door.

Lucia dashed off a text to Cat.

"I was about to come down and make something for myself when I got your message," Cat said when she walked into reception a few minutes later. "Did you eat yet?"

"No, but I had more than a banana eight hours ago."

Cat shook her head. "She gets like this every harvest. It's a good thing we're all living back here now, or we'd come for a visit one day and find her lying out in one of the fields dead from starvation and heat exhaustion."

Lucia cringed.

"I'll make us all something. It's just as easy to put three sandwiches together as it is one."

Lucia looked thoughtful. "Antonio had to go out earlier, and I just realized his nonno probably hasn't had lunch either, and he doesn't have a car to go get himself anything. Do you—"

"Done," Cat said before Lucia could finish.

"Thanks." Lucia smiled appreciatively. "And when you take Marcella's out to her, make sure she eats it if you have to stand over her until she takes the last bite."

The afternoon flew by. Pickers were scheduled, brochures were stocked, fresh flowers picked to refresh the arrangements in the library and lobby, and since guests had already started arriving for the weekend, Lucia set out complimentary cookies and lemonade on the refreshment bar.

Antonio had been out since mid-morning. He'd told her when he left that he was going to run a few errands after his meeting but hoped to get back to the inn in time to get in a couple of hours work before dinner. She glanced at her watch. Unless he was planning a late dinner, she didn't think he was going to get much work in.

Lucia looked up and there he was, standing over her, his beautiful eyes locked on her, so deep, so sexy, so blue—eyes she never tired of looking into.

"Hey."

"Hey yourself. You were deep in thought."

"I was thinking about you...and that you weren't going to get much done today if you were gone much longer." She set aside the to-do list she'd been working her way through and pushed up out of her chair, came around to the other side of the desk, and gave him a quick kiss.

He wrapped an arm around her waist, started to pull her in, but she put her hands on his chest and stepped back, avoiding the temptation. "Guests already in residence," she said by way of explanation.

"I guess that means no sleepovers until next week." He angled his head and watched her a moment, and then said, "If you're not too tired after last night, do you want to get together for a glass of wine on the terrace after your charges are settled in for the night?"

"That'd be nice. Maybe we can have a late dinner...raid the kitchen again, or order pizza."

"Sounds good. I should try to get in a little work. My meeting this morning went well; I think there's a good chance they may offer me the job."

Lucia crossed her fingers in the air. "Good luck."

"Thanks. By the way, have you seen my grandfather today?"

"Not to talk to. He came down this morning for some fruit and cereal, and then went for a walk. He was gone for a couple of hours. I was starting to worry and thought about sending someone to look for him, but he came back on his own, looking fine and fit."

Antonio chuckled. "He's used to doing a lot of walking. Back home he walks into the village several times a week, a couple of miles each way. For his age, he's very hardy."

"It's probably because he stays so active. In any case, Cat made him a sandwich for lunch and took it up to him since he doesn't have a car to get out on his own, but you'll need to see to his dinner."

"Thanks for looking out for him. I'll see what he's hungry for and pick it up before we get together later."

Lucia sat down and looked up at him. "Why don't you see if he'd like to join us on the terrace instead," she suggested. "I know it's not what you had in mind, but he's been alone all day, and I'm sure he'd enjoy the company."

Antonio cocked his head, regarded her, and she wondered at the emotion she saw in his beautiful eyes.

"You've a soft heart, Lucia. Are you sure you want to spend the evening with him, especially after last night?"

"I do. It was embarrassing, but as you said, we're all adults, so I'm not going to avoid him because of it. Besides, I like your grandfather. He's delightful, and tells a good story, and in some ways he's kind of like family. My grandfather would have wanted us to make him welcome."

"You have. And I think he'll be delighted." He looked around the lobby and seeing no one within sight, came around the desk, leaned down and kissed her, short, but sweet it was.

"Thank you," he said, and left her sitting there to watch him walk away, a smile on her lips and feeling surprisingly happy with herself considering she'd just given up an evening alone with Antonio.

ELIANA MADE IT a foursome. Lucia got out a large platter and they arranged some Grana Padano, Gouda, some Brie and biscuits, some prosciutto and fruit. They warmed one of the loaves of crusty Italian bread Caterina had baked the day before.

Antonio worked beside them, cutting thin slices of soppressata and summer sausage, then the bread, although not nearly as thin.

Vincenzo wanted to help, to be a part of the preparing together, so Eliana got out four wine glasses, gave him a key, and left him to the opening and the pouring, telling him he had the most important job of them all, as they could all do with a glass and wasn't it time they had one.

They took everything out to the terrace. The sun had already dropped behind the Blue Ridge, but the sky still held on to some color, pinks blushed with purple and blue that faded into grey before giving itself over to a night filled with stars.

Vincenzo raised his glass. "Salute."

"Salute," they all echoed and chinked glasses.

"What's this?" Caterina walked through the solarium's open French doors out onto the terrace.

"An impromptu celebration," Lucia said. "I didn't expect you home until later. Is everything okay?"

"Katie started to get a migraine so we cut the evening short. We hadn't ordered dinner yet, so I told her we'd get together next week sometime and that she should go home and rest before it got too bad. I know too well how fast one can turn vicious."

"Sorry to hear about Katie. Since you're here, though, you can join us." Eliana pulled a chair over from one of the other tables and slid it in between her and Lucia.

Cat sidled in. "What are we celebrating?"

Lucia wrapped an arm around her sister's shoulders. "A beautiful night. Good food, friends, and family. And wine, which you will need some of."

"That's my job," Vincenzo insisted, standing up. He looked at Caterina and winked. "And the most important one according to your lovely sister."

"Which one?" Cat looked at Lucia, then El, then Vincenzo, and smiled broadly.

Vincenzo chuckled. "Eliana, but you're right, you are all lovely. Now I'll go get another glass and another bottle of wine." He looked at Eliana, who had begun to push back her chair, and motioned for her to stay where she was.

"I know where they are. I saw you get the other ones, and you said the wine was my responsibility, so sit."

Eliana looked at Antonio. "Is he always this bossy?"

Antonio's eyes danced with humor. "And then some!"

When Vincenzo returned with another glass and full bottle, he poured Caterina's wine with a flourish, bent at his waist in a slight bow when he handed it to her. "*Per te bella signorina.*"

Antonio rolled his eyes, which made Lucia laugh.

"Your grandson rolls his eyes." She regarded Vincenzo with a smirking grin. "But truth be told, there's more of you in him than he realizes."

And so the night went, with much joking and laughter. Vincenzo wanted to hear stories about them and their parents, the winery, and their future plans. He told a few stories of his own, mostly about Antonio when he was growing up, to a few groans and more eye rolling from that one.

They said their goodnights coming up on midnight. Lucia knew she'd regret the late hour when six rolled around tomorrow morning, but if she had it to do over, she would.

She climbed into bed. Yes, she thought, it had been a wonderful night. There was a special magic that existed in the ties between family and close friends, and it had surrounded them all this night. She rolled over and closed her eyes. A soft humming drifted past her ears, a now familiar tune. She smiled softly.

"Goodnight, Rosa," she whispered into the shadows.

Eighteen

The sound of a kiss is not so loud
as that of a cannon,
but its echo lasts a great deal longer.

Oliver Wendell Holmes

he last guests checked out Tuesday morning, and as they walked out the door, Lucia laid her head down on the reception desk and moaned.

She had a headache the size of Texas. She rarely got them, unlike Cat who'd been prone to migraines since junior high, but when she did they were usually doozies. Right then, her stomach was nauseous. Her head felt like it was inside a giant clamp that kept compressing tighter and tighter.

"Are you all right, Luch?" she heard Cat say from behind her.

Lucia lifted her head. A wave of dizziness washed over her, and she closed her eyes until it passed.

"Not," she said.

Caterina stooped down and studied her at close range. She reached out and massaged the back of Lucia's neck. "What's wrong, honey?"

"I didn't get any sleep last night. Now I've got a killer headache, and it's making me feel like I might vomit."

"You need to go up and lie down."

"Can't. El's out, Marcella's too busy, no one to cover."

"Come with me, Luch. I'm taking you upstairs. We don't have any guests and I can handle things down here."

Lucia shook her head and the pain spiked. "You're supposed to—"

"Hush. All I've got is a meeting with John Edward at one to go over the menu for his art show. I'll give him a call and ask him to come here instead of meeting in town. It's not a problem, so no arguments."

"Are you sure?"

"Positive, now it's upstairs with you, and you're not to get out of bed until you're feeling better."

Before leaving her to rest, Caterina gave Lucia something for the headache, pulled all the shades down over the windows to darken the room, and then quietly shut the door behind her as she walked out.

Lucia tossed and turned, tried to find a position that might ease the throbbing in her head, the roiling in her stomach. She rolled to her back and tried to imagine her body floating, tried to focus on something other than the pain. As she did, she imagined she felt fingers against her temples, light as a whisper, rubbing gently, soothing away some of the hurt, and the faint humming of a lullaby she might have heard as a child, softly calming. She began to relax.

Sleep rescued her and she slept, deep and sound, and dreamt. She was on a horse, riding along a path through the woods, similar to where she and Antonio had gone hiking. Somewhere nearby was a stream; she could hear it. She imagined the water would be cool, refreshing, and suddenly felt very thirsty.

She turned off the path, following the sound of the stream. She knew if she found it the water would taste like a glass of heaven, clean, crisp...better than any she'd ever tasted.

After what seemed like hours, she came upon the stream. As she pulled up the horse, she startled a snake coiled on the side of the path. It struck out, hissing, and spooked the horse.

It reared. The reins jerked from her hands and she began to slide. Her arms flew over her head. Then she was falling. Everything changed, the horse, the stream, the woods disappeared. All around her was empty space, an abyss through which she continued to spiral downward. Down, down, down—

Lucia woke with a jerk, a startled scream caught in her throat. Her skin was clammy, her heart was racing, and no wonder. Slowly, she sat up, rolled her head from side to side, cautious not to spur the pain, reached out with her senses for the headache that had forced her to nap away an afternoon, but felt no trace of it.

She sighed in relief. Her head and stomach seemed to have recovered without any lingering effects that might steal the rest of the day from her. She slid her legs over the edge of the bed, got up, and went into the bathroom to splash some water on her face.

When she went back into the bedroom, she heard footsteps overhead. Antonio, she thought, and smiled. She glanced at the clock and gasped. It was almost five. She really had slept away the afternoon!

She opened the window shades. Outside, she could see Marcella, moving along a row of vines with her lug, picking clusters of grapes and dropping them into the tote, working right beside the other pickers. They had workers enough to do the job. It didn't matter, nor would it matter if they had two dozen more. Marcella would still be out there—her vines, her grapes, her wine. And she would toil tirelessly until the last of the harvest come October, when she could focus more solely on turning the fruits of the labor into liquid poetry.

Picking up her cell, Lucia texted Caterina to let her know she was awake and feeling much better. Cat messaged back that all was quiet and since nothing was happening, she'd cover the lobby until six and then leave the placard on the reception desk instructing anyone who might wander in to ring the house phone.

Taking advantage of the offer, Lucia decided to go up to the attic to see if Antonio had any plans for dinner. He was probably going to take his grandfather out, as he'd done most evenings since Vincenzo's arrival, so she'd see if she could tag along.

As she climbed the stairs, she was amazed how much better she felt. The sleep, weird dream aside, had been a real balm. She would have to ask Cat what she'd given her for the headache because it had really knocked her out.

A memory flickered through her mind—soothing fingers gently easing away her pain, an elusive lullaby floating on the air—*Rosa?* Lucia blinked. Had her aunt somehow sensed her pain and tried to comfort her? Or had she just imagined the sensations?

When she rounded the landing to the attic, she heard voices and wondered if Antonio had the new television he'd bought for his office turned on. The attic door was open. She cocked an ear and recognized one of the voices as Vincenzo's.

She stopped just outside the doorway and saw Antonio and Vincenzo sitting in the two club chairs that faced the window on the opposite wall. She lifted her hand to knock, but hesitated when she heard Antonio's grandfather mention the betrothal contract between him and her grandfather Rodrigo.

IN TRUTH, IT surprised Antonio that his grandfather waited this long to bring up his relationship with Lucia. When he'd walked in on them in the kitchen last week, found them kissing and then some, Antonio had expected to hear about it the next day.

"It gives my heart such happiness to see the two of you together," Vincenzo said. "I've known all these years, as surely as Rodrigo and I did when you and Lucia were born, the two of you were destined to be together. And after what I've seen during my visit here, I am even more convinced of it."

Antonio leaned forward, rested his elbows on his knees. He had a notion to argue, purely from habit, to poke him because it was the way of them, and because the old man didn't deserve to be let off the hook so easily when he'd tried to blackmail him into honoring an agreement Antonio hadn't even had a say in.

"And what a fine, fine woman she turned out to be." Vincenzo continued to wax over Lucia. "Not only is she lovely to look at, she has a lovely soul to go with it. You are a very fortunate man, Antonio. I couldn't have chosen better for you." He glanced at him, gave him a raised brow, an *I was right all along, wasn't I?* look.

His grandfather chuckled softly. "Oh, Rodrigo would be as delighted as I." He glanced up toward the ceiling. "We were right, my old friend...we were right. The lad fought me on it, told me we were just two sentimental old men who turned a coincidence into a sign from the heavens with the help of too much wine. But—" He looked back at Antonio with a nod of conviction. "We were right. It was destiny the two of you join our families through blood."

Antonio knew he'd fallen in love with Lucia of his own will, because of who she was and who they were together. He didn't believe fate had any more to do with it than the chair he was sitting in. The only reason he'd come to Virginia was to get his grandfather off his back once and for all about fulfilling his destiny. There was no denying they'd been instantly attracted to each other—but that had been physical. And although he'd liked her right off, he hadn't fallen head over heels in love with her, the depth and soul of her, until later, after he'd gotten to know her.

His grandfather wouldn't believe that, no matter what Antonio said or did. He'd hang it all on destiny.

Antonio couldn't help himself; he had to rib him just a bit, if only because of the smug grin on his grandfather's face. He had to poke him. And when the poking was done, he'd admit the truth and thank the old man, because despite his methods, if it hadn't been for his nonno, he probably never would have met the woman who'd captured his heart so completely.

"It seems you'll get your way after all, Nonno. I'm going to ask Lucia to marry me." He sat back and crossed his arms over his chest. "But my decision has nothing to do with love or destiny."

Vincenzo furrowed his brow. "What other reason could there be, Antonio?"

"Are you forgetting the trust? Or the stipulation you and your friend put on it? If I don't marry her before I turn thirty, I'll have to wait another ten years to get my hands on the money.

"By withholding that condition until after you convinced me to let you loan me the money to start up my firm and telling me I could pay you back when the distribution was made, you leave me no other choice."

"I had to do something to force your hand, Antonio. It was in your best interest. You're a stubborn lad, too stubborn for your own good. You never would have come to Virginia to meet Lucia if I hadn't forced the issue."

"No, I wouldn't have, but what you did was akin to blackmail. You put a noose around my neck and you've been tightening it ever since."

"What can I say? I needed to take drastic measures." Vincenzo shifted in his chair. "And would it be so horrible to marry one such as Lucia? You're not likely to find another as beautiful, or with a heart as kind. And from what I've observed, she cares a lot for you."

Antonio was having trouble maintaining the farce, but he decided to give his grandfather one last nudge before giving it up.

"No, I suppose I could do a lot worse in a wife. I hadn't planned on getting married so soon, but two hundred and fifty thousand dollars will go a long way to take some of the sting out of being coerced into it before I was ready. And I won't be able to pay back your loan in time without it. I'm not willing to risk losing the firm and everything I've worked so hard for."

Antonio could barely hold on without cracking a smile. "So you win, I'll ask her to marry me. It's the only way I see to get out of this untenable financial burden you've put on me."

They heard a noise behind them, and Antonio and his grandfather both looked over their shoulders to see Lucia standing in the open doorway. Antonio's first reaction was one of pleasure at seeing her, but as he took in her shattered expression, his enjoyment plummeted at the realization she must have overheard everything he'd just said and taken it as fact.

"Lucia," he said, the hurt in her eyes filling him with regret over his careless joke, even though there hadn't been a shred of truth in any of it.

He stood and rounded the chair to go to her.

"No!" She held her palms out, then spun and darted off. He heard the sound of her feet against the wooden floorboards as she ran. When he reached the doorway, there was no sign of her, and a few seconds later the sound of a door slamming shut echoed up the stairway.

He pushed his fingers through his hair. What an idiot. He could try to explain he was just yanking his grandfather's chain, but what if she didn't believe him. Oh Christ, what had he done?

"I knew you were stringing me along that whole time, lad. I've seen the way you look at her and I know love when I see it." His grandfather pushed himself up out of his chair. "I'll admit I probably had that coming after what I did, but unfortunately, from the look on her face, Lucia believed what you were saying. I suggest you go talk to her right away and set things straight before the seeds of doubt are allowed to grow and do even more harm."

Antonio was afraid his grandfather was right. He needed to get his ass downstairs and clear everything up before there was any chance it caused a bigger problem.

His heart clenched at the thought she might not believe him. The look on her face when he'd turned and saw her there stabbed at him. She had to believe him. She had to because if she didn't, he didn't know what he'd do.

"Wish me luck, Nonno." Antonio fisted his hands and walked down the short hall to the stairway. He couldn't lose her over this.

LUCIA SAT ON the floor at the foot of her bed. She brushed away a few more tears, tried not to cry. The tears were single-minded, wanting their own way, resolute in their attempt to make her feel even more foolish. Stupid and foolish because she loved him so much and he'd just been using her. A means to an end, that's all she'd been.

She thought he loved her, or in the least, cared deeply. That he might have an ulterior motive never crossed her mind. Why would it? It seemed so ridiculous even though she knew differently now. She never suspected, imagined, but...

If she hadn't heard the words coming out of Antonio's mouth, she wouldn't believe it, not if a dozen people tried to tell her it was true. He'd said them, though. She *had* heard them, and as hard as it was to accept their meaning, she couldn't deny what they meant. He didn't love her, never had and never would. She was nothing more than a pawn he'd played so he could get the money from some trust. Oh, and he'd played her well, hadn't he?

And now what? Would he try to convince her he didn't mean it, the words he'd said—the words she'd heard—in an attempt to secure the money he'd been willing to marry her to get?

She squeezed her eyes shut behind her palms, cursed the tears that refused to halt their flow. You'd think she could convince them he wasn't worth it, convince her heart it shouldn't be breaking over a man who would pretend to care about her just because—

There was a knock at the door.

"Lucia." Antonio called to her, and the sound of his voice inspired her eyes to well up even more.

She couldn't talk to him, couldn't face him until she knew she could control her emotions better. If nothing else, she wouldn't fall apart in front of him, would never let him know the heart he'd managed to deceive was crumbling, breaking apart piece by jagged piece because he'd succeeded.

"Go away!" She hugged her knees and buried her head against them.

"Lucia, please...let me in so we can talk."

"Leave me alone. We have nothing to talk about."

"*Mia amore*, what you heard, it was nothing. I was only...this is a huge misunderstanding. Please let me in so I can explain."

She didn't need him to explain, to try convincing her he loved her when she knew the truth. She'd heard him tell his grandfather he intended to marry her. Well, he'd never asked her, never gave her any indication he was even thinking of it. Didn't that prove he was more motivated by letting his grandfather know he was going to honor that stupid betrothal contract so he could get the money from his trust than by anything he felt toward her?

She shook her head, remembering how her heart leapt, had wanted to burst with joy and excitement in that brief second, when he said he intended to marry her...before she heard why. How could she have been so wrong about him? How could he have fooled her so completely? Hadn't she gained any better insight into men after Brad? Apparently not. Apparently she was still a horrible judge of character.

She heard the door rattle and was glad she'd locked it when she came in. She'd wanted to be alone in her misery, at least until she could pull herself together so everyone didn't know how utterly devastated the knowledge of his betrayal made her feel.

"Lucia, please darling. Please let me in."

She spied her shoes lying by the side of the bed and leaned over and grabbed one. She hurled it at the door, felt a small sense of satisfaction when it banged into it with a heavy thud before falling to the floor.

"I said leave me alone, Antonio."

"I'm not leaving until you open this door."

Lucia growled. She got up and stomped across the room. Turning the lock, she flung the door open, and almost fell back when she saw the sorrow in his expression. But it was a ruse, a practiced ploy to deceive her again. Her heart would be all too willing to let him—it loved him, it wept for him, it wanted to believe him—but her head knew better. Her head wasn't as anxious to be tricked again; it wore no rose-colored glasses.

She reached out with her palms and gave him a slight push. "I don't want to talk to you. I don't need or want your excuses, your explanations, anything. I know what I heard, and I'm not gullible enough to fall for whatever you came down to tell me to try to convince me otherwise. I'm a big girl. I'm not going to fire you from the job, but as far as anything personal between us, you're going to need to find someone else you can dupe so you can ensure your financial future."

"Lucia, please, don't be foolish. I promise you this is all a misunderstanding. I planned to tell you about all this sooner but never found the right time. I don't care about—"

She slammed the door in his face. "I can't talk to you right now. Just please, go away."

Lucia walked back to the bed and sank down onto it, cursing herself because she wanted to believe him so badly. She was a fool, but no matter how much it hurt, no matter how hard it would be to banish him from her heart, she would.

LUCIA DIDN'T GO downstairs that night. She texted Caterina, told her the headache she'd had earlier had left her exhausted, and she was going to go to bed early. Asked her to let their sisters know, but no need for anyone to worry, she just needed some more rest.

She spent the evening alone, did without dinner, organized her closet and cleaned out her bureau drawers, made a pile of things she didn't wear anymore to donate for someone who might, anything to try to keep her mind off the unbearable loss she felt.

She tried reading but couldn't get into the romance, not when her own had just fallen apart because the man she'd thought was such a romantic had turned out to be a fraud.

With nothing left to do in the confined space of her room, she crawled into bed and curled into a tight ball under the comforter. It was barely ten, earlier than her norm, but her heart had taken a beating and she was more tired than she otherwise would have been. Sleep would help. Sleep would give her a temporary escape from the pain.

JUST BEFORE LUNCH the next day, Antonio and Liam came into the inn together and approached the reception desk where Lucia was going over the room schedule for the upcoming weekend.

She steeled herself against the emotional onslaught seeing him whipped up. She wouldn't let him see her pain, and she most definitely would not shed a tear, at least not in front of him.

Antonio waved an envelope in the air. "We got the permits. Liam picked them up earlier this morning and drove out here to give them to us."

Lucia looked at Liam, managed a smile. "That's great. Thank you for whatever you did to speed up the process."

"No problem. It helps to have a good relationship with the people in the permitting office. It also helps that they aren't too swamped right now, and they're coming through as fast as I've ever seen."

She kept her focus on Liam who posed no threat to her shredded heart. "Whatever the reasons, I'm glad we cleared that hurdle and can move forward."

Antonio dropped the envelope onto the desk, and it landed in front of her. Lucia picked it up, slipped it into the top drawer for safe keeping, and then looked at Liam again.

"I'll keep it here in case we need it for any reason."

Liam nodded. "Once the building goes up and we get some windows in, we can post it on-site, but that'll do for now."

"Liam still hasn't met Caterina," Antonio said, trying to draw her attention. She continued to smile at Liam.

Antonio shifted his stance. "If she's around, we could try to remedy that now. Since you don't have any guests, maybe the four of us could get a quick lunch and talk about next steps."

"Would you like me to see if she's available to meet you, Liam?" Lucia picked up her cell phone, continued looking at the contractor. "I don't know what her plans are for the day, but if she's free I'm sure she'd love to join you for lunch to hear the plan."

"We can go into Middleburg, Lucia." Antonio persisted, using her name to deliberately try to get her to look at him. "You told me there was a restaurant there you liked."

"I won't be able to join you, Liam, but Cat—that's my sister's nickname—she can fill me in later."

Liam cast an uncomfortable glance at Antonio before answering. Yeah, she was probably being totally obvious, and maybe a bit immature, but she was also trying very hard not to break down in tears or end up screaming at the man who'd stolen her heart for his own selfish purposes.

"Well, I've never started a job without meeting the client first, so if you want to see if she's around—"

"Sure thing. Hold on a sec." Lucia dashed off a text to her sister and received an immediate response: *I was just on my way down.*

Lucia held the phone up for Liam to read the message. Antonio leaned over and looked at it too. Her eyes betrayed her, strayed to his face. She was met with blue ice that froze her where she sat for the course of four or five seconds before she got her wits back, tore her traitorous gaze from his.

He wasn't happy that she was ignoring him. Well, that was just too damned bad. She wasn't the one who'd pretended to be someone they weren't and undermined their relationship. She wasn't the one who lied. *But did he...did he really lie to you? You never gave him a chance to explain.*

Oh, there went her heart again. Being foolish. Wanting to believe he loved her. Trying to tell her she owed it to herself— and to him—to listen to what he had to say before passing a final judgment. It urged her to trust her original instincts about him, but how could she when all she needed to do was remember what she'd heard him say with her own ears to know the truth.

She knew better, she wasn't stupid, and she didn't plan on giving him an opportunity to fill her with false hopes only to crush them once again.

Despite her resolve, her eyes betrayed her and stole another glance at him, at his beautiful face, and behind the irritation she guessed stemmed from her refusal to acknowledge him, she saw something else. Something in his eyes that made her wonder if she should trust her heart a little more, that maybe it was smarter than she wanted to give it credit for right now.

Yes, she'd been hurt by what she heard him tell his grandfather. But what if it hadn't been what it sounded like? She couldn't imagine how it could be otherwise, but what if...? What if, despite his original intentions, he'd really begun to care for her?

Wouldn't the mature thing be to let him tell his side and then decide if she wanted to believe him? Isn't that what a reasonable adult would do?

She was about to change her mind and say she'd join them for lunch if her sister was able to go when Caterina rounded the corner from the hallway, and the energy in the room shifted all over again.

Nineteen

We shape our buildings;
thereafter they shape us.

Winston Churchill

"Maybe he was having an off day, but I have to tell you, I don't get why you, El, and Marcella were all so dead set on hiring that man as our contractor." Caterina walked into the inn in front of Lucia after they returned from having lunch with Liam and Antonio.

"His resume looks good on paper, and his references checked out...although I'm sure he wasn't going to give us any bad ones," she continued, "but the man's about as personable as a stone."

Lucia closed the door behind them. "I think you're rushing to judgment. He's been very personable every other time I've seen him, so maybe you're right and he was just having an off day. Maybe he's got things on his mind and it was affecting his mood." Like wondering what the hell was going on between her and Antonio and whether it was going to be a problem on the job.

She hadn't said a word to him at the restaurant. If he aimed a question or comment in her direction, she turned to someone else to respond. It was impossible to ignore him completely—he'd been sitting right beside her—but she'd done her best, although not as successfully as she'd have liked.

He'd done everything he could to draw her attention short of physically putting his hands on her shoulders and turning her to face him. The few times she hadn't been able to avoid eye contact with him her heart wept. It wanted to believe what she saw when their gaze connected was love, and behind it sorrow, and a reflection of the same pain that made her want to curl up in a ball and shut the world out until it went away.

It was all a scam, though, no different from the lines he'd used when she believed he cared about her, the romantic musings and playful flirtations. They'd all been part of a game he'd been playing to make her think he cared.

He does care. Lucia pushed the traitorous thought from her head. If he truly cared, he would have told her about the trust up-front. She might have understood. If he'd told her, at least she would have known he respected her enough, cared enough, to be honest with her. But he hadn't, and now he wanted to, but how could she believe anything he'd say when she knew his driving motivation was financial gain?

Caterina picked up the mail that was sitting on the front desk and started leafing through it. "He doesn't like me."

Lucia glanced at her sister as she walked around to the chair. "Who doesn't like you?"

"Our new contractor."

"Don't be ridiculous. Why wouldn't he like you? Aside from looking down your nose at him a couple of times over lunch, you didn't do anything to offend him."

"I never looked down my nose at him."

"You looked at him like this." Lucia hiked her chin and then glanced down the length of her own nose, across the desk at her sister, through half-lowered lashes.

"That's not what I did. And if I gave him any kind of look, it was probably because I was trying to figure out why he would randomly decide not to like me."

Lucia shook her head. "You're imagining things."

"Fine. Like I imagined the sneer that curled his lips when I went to take a sip of wine and saw him watching me from across the table."

"I didn't notice him sneering at you. Like I said, I think it's all in your head."

Caterina snorted. "Yeah? Whatever, but I'm telling you he's got some kind of problem with me. And anyway, I don't put much faith in anything you noticed or didn't notice. You and Antonio were both acting weird from the time we left until we got back. In fact, I think I was the only one at the table who didn't seem to be fighting some internal demon over their crab cakes and fries."

When Lucia didn't comment, her sister cocked her head and stared her down. "No problems in paradise, I hope."

"Everything's fine. I'm still just a little worn out from that headache I had yesterday." Lucia fudged, not wanting to say anything about what was happening between her and Antonio until she could do so without breaking down into a pool of tears.

"Okay, well good. I'd like to think out of the four of us that at least one sister has managed to get involved with a man who's worth the effort."

ANTONIO PULLED INTO the gravel parking lot after taking his grandfather out for pizza. As they walked toward the winery's inn, he heard an owl hooting and was reminded of a night a couple of months earlier when he and Lucia had been sitting out on the terrace sharing some wine and a scavenged meal. A night when she still believed in him, trusted him.

He had to find a way to make things right with her. It had been three days since she'd overheard him playing his grandfather and mistakenly taken everything he'd said as truth, and he hadn't been able to put a dent in her armor since. The longer this rift continued, the more he feared it would grow.

The one person he most wanted to please, to make happy, to love and be loved by, he'd hurt. Not through any desire on his part, but still, he'd hurt her deeply, and he might only have one shot at restoring her faith in him.

"So if it won't be a problem to change my tickets, then I'll make arrangements to stay another week," his grandfather said from beside him, continuing the conversation they'd been having on the drive back from the pizza parlor.

"It shouldn't be a problem. I'm just surprised you're not in more of a hurry to go home."

"I miss it, and I'll be happy when I get back, but I've enjoyed my visit, and it might be a while before I see you again. Another week suits me fine."

Antonio was glad he'd have a bit more time with the old man. In spite of their propensity to argue, they were family, and the love they had for each other had deep roots. He had to wonder, though, if his nonno's sudden desire to stay longer had anything to do with the mess Antonio had made of things with Lucia.

When they walked into the inn, Lucia was in the library talking with Eliana and Marcella. It was one of the few times he'd seen Marcella in the last couple of weeks. He nodded in greeting, his eyes touching on each of her sisters a moment before resting on the woman he loved, where they chose to stay.

"Good evening, ladies," Vincenzo said, walking right over and embracing each of them as if they were his own daughters. "I've some news to share."

"What's that?" Eliana asked, a smile dancing on her lips. His nonno had managed to charm the entire Bonavera clan, and they all seemed delighted with him whenever he was around.

"I've decided to stay in the States another week so I can visit with Antonio a while longer before returning home." He turned toward Lucia. "What is the chance I might be able to stay another week at your lovely inn?"

Lucia graced him with a beautiful smile, one that made Antonio covet being in her good graces again. "I think we can arrange that," she said, which earned her a kiss on the cheek from his grandfather.

"Wonderful. Now, if you don't mind, I'm of a mind to stretch out with a good book. If it's my good fortune to do so, I will see all of you tomorrow."

As his grandfather started across the lobby to go upstairs, Antonio turned and caught Lucia looking at him. He held her gaze, refusing to let it go, and begged her with his eyes to give him another chance.

She jerked her head away and walked out of the room, through the solarium doors, apparently not wanting to be anywhere near him.

Antonio wondered if it might be a chance for him to get her alone. He hurried after her and saw her duck into the kitchen. He followed.

She must have heard the door close and spun around to face him.

He saw her eyelids flutter, as if in annoyance. "Please leave," she said, and he thought he heard a tremble in her voice. "There's nothing you can say that will change anything now. I just want you to leave me alone. I came in here because I didn't want to see you right now. So please, just go and honor my wishes."

Antonio flinched. "I'm sorry but I can't do that, not until you hear me out."

Lucia fisted her hands at her sides. "Fine, if you won't leave, then I will."

She made to pass him and he caught her arm, halting her progress.

"Lucia, please give me five minutes to try to prove everything you heard the other day was a lie," he pleaded quietly. "Just five minutes. Please."

"I'm not interested."

"Please, *mia amore*."

She gave him a look filled with daggers.

Antonio sighed deeply, let her go, and she walked away from him.

"Are you kidding me!" he heard her exclaim.

Antonio turned around to see Lucia tugging on the kitchen doorknob.

"I can't," she grit out, and pulled harder, "freaking believe this."

When the door still didn't open, she growled and jerked around.

Antonio walked over and turned the knob with no more success than she'd had.

Lucia ground her teeth and glanced up toward the ceiling. "Is this your doing, Rosa?"

The lights flickered on and off.

Lucia tried the door again but it remained closed tight.

After a few moments of silence, she crossed her arms and swallowed. "I don't really feel like talking to you, but apparently my meddlesome aunt has other ideas."

Antonio sent Rosa a silent thank you.

Lucia shifted and looked around the room. "Since it seems you're going to force me to listen to him, can we at least go out on the terrace? Someone else might want to get something in here, and since you'll probably just lock us in another room when you get the chance, I promise he can have his five minutes."

The lights flickered again.

Lucia tested the knob once more and the door opened. She threw Antonio a none-too-happy glare.

Lucia walked out in front of him. Antonio slipped his hands in his pocket and followed her out onto the terrace.

She sat down at one of the tables and he joined her there, locked eyes with her when she glanced his way and tried to tell her through a look what he felt in his heart. He saw her swallow.

"Since we're going to be working so closely together, it's probably a good idea to clear the air between us, come to some kind of understanding, so say your piece, Antonio." Lucia seemed to steel herself. "I want you to promise something, though. If after you say what you want and I don't feel any differently, you'll agree to forget about what happened between us. Our relationship from here on out will be strictly professional, and you won't bother me unless it has to do with the job."

He'd agree to anything just for a chance to try and win her back. He'd never give up on her, though, not when they belonged together. He hoped she'd believe him when he showed her what he had in his pocket.

"I need to move on with my life," she continued, before he had a chance to say anything. "To do that, I need you to be honest with me. Whatever your reasons for changing your plans and taking on our project, getting involved with me—I don't care anymore. If you never loved me, fine, whatever, I'm still standing. The truth won't destroy me, but it will allow me to make better choices. And I think if nothing else, you owe me that."

She paused a moment, stared at the table and then back at him. "I need to know what's in your heart, Antonio. If it's not love then please, just be honest with me."

She was going right for the core of things, to what mattered. She wanted him to put his heart on the table, to expose all he held there; she wanted his truth. He would give it to her.

"And so you shall, *mia amore*."

LUCIA FROWNED WHEN Antonio took some papers out of his pocket, unfolded them and smoothed them out on the top of the table. He drew in a breath and slid them toward her.

"What's this?"

"A document I had drawn up with a lawyer. It states that when the funds in the trust are distributed, they're to be given to you, whether you agreed to marry me or not. The date at the bottom is from a couple of weeks ago, before this whole mess started, before you'd ever even heard about the trust."

"What!" Lucia stared across the table at him, her expression one of shock and confusion. "Why would you do such a thing?"

"For one very simple reason." He reached out and took her hand, breathed thanks when she didn't pull it away. "I love you, Lucia. When I realized how important you'd become to me, I wanted to try to eliminate any possibility you might doubt that love. I was planning to tell you about the trust the night Mitch showed up. If you remember, I told you there was something we needed to talk about. Once you knew the truth, I was hoping you'd forgive me for waiting so long to tell you, and if you did, I planned on asking you to marry me."

He rubbed his thumb over the top of her hand. "My deepest regret is that we never got the chance to talk before you overheard my grandfather and me. What you heard was nothing more than me trying to turn the tables on him for holding things over my head for so long. He saw right through what I was doing, knew all along there was no truth in it, but you didn't. You believed it, and it hurt you. For that I am sorrier than you could possibly know."

Antonio held her gaze, his eyes full of emotion. "We're meant to be, *mia amore*. I truly believe that. Whether through destiny or choice, we're meant to be. You said you needed to know what's in

, Lucia. For you and only you, and I'll spend the
ing to prove it to you if I have to. Please believe

wed, got weepy for about the hundredth time
since overhearing his conversation with his grandfather what
seemed like a lifetime ago. But these tears flowed for a different
reason. These tears were full of hope and promise. He'd opened his
heart to her, told her what it held, and she'd seen the truth in it.
And she couldn't deny the papers on the table that proved it.

"I believe you."

His sigh came heavy, full of relief, she realized. Lucia smiled
lightly, her eyes drinking in his beloved face, and in his eyes she
saw love, a love she would have seen all along if she'd only trusted
her heart more. She had no doubt now, though, as she looked at
him. Antonio really did love her.

He stood up, reached down and took her hands, and in the
next instant she was in his arms. He brushed his lips over hers, a
kiss light as a whisper, endearing, full of promise, and then rested
his forehead against hers.

"Maybe you're right," she said softly. "Maybe we are meant to
be together, because right now my heart's telling me together is
right where we're supposed to be."

His arms tightened around her. "I don't know what that says
about destiny, fate, whatever you want to call it. All I know is I
love you. I love you with no effort, with no thought, with every
heartbeat. I didn't make a conscious choice to love you, although I
would choose you over and over, a thousand times I would choose
you if the choice were mine. My heart decided on you before I even
had a chance to think about it."

He looked down at her. "Was it destiny? I don't know and I
don't care. The only thing that matters to me is that you know now
and believe what's in my heart."

"I do believe, Antonio."

His grin came quick and full of joy, and made her laugh.

"You know, I have to tell you, I'm developing a real fondness for your Aunt Rosa. If she hadn't locked you in the kitchen with me, there's no telling how long it would have taken for me to convince you to talk to me."

"I'm beginning to warm up to her too. Maybe she really is just watching over us, trying to take care of us. I don't know why, but she made it clear she wasn't about to let me walk away from you when I should be holding on with everything I had."

Antonio caught his lip. "We still haven't discussed the other thing you overheard."

Lucia tilted her head, thought back and tried to remember if there was something else but came up blank. He loved her. She hadn't been wrong in that. What else mattered? She furrowed her brow, thought a moment more, and then shook her head.

"You've got me," she said.

He tightened his arms some more. "And I don't intend to let you go."

"Good, because now that I know the truth, I've decided to keep you, too."

"Which brings us to that other matter."

He took a step back and asked her to sit down again. Keeping her hands in his, he got down on one knee and looked into her eyes.

"Lucia Bonavera," he said, his tone serious, almost reverent, and her eyes filled up because she suddenly remembered the other thing she'd overheard.

"Will you do me the honor of walking through life with me, hand in hand, heart with heart, as my partner, my wife, as my love?"

Her answer echoed in her head, *yes, yes, yes,* but the words got stuck in her throat, too full of emotion to get them out, so she threw herself at him instead, wrapping her arms around his neck and knocking him over. They tumbled onto the terrace slate.

Antonio hugged her to him and pressed his lips against her ear. "Can I interpret that as a yes?"

Lucia laughed, nodded, and lifted her head. "Yes," she said, able to get it out now that she'd knocked the word loose. "I will walk through life with you, hand in hand, heart with heart, with you as my partner, my husband, as my love."

"Oh my God, that was one of the most romantic things I've ever seen! Except for you knocking Antonio over, Lucia."

Lucia and Antonio looked at each other and then both turned their heads toward the open solarium doors where Marcella and Eliana, who'd been the one to announce their presence with her declaration, stood.

Eliana clasped her hands to her chest, over her heart, a dreamy look on her face. Marcella was grinning, apparently not immune to the moment, and from what Lucia could tell, neither looked like they were going anywhere soon.

Antonio rolled Lucia to his side, stood up, and then reached down and took her hand. He helped her up and then grinned over to her sisters, apparently not the least bit embarrassed or annoyed they'd witnessed his proposal.

Eliana rushed over and threw her arms around them. "Oh, oh, oh! I'm so happy for you guys! Congratulations. This is so exciting! You are going to let me plan the wedding, right?"

Lucia looked at Antonio and rolled her eyes. He only laughed. Marcella came over then, gave them each a hug that was a little less effusive, more in keeping with her quiet nature, and said, "Yeah, I saw this coming."

"Okay, so we need to open some wine and celebrate," Eliana declared, having apparently decided this was now a group event. "Cel, call Cat and tell her to come down here, and Antonio..." She looked at him. "Do you want us to see if your grandfather's still up so he can join us too?"

Antonio dipped his head toward Lucia, arched a brow. His eyes sparked crystal blue amusement and her heart did a little dance in her chest. Lord how she loved this man. He was everything she wanted, needed—smart and good and sexy as hell—and he didn't look at all like he wanted to strangle her sisters, so that was a bonus since she was stuck with them.

"I agree a celebration is in order, and what better way to celebrate than with those we love, with family." He leaned down, kissed her forehead, then pushed the hair back from her ear, kissed her there, and whispered for her ears only, "And after, we'll celebrate with just us two."

The warmth of his promise flowed through her veins, and she smiled. She was loved. Her heart had been right all along.

ANTONIO TURNED THE latch on the bedroom door and put his hands on Lucia's shoulders. "There are some things I'm not willing to share with your sisters."

"Even they wouldn't dare open that door tonight."

She wrapped her arms around his waist, so grateful for the man he'd proven himself to be. "You were very gracious this evening, celebrating with my sisters and your grandfather at Eliana's suggestion." She bobbed her head. "Okay, hijacking of your proposal and turning it into a party. I'm not sure most men would have been as understanding."

"They're yours. They love you as you do them. They got caught up in their happiness for you, for us, and as I believe it was that which motivated them to...umm, seize the moment and want to share in it with us, how could I not indulge them? They have always been and will always be your sisters. Because I love you, because I'm yours and you're mine, I view them as part of the package."

He dropped his hands to her waist and moved against her. "With the aforementioned exception."

"Our private celebration."

"Umm hmm." He started walking toward the bed, smoothly urging her backward as he went, his hands never leaving her sides.

"After we celebrate, we're going to need to talk about logistics."

Antonio chuckled. "I love it when you talk common sense. It's such a turn-on."

"Well, we will, you know. We live in different countries, or did that not-so-little detail slip your mind in all the excitement?"

"It didn't slip my mind. I've given it a lot of thought." He stopped when the back of her legs met with the bed.

"And the trust. We're going to need to talk about that. I appreciate what you did and understand why, but I don't feel right about it. It should be distributed more fairly."

He kissed her, his mouth gliding over hers, holding back even as she could taste his hunger on them.

"I don't care what you do with it. Put it into Serendipity, split it among your sisters, it doesn't matter to me."

He reached around to the back of her dress, found the zipper, inched it down, the pad of his thumb trailing over her skin as he did like a matchstick lighting the embers of her desire.

Logistics could wait, talking about the trust could wait. She needed the touch of his skin against hers, the feel of his mouth, his hands, giving, taking, holding nothing back. For a brief space in time she thought she'd lost him, but he was here, now, and would be always.

He eased her dress off her shoulders, slid it along her body, stopping to lavish her breasts with kisses, her stomach, lingered over her hips, and then slipped it the rest of the way off before working his way back up to her waiting mouth.

She found the hem of his Henley and pulled it up, over his well-toned chest, the broad shoulders, and above his head, then tossed it aside. He toed off his shoes, undid his jeans, and worked them off along with his boxers.

Free of all that kept them from their desire, Antonio gently eased her down onto the bed, followed, and brought the words he'd given her earlier to life. With his mouth and his hands and his body, he showered her with love.

ANTONIO WAS ON fire, and the accelerant stoking the flame to burn out of control was named Lucia. The taste of her, the scent of her, the feel of her body moving under him, against him, with him, all combined to fuel the blaze to flare higher.

Surely no other woman could ever bring him to these heights of desire, to incite this need to join with her, to claim her as his, and to give her all that was within his power in return.

He molded his hands over her breasts, stroked the erect tips that pleaded for his attention until she cried out, and then he gave her more, leaning down and taking them into his mouth, one after the other, as she tossed and turned beneath him.

"Please," she moaned, the word laced with need.

He drove her up, over and over, wanting her to feel as desperate as he did, until he could bear no more and slid his hand down between her legs. She was wet and warm, and when he drew his finger over the center of her pleasure, he thought she might fly off the bed.

"Now, Antonio," she demanded. "Please, I need you now."

And what was a man to do when the woman he loved asked so nicely? He slid up to take her mouth with his, his tongue hungry to mate with hers, to taste the desire there as he nudged her knees apart and slid into her heat.

He filled her, got swept up in the love, the lust. Pleasure inundated him. He opened his eyes, saw the love in hers, the miracle of what she offered, and he knew there could never be another for him.

They rode out the storm, a tempest that raged until they both burst like a million fireworks lighting the sky. When they came down, they laid in each other's arms in silence, both shaken to the core by the intensity of what they'd just shared.

Antonio reached up, stroked her head, wrapped a length of her hair around his hand.

"My heart is yours, *mia amore*." He laid his lips against her temple. "Now and always."

Twenty

Few men have imagination enough for reality.
Johann Wolfgang von Goethe

*I*n the week and a half that followed, in between meetings with Liam and the two new clients he'd picked up through referrals, Antonio spent as much time as he could with his grandfather before his return trip to Cortona.

Lucia joined them whenever possible, and on two occasions when Antonio had other commitments but she was free, she and Vincenzo went out to lunch together, just the two of them. She cherished the time, getting to know him better, listening to stories about Antonio as a boy, a younger man, and to learn more about her own grandparents.

He left on a Monday. Most of her weekend guests had checked out the prior afternoon, with only two couples staying over through Tuesday. Eliana volunteered to cover reception so Lucia could go with Antonio and his grandfather to the airport.

"I'm going to miss him," Antonio said on the drive back to the winery.

"I know you will. I'll miss him, too." Lucia reached over and rested a hand on his knee. "But he said he'd come back at least once a year to visit, and you'll be going there for a week in November, so you'll see him again in three months."

"I'm surprised he wants to come back, given how he said he'd never come to the States again after his only other visit."

"You'll be here now, so he has a reason."

Antonio shot her a glance across the front seat, his lips twitching. "And so are you and your sisters. I think the main reason is because he enjoyed being fussed over by the four of you."

They had spoiled him, but it had been hard not to. He was a delight, full of charm, a compliment to brighten your day, and a story if you had the time. And at his age, she thought he deserved a little spoiling.

Vincenzo had sat down with Lucia and Antonio early that morning to tell them he hadn't been completely honest about the stipulations of the trust he and Rodrigo had set up. When she learned about it from Antonio, he'd explained that his grandfather told him a trust had been set up for Antonio for two hundred and fifty thousand dollars that would be distributed to him when he turned thirty. He didn't mention that it had been set up by him and Rodrigo, or that it was connected to their betrothal contract.

Antonio had assumed the trust was connected to his parents' estate, a logical assumption. When he decided to start his own architectural firm several years earlier, his grandfather offered to lend him a hundred and fifty thousand to do so, and Antonio signed a promissory note that he'd pay him back within one year of his thirtieth birthday. That would have given him twelve months after he received the money in the trust.

It had been a no-brainer for him, until a year ago when his nonno decided Antonio, who'd refused up to that point to consider even going to the States to meet Lucia, needed a little motivation. And that was when he found out the trust had been set up by their grandfathers as an incentive, should they need one, to bring their progeny together. It stipulated that Antonio needed to marry Lucia by his thirtieth birthday. If the two failed to marry, the funds wouldn't be distributed until he and Lucia turned forty and would be divided equally.

"What's going on in that head of yours?" Antonio asked.

Lucia glanced across the seat. "Oh, I was just thinking of our grandfathers' agreement, and the trust. Did you really think your grandfather was going to stick to the original terms?"

"He's a stubborn old man, and he and your grandfather swore a pact. He felt like it was his duty to honor it. He didn't have any siblings, and he told me on several occasions that Rodrigo was like a brother to him.

"I always knew my grandfather loved me, which is why a part of me couldn't believe he'd maneuvered me into a financial debt that I couldn't repay if I didn't do as he asked."

Lucia took her water bottle out of the cup holder and screwed off the lid for a drink. "You didn't seem that surprised this morning, though, when he told us he'd changed the terms of the trust years ago."

Antonio grinned. "Not totally. I think deep down I knew he'd come through and do the right thing. As close as he was to your grandfather, it was hard for me to believe he'd let his best friend's grandchildren get nothing from the trust while I got it all. When I came up with that crazy plan for a temporary marriage, my original thought was that if you went along with it, I'd split everything equally among the five of us.

"The idea seemed like a good way to meet the stipulation, get the distribution, and be done with their contract once and for all. I'm not wealthy, but I have enough money that I figured with my share I'd be able to repay my grandfather and be done with it. It never would have worked, though."

"What wouldn't have?"

"My plan. It had a major flaw."

Lucia tilted her head. "Aside from the possibility I might have turned you down, which was unlikely, what part of it was flawed?"

He looked across at her and grinned. "I was already in love with you. If you'd agreed to marry me, I never would have been able to give you up."

Lucia melted. "That's nice to know, and a good thing, because I don't think I would have let you."

"Marry you?"

She chuckled. "No, Antonio. Give me up."

THEY DIDN'T HAVE too much more to drive before they'd get back to the winery when Lucia looked at Antonio and was surprised to see him frowning.

"You're grimacing. What's that about?"

"What? Oh." His hair fell over his forehead and he pushed it back. Lucia smiled. She loved his habit of doing it. It was such a simple thing to find endearing, but she did...and that was the all of it.

"You're not going to believe what my grandfather told me when I went into his room to get his suitcases this morning."

She waited, and when he didn't elaborate, she said, "Okay, what?"

"He saw Rosa."

"What!"

"Rosa...your ghost aunt, he said he saw her. Told me she appeared in his room when he was waiting for me to stop by for the bags."

"He *saw* her! Wait, I didn't know he knew about her, but he told you he saw our dead aunt?"

"Not exactly, he didn't know who she was. He asked me if you and your sisters knew you had a ghost in residence." Antonio looked over his shoulder and then merged onto the John Mosby Highway. "He was all packed, sitting on the bed waiting for me, and he said he looked up and she was just standing there, watching him."

"And that didn't freak him out? I mean, was she a solid woman...or see-through...or...what?"

"No, he didn't seem upset by it at all. He said she seemed serene. Supposedly, she was smiling at him. I didn't think to ask him if he could see through her, but he did say she was only there for a few seconds and then she disappeared, which is why he thinks you have a ghost living in the family house."

Lucia stared across the front seat, incredulous. It wasn't that she didn't believe Vincenzo's story, but in all the years when she'd been growing up or since she'd moved back home, their dead aunt had never chosen to make her presence known to her until recently. And she'd never *appeared*.

"So, and don't take this the wrong way, but why do you think Rosa would choose to materialize in front of your grandfather when she hasn't done so with any of us? I mean, she's our relative, right?"

She saw him grin. "Are you jealous, *bella mia*?"

"Of course I'm not jealous," she objected. "I'm just trying to understand why. Doesn't it seem weird to you she'd show up in his room and smile at him when he didn't even know anything about her?"

"Maybe she stopped by to introduce herself before he had to leave."

Lucia's lips parted and she shook her head. "That doesn't make any sense. Why would she do that?"

Antonio shrugged. "I haven't really studied up on ghost motivations, so I can't say. Maybe she wanted to check him out since you're going to be marrying into his family, see if she approved." He shot her a teasing grin. "Looking out for her charges."

Lucia looked out the window, the landscape changing as they got further from the city, giving way to more open spaces, more trees, and gently rolling hills. "I think I'd like to do some research and see what I can find out about Rosa. Maybe it'll help us figure out what her ghost is doing hanging out at the winery."

"I'd be game if you want help researching, and your sisters probably would be too."

"We should then. As soon as the harvest's over and things aren't so crazy. I just hope we don't stumble upon anything we wish we hadn't known." She caught a strand of her hair and twirled it around her finger. "You know what they say, be careful what you ask for."

AUGUST ROLLED INTO September with no more ghostly activity and little time to think about it. Everyone was busy. This was the winery's most demanding time of the year, with harvest in full swing, tourism up, and fall being everyone's favorite season to do tasting tours and enjoy northern Virginia's beautiful scenery.

Liam's crew was getting ready to break ground, adding to the hectic schedule.

Lucia and Antonio had set a May wedding date. She wanted to get married in spring. She loved all the seasons, but that was her favorite. Summer would be too hot, winter too cold, and fall, although a lovely time of year, was simply impossible. She had plenty of time to plan for that, though, especially since they decided they wanted to get married at the winery, and Eliana would be handling most of the details.

The new construction wouldn't be completed yet. Liam was estimating late August unless they ran into unexpected delays.

Lucia pulled the pruners out of her garden apron and cut some hydrangea blossoms for the arrangements she planned to make that afternoon, humming as she did. By the time Serendipity opened for business, she and Antonio would already be married. A warm glow of contentment flowed through her as she snipped off a bloom.

Antonio came out of the inn and jogged down the front steps. "Hey," she said. "I was just thinking about you."

He walked over, took a moment for a kiss. "How you can never get enough of me and no other man will ever be able to make you as happy as I do?"

"Something like that."

He chuckled. "I'm going over to the site to meet with Liam. They started the digging for the basement. I'd like to see how that's going, plus there are a few things he and I need to go over."

"Thought that's where you were off to considering what you're wearing." Lucia looked him over, trailed her eyes down the denim shirt, jeans, and the Wolverines she'd helped him pick out last week for when he was on-site.

"You know I think you're gorgeous. You've got this amazing style without even trying, but I've gotta say, I'm kind of digging this rugged, hunky, worker-dude look you've got going right now."

He pinned her with his sexy cobalt blues and gave her a suggestive grin. "Maybe I'll rub some dirt on my face while I'm over there and search you out when I get back. We could sneak up to your room, and I can throw around some construction terms."

Lucia patted her chest. "Be still my heart."

"So it's a date?"

She laughed at the hopeful tone in his voice. They'd both been so busy lately they'd had little time alone the last week. She missed the comfort of his arms, of making love to him and then lying together in the aftermath, in their own small cocoon, content to close out the rest of the world for a brief time and just savor each other.

"Yes. But don't bother with the dirt; you know I'm not really into that whole mud thing."

He left her with the delightful prospect of an afternoon tryst, something she wouldn't normally consider but felt wickedly satisfied she'd agreed to.

LUCIA KEPT BUSY the rest of the morning making sure everything was in good order. Three of the six guest rooms were occupied, but she'd seen and spoken to all of the guests when they'd come down to take advantage of the inn's breakfast and knew they all had plans to be gone for the day and wouldn't be returning until sometime after dinner.

Antonio got back just after noon. "Are we still on for this afternoon?"

"Yes. The guests are all out and about for the day, so it looks like we can actually pull off a couple of hours together."

"Why don't I run out and pick up lunch? We can have a picnic in your room."

"That sounds like fun, and since neither of us has eaten yet, that'll give us a little more time together."

"We can eat naked if you want," he suggested, "be even more efficient with our time."

Lucia winced. "Nyeah, naked and *pass the truffle spread* don't really go together that well for me. Let's eat first, then we can get naked."

"Okay, as long as there's going to be some nakedness in there somewhere."

Caterina interrupted their banter when she came in a moment later.

"Hey, Cat," Lucia called over to her. "Antonio and I were going to try to have lunch together since all the guests are out. Are you going to be around for a bit?"

"I don't have any plans. Did you want me to hang out down here until you get back?"

"That'd be great. Say in twenty minutes? There shouldn't be anything happening, so you can just check in and out if you want."

"Okay. I might take a book out to the porch. That way if anyone comes by, I'll know. It'll also let me telepath *screw you* messages across the vineyard and down the road to that ill-tempered builder we hired." Cat gave a light snort. "I don't know how the two of you put up with that attitude of his."

She didn't give either one of them a chance to answer. Turning on her heels, she walked toward the hallway, calling over her shoulder, "I'm going to go wash this dust off my face and get a book, and I'll be back down in a few."

Lucia glanced up at Antonio. "Was she over at the site when you were there?"

"Yes, she stopped by on her way back from somewhere. Parked on the road and picked her way across the lot in her heels to see what was happening." He reached up and rubbed the back of his neck.

"Did something happen with her and Liam?"

"I wouldn't say something happened, but I don't think he liked her poking around an active site. She was walking the perimeter where the foundation will go, checking things out. He went over to her and made some kind of comment about appropriate attire. I couldn't hear exactly what he said, or her response, but neither of them looked too pleased with the other."

"I don't understand it. Cat's not that hard to get along with, and Liam seems fairly easygoing to me, but she insists he doesn't like her for some reason. On the few occasions I've seen them together, the air does seem to get a little thicker."

"Well, I hope whatever issues they have with each other, they'll figure a way to work them out." He pulled out his keys. "I don't plan to worry about that right now, though. I've got to go pick up some lunch for a hot date with my fiancé."

Caterina came back down ten minutes later, and Lucia went into the kitchen to get a bottle of Viognier. When she walked back through the reception area, Cat said, "I thought you two were going out for lunch."

"Antonio's picking something up and we're going to have a picnic up in my room."

Cat raised her brows. "Sounds kinky."

Lucia shot her sister a sideward glance and grinned. "Hopefully."

Twenty-one

And think not you can direct the course of
love, for love, if it finds you worthy,
directs your course.

Kahlil Gibran, *The Prophet*

Lucia spread a blanket on the floor, some of the throw pillows from the bed. She took the small vase of roses and hydrangea off her bureau and put it in the middle, set out some candles because even more than she, Antonio was a romantic.

Whenever she thought about their relationship, she still had to shake her head over the irony. Even in her wildest imaginings, imagining that when he showed up at the winery that night almost five months ago it would change the course of their lives wouldn't even have made the wild imaginings list.

They'd been connected since the day they were born, even if it hadn't been through any choice of their own. Still, that old pact had been what brought them together.

Maybe some things *were* meant to be. So many different pieces had needed to fit into place for them to end up where they were.

Was it all just chance, coincidence, or was it possible there really was some greater force at work?

There was a tap on the door. It cracked open and Antonio poked his head in. "It's me."

"So I see," Lucia said softly, her eyes roaming over his beloved face. She would never tire of seeing him walk through a door, toward her, to be with her...whether for a moment, an hour, or the rest of their lives.

He held up two white paper bags. A baguette stuck out of the top of one, and she knew he'd gone to his favorite local deli, knew they'd be dining on cheese and meats, some jam and bread, and if they'd had any, sharing some tiramisu...the man had a sweet tooth.

Antonio looked across the room to where she'd set up for their picnic, including the pretty plates and wine glasses she'd brought up from the kitchen. She'd lit the candles that were set out around the vase of flowers, and the flames danced and reflected off the crystal.

He smiled, one corner of his mouth lifting slowly, and then shifted his eyes back to look into hers.

Lucia extended a hand. "Our table awaits us."

Her blood heated as he walked toward her, trapping her in his blue gaze. When he reached her side, he took her hand and brought it to his lips. "I love you," he stated simply.

The honest, straightforward feeling in his voice touched her heart, filled it, and she knew it would belong to him, always.

"I love you too," she said warmly, and swallowed back the emotion rising up the back of her throat. She tugged on his hand, pulled him toward the blanket so they could sit down and eat before she started tearing up.

He fed her, took pleasure in doing so, turned it into a seduction, and she let him. He wasn't the only one who enjoyed it. The way his fingers caressed the corners of her mouth as she took each bite, how his eyes traced the path of her tongue when she ran it over her lips to catch a stray crumb, and the desire she saw there— all touched her senses, turning their little picnic into foreplay.

When they finished eating, they left everything on the blanket and Antonio led her to the bed. He hadn't changed his clothes from when he'd gone over to the work site earlier in the day. Lucia ran her hands up the denim shirt, rested them over his chest where his heart beat, strong and fast, making her own race with the anticipation of loving him.

They undressed each other slowly until all that remained were his boxers, her bra, and matching panties. Lucia ran her finger along the waistband of his shorts. "Navy blue silk with denim and work boots..." She looked up and touched the tip of her tongue to her upper lip. "I do like your style, mister."

He reached behind her back and unhooked the lace bra, slid the straps down her arms, and tossed it over his shoulder. "And I like yours, but I like you au naturel even better."

Lucia lifted up on her toes and kissed him. "Antonio," she said, breaking the kiss and angling her head back so she could see his eyes. "After everything that's happened, do you think our grandfathers might have been right? That we were destined to be together, and no matter what road each of us had chosen to go down in life, that at some point our paths would have intersected...because, well...because they were meant to?"

He smiled down at her, his eyes blue crystals that shone with affection. "I don't know what I believe anymore. Did we arrive in this place because we made conscious choices along the way that brought us here, or would whatever choice we made keep throwing us into each other's path until we ended up where we are? Either way, I like the outcome."

"I don't know what I believe anymore, either. But I've been wondering more and more about this, if maybe there is a guiding hand that tries to nudge us in the direction we're meant to go—

the direction that will bring us the most satisfaction and happiness in our lives."

Lucia sat down on the bed and he sat beside her. "Maybe," she mused, finding she was more open to possibilities than she used to be, "it's a combination of the two. Destiny and choice. Our lives are a story that can have different endings, each one its own destiny, and depending on what choices we make, that determines which of our destinies we fulfill."

Antonio leaned back and pulled her with him. "Do you think making love to you is in my destiny right now?"

She ran her hands over his chest, up to rest against his cheeks, and smiled. "I think it is."

He rolled her over to her back. "Good, because I don't think I can wait much longer." He captured her mouth, took it hostage, and struck the match to her blood that set her on fire.

Lightning quick, he inflamed her and all talk of chance or choice was forgotten. They just were. The two of them, heart, soul, and body, and nothing had ever felt so right or perfect to Lucia.

It didn't really matter what had brought them together. All she knew or cared about was that they loved, that she would be sharing her life and growing old with this man, and whether it was by fate or chance she couldn't be happier.

The afternoon waned as the sun washed down over the Blue Ridge like liquid gold, and as it did, Destiny smiled—two of her charges had made the right choice—but her work was never done. She turned her gaze toward two others, two who had lost their way and needed a nudge in the right direction.

It's your turn, Caterina, my dear.

Dear Reader

Thank you for reading *Lucia*. Researching northern Virginia, the setting for the Bonavera series, has been a wonderful experience. It's such a beautiful part of the country, oozing with history and charm, and learning about its flourishing wine industry is proving to be both fun and informative.

I hope you enjoyed getting to know Lucia and Antonio and travelling with them to their very own happily ever after. If so, I've got a lot more love in store for you with Caterina, Eliana, and Marcella's stories, as each sister traverses that sometimes rocky, but wonderful and emotionally satisfying road that leads to true love.

If you enjoyed *Lucia*, would you please take a moment to leave a review on Amazon. Reviews as extremely important to authors, and I'd be so grateful if you could leave a brief sentence or two.

As always, thank you for taking this journey with me, and until the next one...bon voyage.

Sincerely,
Patricia Paris

About the Author

Patricia Paris lives in the Chesapeake Bay area of Maryland, which provides much of the inspiration for her writing. When not writing, she spends much of her free time exploring the bay, battling the weeds that insist on invading her gardens, or experimenting with a new recipe in her kitchen. She is an unapologetic romantic, and loves to give her readers that happily ever after, every time.

Award-winning romance from
PATRICIA PARIS

All titles available in trade softcover and eBook

Alexisvictoriasbh@gmail.com